Praise for *The Joshua Files*

"A gripping survival story ... a fantasy of
pyramids, caves and tunnels"
Daily Telegraph

"Fast-paced and exciting, this is one for fans of Alex Rider
and Young Bond"
The Bookseller

"A splendid adventure story"
Mail on Sunday

"It's the Mexican and Mayan flavourings that give Harris's
adventure yarn that bit of extra bite as she weaves a
satisfyingly twisty plot around the science fiction staples of
UFOs and time travel"
Financial Times

Also by M.G. Harris

The Joshua Files
Invisible City
Zero Moment

M.G. HARRIS

THE JOSHUA FILES

ICE SHOCK

SCHOLASTIC

In memory of my Aunty Jose, who told me to go to Veracruz

First published in the UK in 2009 by Scholastic Children's Books.
This edition published by Scholastic Children's Books, 2010.
An imprint of Scholastic Ltd
Euston House, 24 Eversholt Street
London, NW1 1DB, UK
Registered office: Westfield Road, Southam, Warwickshire, CV47 0RA
SCHOLASTIC and associated logos are trademarks and/or registered trademarks of
Scholastic Inc.

Text copyright © M.G. Harris, 2009
The right of M.G. Harris to be identified as the author of this work
has been asserted by her.

ISBN 978 1407 11610 5

Printed in the UK by CPI Bookmarque, Croydon, CR0 4TD
Papers used by Scholastic Children's Books are made from wood grown in
sustainable forests.

3 5 7 9 10 8 6 4

This is a work of fiction. Names, characters, places, incidents and dialogues are
products of the author's imagination or are used fictitiously. Any resemblance to actual
people, living or dead, events or locales is entirely coincidental.

www.scholastic.co.uk/zone

Time is a river which sweeps me along, but I am the river; it is a tiger which destroys me, but I am the tiger; it is a fire which consumes me, but I am the fire.

Jorge Luis Borges

News for the English-speaking community of Lebanon

Paragliding daredevil steals ancient Sumerian artefact

Paragliders enjoying the views from Mount Lebanon near Beirut were the first to spot the lone American who launched his flight from behind the mountain's cedar trees.

Under an electric blue canopy, the thief with a taste for a daredevil stunt rode the air currents until he reached the luxurious villa owned by successful banker Abdul-Quddus Al-Thani, 52.

Under the nose of Souraya, 32, the wife of Abdul-Quddus, as well as six armed security guards, the paragliding madman swept over the high perimeter walls of the property, cut himself free of the canopy and landed in the azure waters of the villa's 20m swimming pool.

The reckless bandit then held the terrified wife of Abdul-Quddus at gunpoint with a Beretta 92F pistol and forced her to pour him a glass of her husband's liquor, before helping himself to the wealthy banker's most prized possession – an ancient Mesopotamian artefact rumoured to be protected with a magical – and deadly – curse.

A curse to which the robber seemed strangely immune. . .

"Once he had the artefact in his hand, no one dared to go near him," Souraya told our reporter. "When the piece was originally brought here, our houseboy died. He got too close to it. Everyone in my household was terrified of that artefact. That's why we kept it behind glass."

However, Abdul-Quddus's wife refused to comment on claims that the object was originally stolen from the Baghdad National Museum during the Iraq War, later purchased by her husband as part of a collection of relics from the ancient Sumerian city of Eridu, near modern-day Abu Shahrain in Iraq.

The theft was captured on closed-circuit TV cameras around Abdul-Quddus's villa. The daring thief made his getaway on a vintage Ducati motorbike stolen from Abdul-Quddus's own collection.

Although the ruthless outlaw wore a helmet throughout, the image proved enough to identify him as US citizen Simon Madison, a suspected terrorist known to be wanted by both the FBI and CIA.

If w
will s
aside o
nately
my r
to get
include
by you
furbis
tion.
from

If w
will
aside
nately
my rec
to get
included
by your
furbishe
tion. I r
from m

The sound of humming gives it away. I'm wide awake within seconds, listening to a sound that I haven't heard for months: the unforgettable sound of a UFO. This time it's hovering above my house. By the time I pull on a sweater and some jeans, the sound has gone. I'm left waiting.

Minutes later, there's the roar of a motorbike riding up my street on a chilly December morning. I lean out of my window to see the outline of a guy in a leather jacket zoom up to my front door riding a Harley Davidson. I peer at him through the early-morning gloom.

"All right, Benicio?" I mutter as casually as I can. But inside I'm fizzing with anticipation.

Benicio here, in Oxford!

The sound of my voice is swallowed by the damp air. My second cousin Benicio pulls off his helmet, shakes his hair free of his eyes. He peers back at me.

"Yes, thanks, Josh, I'm all right."

We stare at each other for a second.

"You gonna come down, then?"

"You're not coming in?"

"I thought we agreed. Safer to go somewhere away from your house. So get a jacket, cos it's *really* cold!"

I can hardly remember what I'd agreed. I mean, when you get a call at two in the morning on a strange-looking mobile phone that you've never heard ring before . . . a phone you thought you'd switched off. . . Well, you're not in the most focused state of mind.

Mainly, you're excited.

A call like that comes in and it shakes everything up – in a good way. In a great way. I needed to be woken up like that. Feel like I've been asleep for months.

Josh, there's something I need to tell you, to show you. Some important news from Ek Naab. And . . . I'm gonna come in person.

Good old Benicio – I can always count on him.

Only a few minutes later I'm squeezing my head into Benicio's spare helmet, wrapping a scarf around my neck (it really is freezing), closing the front door softly and joining Benicio on the back of that Harley.

We zip down our little suburban Oxford street and head out towards the main event – Sunnymead Meadow – where Benicio's hidden the Muwan aircraft that flew him from Ek Naab in Mexico to Oxford.

"I've always wanted to see Oxford," Benicio tells me, his words muffled against the visor.

Well, me too. I've always wanted to see Oxford – from the air.

The bike speeds across the short river-bridge near the meadow; then we're riding over slippery grass in the meadow. I stop for a second, admiring the "UFO". Because deep within the wisps of low cloud, that's exactly what it looks like – a humming object covered in blue and orange flashing lights. Nothing like any airplane I've ever seen.

"How did you land here without anyone noticing?" I ask Benicio as we slide off the motorbike. With a remote control, he opens a panel in the belly of the Muwan. It's parked behind some low, scrappy trees. "We're right next to the ring road!"

Grinning, Benicio pushes the bike into the Muwan and closes the panel. The Oxford ring road is less than fifteen metres away, on the other side of a row of trees and hedge. Even at this early hour it's so noisy that I need to raise my voice to be heard.

"Maybe someone saw me. But UFO sightings are so boring now – most people won't bother to report them." He opens the main body of the plane. "Anyway, Josh, I'm not gonna make a habit of this."

"So why are you here?"

Benicio shrugs. For a second or two, he tries to look serious. "Get in. We need to have a talk."

He takes the Muwan up almost vertically. In just over two seconds we're above the low clouds. I'm in a seat behind Benicio in the Mark II Muwan; in Mayan it means *sparrow-hawk*.

I can't think of it as "Mayan" technology. The people of Ek Naab may be descendents of a hidden tribe of the ancient Maya, but their technology comes from somewhere and someone else. When I was in Ek Naab they didn't tell me from *where* or *who*. Could it be they don't even know?

The Muwan has room for one pilot and two seats in the rear. The cockpit window covers the pilot's seat and extends just over the passenger seats, so I can see up as well as ahead. The glass – if it is glass – is tinted a sort of pinky-gold colour. Or maybe that's a reflection of the Oxford dawn sky? As I watch the cloud layer through the window, it's as though the tint actually changes colour, cycling through pinkish-gold to silver-grey.

"Where do I go for a good view of these 'dreaming spires'?" Benicio says.

I remember my dad once driving me up a hill near a golf course, where he showed me the famous view of the spires of Oxford. "Hinksey Hill," I say.

A few seconds later we drop below the clouds, swoop over the golf course and land in a quiet spot. Benicio gazes at the view before us. The lowlands near the city are waterlogged from recent rain, settled over by thick white mist. The spires seem to rise from the centre of a magical island surrounded by clouds. I can't remember seeing Oxford look so beautiful.

"Wow," Benicio murmurs. "That's something."

I unbuckle and lean forward, touching the edge of his seat. "Yeah . . . Oxford's pretty cool."

He takes a folded piece of paper from his jacket pocket. "It's from Carlos. For you."

I start to unfurl it. "A letter?"

It's not a letter but a newspaper cutting. Still crisp and new – from a recent edition of a newspaper called *The Lebanon Reporter*. I scan it. At first I don't get why Benicio's given it to me. Until I read the end.

"Simon Madison. . .?"

"Carlos is watching every news source in the world. Waiting for any mention of Simon Madison. He made us buy some incredibly expensive software to analyse news – the kind the intelligence services use."

Well, that sounds like the Carlos Montoyo I remember. Totally single-minded – I reckon he'd do anything to protect Ek Naab from being found. And if there's one guy who ever got close to discovering the secret entrance to Ek Naab, it's Simon Madison. The newspaper report makes out that Madison is a suspected terrorist. But until some US secret agents from the National Reconnaissance Office – the NRO –

told me the same thing, well . . . I honestly thought Madison worked for *them*.

"So Madison's back," I say to Benicio. "And what's this artefact he's taken?"

"No clue," Benicio says. "Montoyo wanted you to know that he's on the move. Madison was in Beirut – but he could easily return to Oxford. He broke into your house once . . . so take care."

"We've changed all the locks since then," I say. "And we have a really high-tech alarm."

"Just keep your eyes open," Benicio says. "OK?"

I nod, glancing at the newspaper article again. "Gotcha."

"And, Josh. . ." Benicio sounds a little embarrassed. "There's something else."

"Yeah?"

"Your blog . . . it's gonna have to stop."

"My blog?"

"Montoyo found your so-called secret blog. The one you'd been keeping since you supposedly closed it down."

My mind goes immediately to my last blog post, just a few days ago. Probably the most personal post I've ever written. I begin to turn red. Luckily Benicio isn't looking at me.

"Montoyo found it with this amazing new Web-searching program he bought. If he found it, Josh. . ."

"I get it. If Montoyo found it, then so might the NRO. So might Madison."

And whoever Madison really works for.

I sigh, resigned.

"So I can tell Carlos that you'll delete it?"

I sigh again. "All right."

Benicio becomes brisk. "*Excelente!* OK, good. Now – is there someplace I can take you?"

"Take me?"

"In the Muwan. Do you need to go to school or something?"

I check my watch. "It's a bit early. . ." How can I pass up the chance to fly over Oxford in a Muwan and be dropped off near school. . .? "But all right. Yeah! I'll go wake up my friend Emmy. . ."

Benicio starts up the anti-gravity engine, locks his piloting visor in place.

"That dream about your father," he says. "Your latest blog post, 'Blue in Green'. . ."

OK, here it comes. . . That's a post I really didn't mean to be read.

He pauses. "Quite a revealing dream, Josh. You should maybe talk to a psychotherapist. I think you're having some trouble handling your father's death."

"Well, yeah!" I'm indignant. "I don't even know how he died . . . chased by the NRO in their own Muwans, I know, but . . . after they captured him, who killed him . . . and why?"

Benicio sounds sympathetic. "I'm sorry, buddy. That's gotta be tough."

The Muwan rises with barely a whisper and floats out over the city. The golden stone of the college towers seems tantalizingly close as we drift across the city centre. As we approach the east end of the city, I see the high, doughnut-shaped main building of my school. Benicio dips into the clouds for cover. Then the Muwan drops like a stone to land in the shady park next door.

"You're mad!" I tell him. "We're right in the middle of a built-up area! Loads of people could have seen us!"

Benicio opens up the cockpit and watches me climb out.

"Trust me, nothing's gonna happen. In about three minutes, I'll be hundreds of miles away. There'll be a story in your local paper. Maybe a fuzzy video or photo taken with a mobile phone. Probably not even that. And no one will believe it."

He's dreaming. A flying craft the size of a fighter plane just dropped me off in a public city park! The story has to be bigger than that.

But Benicio seems pretty confident. "Trust me, coz. I've done this many times. And I'm guessing – so have our friends in the NRO."

As the window closes, Benicio takes one last look around. "You're a lucky guy to live here. I sure hope you realize what you've got."

"Ek Naab isn't exactly a dump."

"Small horizons, my friend. Sometimes I think it would be nice to live in the outside world."

With that, the window seals. Benicio grins, does a mock salute, then raises the Muwan slowly over the trees.

And with a sudden whoosh of air being sucked upwards, he's gone.

I tighten the scarf, zip my jacket, check my watch. It's only six a.m. Still buzzing from the rush, I walk out of the park.

Practically floating.

BLOG ENTRY: BLUE IN GREEN

ᚳᛉᚧᛁᛗᚤᛟᛆ�

I've had the dream every night this week. By now I'm pretty exhausted. Here's how it goes.

On a hot, sunny day, I'm taking a stroll. I don't recognize the street, but something tells me that I should. Then I realize what's so strange – there are no cars. I'm walking, then I notice I'm barefoot. The tarmac is warm, feels good on the soles of my feet. The sky is a deep powder blue. Not a cloud in sight. Every garden I pass is filled with rosemary and lavender – the air is thick with the smell. I notice grapevines and fig trees, all plump green leaves. I'm just beginning to wonder where I'm going when I see my house. That's the first time it hits me that I'm on my own street.

The door to my house is open, swinging gently on the latch.

11

There's no one in sight. It feels eerie – there's always someone hanging around in this neighbourhood. Today it's just me.

The door blows open, inviting me in. Faintly, I hear music playing. Miles Davis – a tune from Kind of Blue.

And my heart picks up a beat.

I wander into the kitchen. It's all been cleared, no food in sight. The fridge door too – none of the usual papers or my fading artwork from year five.

There's just one postcard.

There's a noise behind me. I swirl around and nearly faint. He walks through the kitchen door. It's him – my dad.

He's so tall, so alive. Tanned, a picture of health, wearing his usual check shirt and cords, dark hair slicked back with gel. Watching him standing casually in our kitchen, as though he'd just dropped in from college, I can hardly breathe.

Dad doesn't look at me, just reaches for the fridge door.

"Hey, son. Do you ever feel like you forgot something? A little thing? I do it all the time; overlook things. Detail, that's the name of the game. But then, you've already begun."

That's all he says. He pours himself a glass of milk.

Maybe I finally manage to mumble something, I can't remember. Whatever I say, he gives me a quizzical look. "Where've I been? Well, yeah. Been meaning to talk to you about that."

He takes my arm. "Listen, son, your mother and I, we've had some problems. This is how it goes between grown-ups sometimes. You know?"

I shake his hand away, frozen. "I don't know." Mouth dry, I tell him, "I thought you were dead."

Dad looks disappointed. "It wasn't my idea."

"What?!"

"The whole death thing. Not my idea."

He shakes his head now, looking annoyed.

"Then whose?"

"Your mother's."

"And you agreed?"

He pauses, hands on hips. "Yeah."

I stagger, lean back on the kitchen worktop for support.

"You and Mum . . . decided to make me think you were dead?"

"She decided."

"What?!"

He says nothing for a while, just stares at me as though wondering what to do next. "I guess so, son. Like I said, I'm sorry. I was in Mexico."

Now I'm starting to feel furious, betrayed.

"You were in Mexico? Why didn't you call? One lousy phone call? You left me thinking you died?"

His eyes fill with sorrow. I'm totally confused, not to say upset. What kind of parents would deceive their child like that? And how the heck did he engineer that plane crash?

Then (always then), the dream ends; I wake up.

The first few times, it feels so real that I wake up in actual tears, sobbing.

Then in some weird way, I start to enjoy it. Somehow, it's like seeing my dad alive again. Even though we keep playing out the same little scene, it feels real. I sense myself in his presence again. That's way better than nothing. I go to sleep and I'm hoping it's going to happen again, the dream.

My recurring dream is something I don't want to think about. Just remembering that Montoyo and Benicio know about it makes me cringe.

Get some therapy?

It's the last thing I want to talk about. That's why I was blogging . . . so much easier when there's no face-to-face reaction.

And the dream is definitely not something I can discuss with Mum.

Things were better between Mum and me when we came back from Mexico, but only for a while. It didn't take long to work out that she'd been taking extra-special care not to upset me. I really scared everyone, going missing in Mexico like that. Every so often I can almost see the question forming itself on her lips.

What on earth happened to you?

And yet – Mum never, never dares to ask. Not seriously; not in a way that might mean I'd actually tell her the truth.

Mum recovered a fair bit when she found out that Camila was Dad's long-lost daughter, that Dad's murder wasn't connected to any funny business with a woman. We had some nice conversations about Camila and the afternoon that I spent with her. (Unbelievable to think it was only that. . .) A couple of times I got a bit down and Mum would comfort me.

But deep down we both know that we're still in the dark about what happened to Dad.

Maybe Mum made a secret pact, a vow or something, because ever since I came back from Mexico, she's started going to church regularly. Every Sunday, and at least once in the week. I've caught her with rosary beads too. She's asked me to go with her, many times. I always make excuses.

We're coming up to our first Christmas without Dad. I can sense the stress piling on.

"Let's do Christmas in a restaurant this year," she says one morning, just a little too brightly.

"Nah . . . don't fancy that."

"Then let's make a thing of it. Go to a hotel, splash out a bit."

"A hotel, where?"

"The Cotswolds somewhere. You pick."

"OK," I say. "Bibury. That hotel where we had tea that time."

Mum's face drops. "Not Bibury."

Of course she doesn't want to go back to that hotel in
Bibury; it was Dad's favourite. If the point of going away for
Christmas is to avoid thinking about Dad, then Bibury is sure
to spoil her plan.

But I don't want to avoid thinking about Dad. So, I put
my foot down. "If it's not that hotel in Bibury, then I'm not
going. I'd rather stay here – at least we've got good telly."

Mum just blanches. A few months ago I'd have got a
rollicking for talking to her like that. Somehow, not now.
What's changed? Is it Mum, or me?

I can see this argument coming back to haunt me one of
these days.

In the meantime, Mum has another go at getting me
interested in "culture". Culture! I'm still trying to get a grip
on what happened in Ek Naab and all this Mayan heritage it
turns out I have. . . Now Mum wants me to go to museums
and concerts. She's terrified of going anywhere alone, that's
what it is. How can I refuse?

Today, however, Mum hits upon a winning strategy,
a way to ensure I'm not just dragged along in a sulk. She
invites Ollie to join us.

Mum's put her finger right on my weak point.

Ollie had to go away with her family for a few weeks
after we returned from Mexico. And I didn't see too much of
Tyler either. So I've been hanging out with a girl from school

17

called Emmy. We have one of those on-off friendships. Big friends in primary school; then we ignored each other for three years. Now, I can't even remember why we fell out. She's one of those girls who like to watch boys at the skatepark. And like all girls, she talks a lot. Which suits me fine – saves me the trouble.

Tyler, though – that's a tricky issue. We were never what you'd call close friends – we only really met at capoeira. Mexico didn't help. Tyler is still mad at me for the fact that he and Ollie wound up being interrogated by those NRO guys. He's even angrier that weeks and even months later I'm still tight as a clam on the subject of what really happened.

I stick with the UFO abduction story. Well, I think he sees right through that.

I need Tyler, though, that's the thing. He's the best capoeira player in our age range, and I need the practice. We've even had our official "baptisms" now – ceremonies where you get a *corda* and an *apelido* – a colour-coded belt and a capoeira nickname.

Tyler's *apelido* is "Eddy G" after the capoeira fighter from the video game *Tekken*. And I'm "Mariposa" – butterfly. After my favourite capoeira move, *mariposa*, the "butterfly twist". I'm always practising. It's pretty darn tricky.

I'd never have guessed that capoeira could get me out of so much trouble. Even better, I'm beginning to see a real potential for learning to protect myself. For that, I have to practise it as a contact sport and not just acrobatics. At my capoeira school, they'll never allow that.

So, Tyler and I get together once in a while, and we agree – for a few minutes only – to really go for it.

That's how I can tell he's mad at me; I have the bruises to prove it.

Mum called Ollie about this concert Mum's keen on. Of course, Ollie said yes.

I haven't gone out of my way to avoid Tyler, but Ollie? I've been avoiding her.

She's a girl – doesn't like having her questions ignored or dodged. And the girl is gorgeous. Obviously, if she wants me to talk, then I'm going to have a hard time resisting. The only solution I've come up with is to seem very, very busy.

It was working, too, until Mum booked us all to go to this concert.

The performer, a Chilean tenor named Rodrigo del Pozo, is an old friend of Dad's from college or something. I remember him from when I was a little kid. His daughter and I used to play together before they moved back to Chile. I never heard his singing, though, which Mum and Dad always said was really special. Mum insists that we go to his concert. He's a mate of Dad's, so I guess that's fair.

We meet in Turl Street outside the college. People in scarves scamper between the music, art and gift shops, putting in some Christmas shopping. Hefty, wrought-iron street lamps give the streets an orange glow. The sandstone college buildings look even more golden by night. I love Oxford like this.

Ollie wears the North Oxford preppy fashion. Don't ask me where they find out the rules, but somehow these girls all dress the same. Ruffled short skirts, cute little tops, tailored velveteen jackets and pashminas; that sort of thing.

She gives me a big haven't-seen-you-for-ages-and-I've-missed-you hug.

Inside the college chapel, burning candles give the room a solemn, wintry feel. Ollie and I sit a little way behind Mum. The band – there's only three of them – play old instruments; lutes and those cello-like things. I guess I was about ten years old last time Rodrigo was here. Now I realize that he's only a few centimetres taller than me. There are a few flecks of grey in his hair; apart from that he doesn't seem much older, but then he's got a sort of youthful face.

Rodrigo and a pretty, raven-haired soprano sing these romantic-sounding songs in Spanish and Italian. Not my scene at all, but after a few songs I'm actually starting to quite like it.

In fact, after a few songs, I realize that the music is having a strange effect on me. The songs sound medieval, and before long I'm reminded of banquets in castles, horseback quests through forests and beautiful elves. I steal a glance at Ollie, and I'm more than a little surprised to find her staring straight back. We hold each other's gaze for a full ten seconds – it feels like eternity. She takes hold of my hand. I freeze; I simply have no idea what to do.

Ollie leans in close and whispers into my ear, "I keep imagining myself as Arwen from *Lord of the Rings*." When she pulls back, I see she's smiling.

She's given me the line, though, hasn't she?

"So who am I – Aragorn? Legolas? Don't say Frodo. . ."

That wins another smile. I squeeze her hand and try to lean back casually into the hard, uncomfortable pew. But inside my chest, there's thunder. I can't take my mind off the warm, slender fingers holding mine. Not for a single second.

After the concert, Mum wants to wait for Rodrigo. He's delighted to see us both and gives Mum a big hug when they first meet. He also hugs me for ages, saying, "You're doing a good job, Josh."

Mum suggests an Indian meal, which seems to excite Rodrigo. His eyes light up. "Fantastic – let's go!"

Over dinner, we hear about Rodrigo and his family and how they're settling back into life in Chile after all those years in Oxford.

Mum doesn't mention my adventure in Mexico. It's become our embarrassing little secret.

My son ran off to Mexico with a couple of friends when I was in the mental hospital, and then he ran away from them

*too, went missing for a few days and claims to have been
abducted by UFOs.*

It certainly beats the usual story: *My son had a raucous
house party while I was out of town.*

"I was completely amazed to hear about Andres,"
Rodrigo says, sipping his Cobra beer, shaking his head in
wonder and dismay. "And to think that I actually saw him
just before! That gave me a really weird feeling."

We all stop eating and slowly look up, staring at Rodrigo.
Mum speaks first. "You were in Mexico in March?"

Rodrigo smiles, puzzled. "No, I mean I saw him whilst he
was still in England."

"Rodrigo," says Mum, almost whispering, "he was in
Mexico for weeks before the plane crash."

"You're sure it was him?" I ask. "Not just someone who
looked like him?"

Rodrigo shrugs, bemused. "Well, definitely; I spoke to
him!"

It's as though a switch flips within me. Instinctively I know
that Rodrigo's on to something. "What day?" I insist. "Can
you remember the exact date?"

Rodrigo sips his beer again. The sudden tension around
our table seems to get to him. "It was June sixteenth. Yes,
had to be. Quite early in the morning. I had a concert that
evening, and your dad said what a shame it was that he
couldn't be there."

We almost drop our forks.

"June sixteenth. . .?"

Rodrigo nods. "Something wrong. . .?"

"My dad died on June sixteenth," I say. "Sometime that night, Mexico time."

And flew away from the secret city of Ek Naab on 15 June, the night of the UFO sighting – the six Muwans, one flown by Dad, five from the NRO. . .

Rodrigo stares at me, dumbstruck.

I get my question in before Mum can say anything: "Was he with anyone?"

"Yes," Rodrigo says, looking at us in turn, now utterly bemused by our reaction. "A couple of guys."

"What did they look like?"

"Smartly dressed," says Rodrigo. "Shirts and ties. Andres introduced them as fellow archaeologists. From the United States."

"Archaeologists don't wear ties. . ." Mum says. Her voice sounds hollow.

She's right. I knew it – Dad was captured by those evil NRO agents. I can hardly sit still.

Ollie hasn't said a single word so far, but now she speaks up: "Where was this?"

"Saffron Walden," Rodrigo replies, "a little town near Cambridge. We were doing a concert in a church there . . . music from the latest recording. . ."

I want to leave the restaurant immediately, go somewhere quiet and think about this. But Mum's reaction is so extreme that it takes my mind off everything – for the moment.

Mum faints. She literally fades out, right there at the table. It doesn't last long, but when the paramedics arrive, they diagnose low blood pressure and shock. Poor Rodrigo can't believe the effect of his innocent comment.

Mum is driven home in the ambulance. Rodrigo, Ollie and I take a taxi, stopping to drop off Ollie, who kisses me on the cheek when she says goodbye. Back at our house, Rodrigo sits with my mum, making her tea with a dash of brandy. Mum makes a good recovery. Maybe I should be more astonished at the whole event, but somehow I'm not. I've seen this coming, the wearing away of Mum's strength. There's a cloud of worry floating around her these days. I just know it centres on me.

Rodrigo takes me aside. "What's going on. . .?"

If Mum falls apart again, I have to get help – I can't do this on my own. I have to tell someone something. It's like a dam struggling to hold in a flood – something's got to give.

Well, it's no use. I won't be sleeping much tonight, either. The dream is back. Not just that but I can hear my mum snoring next door. The doctor gave her something to help her sleep and it's put her into mega-deep napping mode.

I do what I always do when I can't sleep – Latin homework. Usually works like a charm. But the latest batch isn't that dull – it's a history of Julius Caesar's military campaigns. Apparently he invented a whole new code – a cipher – for communicating with his front line of troops. Since I'm quite getting into codes, it actually keeps me awake.

I came close to spilling the beans with Rodrigo del Pozo yesterday. He caught on to how freaked we were with what he said about seeing Dad in Saffron Walden.

"You know something about this, I can tell," he said just before he left, and gave me a hard stare. "Your mum, she was shocked. Absolutely stunned. But you! You hardly flinched."

"It's probably something to do with that Mayan archaeologist who used to live in Saffron Walden," I said. At least that could be true, so I actually met his eye. "Dad sometimes mentioned him. Maybe he was checking something out?"

Rodrigo's eyes narrowed. "Like what?"

I wanted to tell him, but I didn't. The words just wouldn't come. Where would I begin? Show off my phone from Ek Naab? It looks strange enough, not much like a normal mobile phone. But I didn't. I can't even imagine where that would lead.

Sitting at my desk at three in the morning, I wonder if I should call Montoyo.

"Anytime you feel you need to talk about what happened," he told me when I called to say I'd arrived back in Oxford, "or that you're worried about something . . . or if you change your mind about coming back to us."

Truth is, though, I want to get a little further into this. Montoyo and the others in Ek Naab would be really impressed if I brought back something more concrete than a rumour.

How hard could it be to do this myself . . . I found the Ix Codex, after all. And that was *ages* away from Ek Naab. Saffron Walden is only a couple of bus rides away.

And I wasn't fibbing about where Dad and those agents from the National Reconnaissance Office went in Saffron

Walden. It's obvious; they went to that archaeologist's house – J Eric Thompson. The same place where my grandfather, Aureliano, went forty years ago.

I think back to the day Montoyo told me the history of my grandfather, Aureliano, the last Bakab Ix in Ek Naab. He was the one who finally tracked down the missing Ix Codex – one of the four ancient Books of Itzamna. It turned up in an archaeologist's cottage in an English village. If it hadn't been for Aureliano's attack of asthma on his way back to Ek Naab, they'd have had their precious Ix Codex back years ago. Me, my dad, we'd never have found out that we were both "Bakabs" – protectors of the Books of Itzamna.

My dad would still be alive.

I pick up my dad's copy of Thompson's *The Rise and Fall of Maya Civilisation*, open it to the acknowledgements page. Thompson ends with his address: "Yale", Ashdon, Saffron Walden.

A house named "Yale" in a tiny little village like Ashdon – shouldn't be hard to find. I return to bed, already putting together a plan.

The next morning is Saturday. Despite the insomnia, I still wake at seven-thirty, same as any other day. I can hear that Mum is already downstairs, washing dishes as though nothing has happened.

I make myself a stack of toast and jam, a mug of tea, and sit down opposite Mum, watching her bustle.

It's not a good sign when she bustles this early. Something's brewing, that's for sure.

And here it comes. . .

She turns around, breathes a deep sigh, leans against the sink and stares at me.

"I can't take this any more."

I try to look clueless.

"You. Me. What's happened to us. I know you're hitting your teens now, but honestly. . ."

"What. . .?"

"Is it really necessary to be so uncommunicative? It's been clear to me since you came back from Mexico that you know something about your father's death. Something you aren't sharing with me. Maybe something you're not even sharing with the police. I've gone beyond caring what it does to me. I have to know what *you* know."

Whoa. Sounds as if that's been brewing for a while. . .

I hang my head for a second, wondering what I can say to get out of it. Nothing. I don't want to, either. I want to tell her everything.

But slowly. Carefully.

"Sit down."

She gives me this slightly surprised look, and sits.

"When I was questioned by those NRO guys – the agents from the National Reconnaissance Office – I got the impression that they'd seen Dad before he died."

"Got the impression. . .? Josh: just give me facts."

"They asked me a lot of questions. About Dad, what he was doing, what he was searching for, who he knew. Why ask all that? They didn't seem interested in the plane crash at all. Why not? Only about things he did in Oxford before leaving and things he's done in Mexico."

Mum looks puzzled. "I thought they interrogated you about your abduction?"

"Well, that too."

"Josh . . . were you abducted?"

A long pause. "Not exactly. I was in a sort of spaceship thing, but it wasn't against my will. . ."

I don't get any further. Mum just rolls her eyes. "Oh, Josh, you're not still going on about the spaceships? I don't believe this."

So there it is. I could cry with frustration, but instead I feel myself freezing up again. "All right, all right! Maybe it's best if we don't talk about that. Just about Dad."

Mum stops talking, looks at me carefully.

"It wasn't just me they asked about Dad. They interrogated Tyler and Ollie too."

"Yes, I know all about that, I had Tyler's parents complaining to me about it. To me! As if it was anything to do with me. If anything, that Ollie's father should take the blame – he's the one who bought your tickets to Mexico. I was in no state to make a decision to let you do something like that!"

Of course, Mum was in a psychiatric hospital at the time, and Ollie did persuade her dad that we'd only be gone a week. I take her point, though. Tyler's folks had been a tad unhappy too. I guess Ollie's parents didn't feel like they had a right to complain, since they authorized the trip. I bet they felt angry just the same.

"The NRO weren't interested in the plane crash, or anything about Dad's death, because *they did it*. Don't you see, Mum? They're the ones. They wanted something that he was looking for, or maybe something that he had. And when they couldn't get it from him, they killed him, to keep him quiet. They put his body in a plane on the night of June sixteenth, to make it look like an accident. So when I turn up in Mexico, they assume I know something too. That's what the interrogation was about."

"But you didn't know anything?"

Well, I persuaded them I didn't, but I can't tell Mum that.

"I couldn't tell them what they wanted to know, whatever that was."

Mum slumps into a kitchen chair, pondering. Eventually she says, "I need to get away from this house for a bit. I just don't know how you're supposed to cope with bereavement when things like this happen. All the uncertainty."

"Imagine what it's like for soldiers' families when they go missing in action in a war. . ."

Mum looks irritated. "I'm sure it's awful, Josh. It's good

to see you have some compassion for total strangers. I only wish you could show the same to me; I am your mother, after all."

I can never say the right thing.

Mum takes one of my pieces of toast. She looks thoughtful, tired, sad: a lethal combination. A change is coming, I know it.

I never get letters. I don't get that many emails either.
Apart from the occasional mooch with Emmy down at the
skatepark, I seem to have dropped off the social scene.
There was a time when I had a few mates, but when my dad
disappeared, that seemed to pretty much do it for me. I lost
all interest in hanging around doing whatever it was we used
to do . . . Xbox, guitars and stuff.

Well, this morning, I got a postcard. I didn't look properly
at first, assumed it was to Mum *and* me. It's a photo of
Labna, the site of a Mayan ruin, one I remember visiting
when I was about eight years old. It looks exactly the way I
remember it. A typical rip-off postcard – an old photo.

The card is addressed to me, only me. The writing is
typed, old-fashioned typewriter-style. There's no "Dear Josh"
or anything. Just two words in capital letters:

HOLDS.BLOOD.

That's it.

It was posted about ten days ago, in the Mexican state of Veracruz.

Totally random. I have no idea what it means, if anything. Maybe it's meant to be a threat?

I put the postcard on my desk and turn on my computer. Maybe I'll find someone I know logged into my instant messenger program.

Maybe even Ollie. I keep thinking about Ollie, about that moment in the concert, when she held my hand. How much did I let on that I've got a thing for her? When Rodrigo appeared on the scene, we didn't manage to pick up whatever it was we had going on in the chapel. Like me, Ollie became totally focused on what Rodrigo said about meeting my father in Saffron Walden.

Ollie's not online, but Tyler is. And that gives me an idea.

Want to go on an "adventure"? I type.

He replies: *LOL. Oh yeh. I'm dying to be interrogated again.*

Just to Saffron Walden. It's near Cambridge. We could be back by tonight.

What's in Saffron Walden?

I type: *Meet me at McDonald's in town half an hour from now and I'll tell you. Bring cash for the bus!*

I check my watch. If I hurry I can make it in time for an Egg McMuffin.

Tyler arrives later, orders a cheeseburger and orange

33

juice, sits down. This time of the morning, the restaurant is fairly empty. We sit upstairs, looking out over Cornmarket across at the people in Starbucks, who stare right back. Early winter can be soggy and grey in Oxford, but today is one of the better crisp blue days. Not too cold either. Street entertainers are setting up for a lunch-time busk. Briefly, we watch a juggler hurl a bunch of tennis rackets around his head.

"I'm not saying I'm comin' with you," begins Tyler.

"Whatever. Just listen."

I tell him about Rodrigo, Dad and Saffron Walden. His eyes grow big; he's definitely interested.

"Man, that is *mad*. He was in England on June sixteenth? That means your dad was never in that plane."

I wish. But by now I've thought it through. Rodrigo spotted Dad with those other guys on the morning of 16 June in Saffron Walden. With the time difference, he could still – just – have made it to Mexico that night in time to be murdered and put in the Cessna, which was rigged to crash. I checked on the Web; there's a RAF air base, Lakenheath, about twenty-five miles north of Cambridge. I reckon the NRO guys flew Dad in and out of that air base, had him back in Mexico that night. They wouldn't even have had to use their stolen Muwan technology – with the time difference between England and Mexico, an ordinary military plane could do it.

Which still leaves the question – what was so important in Saffron Walden?

My guess? They were looking for the Ix Codex.

Tyler kisses his teeth in scorn. "What?! I thought you'd given up on that. Seemed like you went off the whole idea after your 'abduction'."

When he says "abduction" it's pretty clear that he doesn't believe me.

"Listen, Ty, it's not about the codex any more. Those people killed my dad. Think about that for a minute."

Tyler looks uncomfortable. "I know, mate," he mumbles. "But what can you do?"

I give a deep sigh. "Maybe I'm kidding myself, you know? Maybe there's no way I can ever find out who really killed my dad. Or why. But if there's *any* chance, any clue. . . Ty – how could I ever forgive myself? Five years from now, ten years from now. . . Knowing that I just gave up?"

"Yeah, man." Tyler nods slowly. "Yeah. You got a point."

"I need to know what he was doing the last day he was alive. Now that I know he was here, I can't just forget it. Could you? I have to know why, what he was doing, to know if there's any connection. . ."

He seems to consider it. "Would you feel this way if he'd died in a proper accident? A real plane crash? Or if he'd fallen off a mountain? He used to climb, didn't he, your dad?"

"I think I would," I reply. "If there was anything strange or mysterious about it, yeah. Like mountaineering. Sometimes they don't find bodies for years. Relatives, friends, they never forget, never stop wondering. That's how it is with me. It's like there's a hole somewhere inside your chest. No matter what you do, you can't fill it. People grow old, wondering. Then they find the bodies, the people they lost. Frozen, still young. Yeah, if he'd died like that I'd want to know what happened. I'd want to see the place where he fell."

They gave me an urn with my dad's ashes, but it's not the same. I need to know the exact sequence of events that led to the end. Mum calls it "closure". We both need it. And now there's a chance to know what he was doing on his last day alive.

Tyler nods a few times. He's still weighing things up. "Why not Ollie too?"

I don't want Ollie involved – I want to protect her. "Not Ollie," I say. "She's always busy these days . . . with coursework."

He shrugs. "What's the plan?"

"We go to a house near Saffron Walden, used to belong to a famous Mayan archaeologist. We ask questions."

"What questions?"

I shrug. "We ask them what my dad was doing there,

what he wanted, who the blokes in ties claimed to be . . .
that sort of thing."

"That's it?"

I nod.

"And if they tell us to get lost?"

"Well, then . . . I guess we might have to get into some
light . . . housebreaking."

Tyler laughs. He thinks I'm kidding.

It takes longer than I'd hoped to reach Saffron Walden.
There's no bus to Cambridge for another hour. We talk a
little, then stare out of the window. Tyler gets a text and
then spends the rest of the time chuckling to himself and
texting. He won't show me the texts. "Private," he smirks.
"From a girl."

I try to ignore him and daydream about Ollie.

The bus takes ages but gets us most of the way, and we
have to catch another to Saffron Walden, then another to
the little village of Ashdon, where Thompson used to live.

It's past sunset, dark, the village centre decorated with
trails of pinpoints of blue lights strung over the trees and
shops, which are about to close. I walk into the pharmacy,
figuring that the pharmacist must know everyone.

"Excuse me, we're looking for a house called 'Yale'.
Used to belong to an archaeologist called Sir J Eric
Thompson."

The pharmacist nods and smiles, her curly brown hair

bobbing. "You'll be looking for the fancy-dress party, then? They have one every year, don't they? First week of December. It's like the start of the Christmas season here."

I pause for just a little too long, but Tyler comes to the rescue. "That's right. We're supposed to deliver some . . . ah . . . costumes."

"Our parents forgot to pick them up," I say. "From some shop nearby. . ."

The pharmacist chuckles. "No costume shops here! There might be one in Saffron."

I groan. If there's a party going on, it's going to be hard to get time alone with the current owner of the house. On the other hand. . .

"Where's the house?" I ask.

She gives me directions – the house is no more than ten minutes' walk from the village centre. Shorter if we cross a field, but in this weather she wouldn't recommend that. "Get all muddy, you will!"

Outside, Tyler and I debate our strategy.

"It's blatant, innit?" he says. "We get some costumes, we sneak in as guests."

I like the plan. We catch the bus back to Saffron Walden, hoping to hunt down some costumes. What worries me is that we don't know who lives there *now*, whether they have any connection with Thompson at all. The fact that the pharmacist recognized the name doesn't mean much – he was a famous archaeologist, after all. It could be his heirs living there . . . or anyone, really.

I'm kicking myself that we didn't ask more questions. I need to get better at this, and fast.

The village bus service makes it to Saffron Walden just as the shops are closing. We rush around like loons asking for the "costume shop". Just our luck – it's as far away as possible, right the other end of town. We arrive out of breath and sweating in time to see the manager closing up. He can hardly make out what we're saying, we're panting so hard.

"Please . . . need costumes . . . tonight."

"Good Lord, boys, take a breather, why don't you? Now then, this would be for the party at the Thompson place?"

Great – a Thompson still lives there.

"Well, as you can see, we've just closed."

We're bent double, trying to catch our breath. With my head somewhere around my knees, I say again, "Oh, go on. Please. We'll get into big trouble with our parents."

The shop manager is a man in his late forties, with a big mop of messy, sandy-coloured hair that gives him a sympathetic look. He hesitates. "OK. But this is just a normal shop, you know. There's no magic portal to one of Mr Benn's worlds, if that's what you're looking for."

He's still chortling away at his obscure joke as he unlocks the front door.

The shop isn't a real costume shop but a charity shop with a few costumes in the second-hand-clothes section. In the window, a child-sized dummy is dressed up like a fantasy hero, with a sword, shield, amulets and everything.

We check through the collection. There are maybe three costumes that would fit me. Two of those are for girls – flowing white dresses.

"That one's multi-purpose," the manager says helpfully. "The Snow Queen, White Witch of Narnia, Arwen from *Lord of the Rings*. Or a ghost, if you take a hood as well."

Tyler turns over a pair of costumes that I realize, the minute I see them, are perfect.

"Hey, look, Josh. Batman and Robin."

"I call Batman!"

The shop manager weighs in. "I shouldn't lend you the Batman. Only the Robin. I already rented out another Batman suit. Bad form to turn up in the same costume as another guest."

Tyler picks up the Batman costume, holds it against himself. "Wouldn't fit me anyway. It's about five centimetres too small."

"That Robin suit is adult-sized," says the manager.

"I'm Robin!" shouts Tyler, before I can say anything. Not that I would, because I can tell right away it wouldn't fit me. Tyler's either fully grown already, or he's going to be a giant. Me, I'm still growing. I check out the Batman suit. It looks perfect.

"Oh, go on, let me borrow the Batman," I wheedle. "Then we'll be a match, my mate and me. Anyway, it's the only one that fits."

"Apart from the White Witch," Tyler says with a snigger.

The manager relents, again. I guess he just wants us out of there.

"Do you know the Thompsons?" I ask as we hand over cash.

"I'm not that old," he replies with a smirk. "Died back in the seventies, didn't he, Sir Eric? Some niece of his living there now. No idea what she's called."

But she's a relative. She might still have Thompson's Mayan stuff. That makes sense – why else would the NRO drag my father there?

"Has she lived there since Thompson died?"

"No," he says, pausing. There's a tiny shift in his attitude towards us. Maybe I'm imagining it, but it's as though the can-do, easy-going nature has suddenly vanished. And it's replaced with an air of conspiracy. . .

"Who lived there after he died?"

"His widow; then the house was empty for a while."

"It didn't sell?"

"It wasn't on the market. Not with that history."

"What history?"

The manager looks me calmly in the eye. "The history that any half-decent research would uncover. The stories from the time Thompson lived there."

We stare blankly. "Like what?"

"Probably a lot of nonsense. As I say, I was too young to remember much. There were people who reckoned that it wasn't only Egyptian archaeologists who came back with curses on them."

Tyler says, "What, Mayans had pyramid curses too?"

"So it was reckoned, round here. Mostly just whispers. All because of that young assistant of Thompson's, the one that disappeared. There were folks who wondered if it was covered up at a high level because – it got a D-Notice, as it was called back then. One of them things the government slaps on a case – making it a national secret. You need someone high up to get a D-Notice. It didn't make the national papers. And that young fella, they never found him."

I gather up the costumes in a major hurry. I've got a hunch that Tyler's next question is going to give the game away.

"We'd better get going," I announce. "Going to be late."

Minutes later, standing in the bus shelter, Tyler says

breathlessly, "Wow . . . what do you reckon to that story? Thompson's Mayan curse could be linked to the Ix Codex, innit? Didn't those blokes who emailed you say it was dangerous or cursed and that?"

He's right, of course. And my mind can't help going back to that news story in the Lebanon newspaper about Madison. How many of these "cursed" artefacts are out there in the world?

"It *is* cursed," I say, shortly. I'm so close to a possible answer – it's time I told Tyler a bit more. "But the codex isn't there any more. Someone got there already, years ago. And my dad would have known that too. What I want to know is, why did he go to the trouble of coming back here? With those NRO men?"

Tyler stares at me. "What are you talking about? How do you know all that?"

"My grandfather found the Ix Codex," I tell him. "And I think I know how – he must have found the stories about Eric Thompson's assistant in the local newspapers. Something must have put him on to Thompson – I guess we'll never know what. But once my grandfather realized that Thompson had some sort of cursed Mayan relic, he must have decided there was a chance it was the Ix Codex."

That's the thing about mysterious disappearances – curious people can't resist them.

Tyler isn't entirely satisfied with my answer, I can tell. But for some reason, he doesn't push it further. He just leans against the shelter, like me. Thinking.

Half an hour later we're back on the bus to Ashdon, clutching plastic bags with our costumes inside, wondering where we're going to change.

"Too bad they got rid of most of those red phone boxes," remarks Tyler. "We could do a *Superman*."

Of course, they didn't completely get rid of them – not everywhere. I cross my fingers that Ashdon is considered cute and traditional enough to keep its original phone box.

A single main road passes through the village of Ashdon. Our luck is in – they've kept their old-fashioned phone boxes and we can change into our Caped Crusader outfits. The house named "Yale" lies along a lane surrounded by fields, lined with trees. There are very few street lights and the sky is layered with dense grey clouds. We have to walk a long way in the cold, foggy dark. It's just as well that it's hard to see us in the murky light, with us dressed as Batman and Robin.

Tyler hasn't said much since I half-answered his question. Finally, he breaks his silence. "This Mayan codex . . . if it was here in Saffron Walden all along, why did no one find it before?"

"I guess no one knew to look for it here."

"But this Thompson bloke, he was a Mayan archaeologist, right? So he must have known what he had, yeah?"

I don't answer, remembering how I dug up the codex

at the shrine of those creepy little statues in the forest –
the *chaneques*. And those two NRO agents; how they
watched me dig, the horrible way they died when they
touched it. . . My guess is that Thompson didn't know
what he had. Because once he'd seen what it could do to
a person, he never would have let that weird volume be
touched again.

Which means that most likely, Thompson would never
have seen inside the box, never looked at the actual codex.

"Maybe he kept it a secret," I suggest.

"Maybe," replies Tyler. But he doesn't sound convinced.
"So what's the plan?"

"We go in, we act natural at the party, we try to chat to
the owners about Thompson. Then we mention my dad, see
if it gets any reaction."

"And if they ask us who the heck we are. . .?"

"Easy," I tell him. "We tell them to try and guess. No one
recognizes their friends in proper fancy dress."

"But we're dressed like Batman and Robin."

"Yeah, so?"

Tyler shrugs. "Seems like a waste to me . . . if we won't
be recognized, we could go unnoticed for ages. We'd have a
chance for a proper snoop first."

"Now that is not a bad idea. . ."

It's easy to see there's a party going on at the Thompson
house. Balloons are strung around the front yard. Christmas

decorations hang in the leafless branches of a small tree. Light blazes from every window in the house, the only light for at least half a mile. It's a big timber-framed country house, with deep brown logs that criss-cross the walls, covered by ivy. The windows look old and rickety. The downstairs windows have tiny leaded panes.

A car passes when we're only a few metres from the gate. It catches us in the full beam of its headlamps for a second, then swings in and parks in the already-crowded, gravel-covered front yard.

We hang back for a minute, waiting. I'm impressed when I see who gets out of the car . . . it's Batman!

Batman according to the latest movie incarnation, mind you. Not the cheesy TV version, like our costumes. Compared to me, this guy is huge, menacing. Batman Suit knocks on the door, glancing around for a second in our direction. I push back against the hedge. But it's pretty likely that he's spotted us already.

Someone opens the front door; Batman Suit steps through. We wait for a few more seconds, then creep up to the door.

"We should go in round the back," Tyler says. "If the hosts have to greet us, there might be questions."

Maybe it's the kind of party where people spill out into the back garden. . . So we slip around there.

It isn't that kind of party. Behind the house it's dark.

48

We try all the doors and downstairs windows. There's an open window. We let ourselves in. The window leads to a utility room, piled high with laundry. Both the washing machine and the tumble dryer are on, so any sound we make is masked. We open the door to the kitchen, wait until there's no one in sight, then sneak in.

The very next second, the kitchen door opens. A woman walks in, dressed as a flapper girl from the Roaring Twenties.

"Lovely, Batman and Robin! You're . . . ooh, wait, don't tell me. You're Poppy's friends, aren't you? You boys lost? Or looking for food?"

"Looking for food!" Tyler says, giving her a wide grin.

She directs us through the large hall and towards the main living room, where the party seems to be in full swing. The room's packed with people wearing elaborate costumes – vicar outfits, girls in bunny costumes with fancy face masks, a couple of Supermen, an Elvis, two James Bonds, a Darth Vader and a whole crew of pirates.

We wait until Flapper Girl is out of eyesight, then turn around and head for the staircase. It isn't easy – the hall is crammed with people drinking mulled wine and talking loudly. From wall speakers, Christmas music blares – that song by Mariah Carey. I spot Batman Suit in the far corner, still by the door, with his back to us. He's with a woman dressed as a Bond girl. At least I assume she's a Bond girl, with such a skimpy outfit and handguns strapped to her thigh.

Tyler and I try to sidle casually up the stairs. Once upstairs, we pad down the corridor, away from the festivities.

"Where are we going?" Tyler asks.

"No idea," I reply, trying a door. It's open. A bedroom. "Not there."

"Look for a library," he whispers.

"Thanks, Einstein, cos I was thinking the bathroom. . ."

"Oh, shut it."

The third door we try leads to a room that's a cross between a study and a library. I switch on the light. Three of the walls are lined floor to ceiling by shelves covered with books and some computer equipment. Against the fourth wall is a huge oak desk, with drawer handles carved into open lions' mouths. Towards the centre of the room, a red leather sofa sits in front of a low coffee table, which is stacked high with magazines. I pick one up – *Architectural Digest.*

"What are we looking for?"

"Anything to do with Mayan archaeology," I say, replacing the magazine. "Look for copies of Thompson's books."

"How's that going to help?"

"I dunno! I just want to see if they've kept anything of his. If they have, then maybe he has notes, or a diary. It's what my dad would have been looking for, if he really did come here."

We continue searching. I've just discovered a rich seam of books about the Maya when we hear a sound from the corridor. Footsteps and voices, definitely approaching this room. With barely a second to glance at each other, we turn out the light, throw ourselves into the only hiding place – under the desk. The front and sides of the desk go all the way to the floor, so unless someone actually tries to sit at the desk, we'll be OK.

The door opens, light turns back on and we hear two voices – a man and a woman. My blood runs cold when I hear the man.

I recognize the voice.

"What a nice room," he begins. "My father's study is just like this."

It's the guy who chased me in the blue Nissan – Simon Madison, or whatever his real name is. The man who killed my sister.

The woman sounds quite elderly and speaks in a clipped accent that I don't quite recognize. It's somewhere between Australian and South African.

"Professor Martineau? Oh yes, I'm not surprised. D'you know, we've kept this room almost exactly as my uncle had it. Course, we couldn't bring all our books from Rhodesia."

"Do you miss Africa?" Madison asks her. There's a tone to his voice that I don't recognize at all. This is him being charming. No trace of the bullying, threatening voice he used with me. He sounds quite believable, in fact. But I know what he really is – a violent thug.

"Wonderful place. D'you know it at all?"

"I'm afraid not," Madison says politely.

"Now, my uncle taught your father, have I remembered that right?"

"My father accompanied him on one excavation, I think," says Madison.

"D'you mind – could I ask you to take off the mask? It's just . . . you look kind of intimidating!"

Madison laughs. "Sure!"

There's a rubbery squidging sound.

"There ya go," the niece says. "Much better!"

That rubber mask . . . Madison is Batman Suit!

"Now d'you know, it's funny you should ask about these papers, because only a few months ago some other people came by, asking exactly the same. Well, I wasn't around. My husband – he hasn't a clue where we keep them. We had to turn those people away empty-handed."

Madison might suspect that one of those "visitors" was my dad. If he does, he makes a good job of covering it up with a casual, "Oh, really? I wonder who that could have been."

"One of your father's lot, I imagine."

"From the Peabody Museum?"

"I don't think so. But they did say they were Mayanists."

She pauses and then exclaims with satisfaction. "Now then! Here it is. I'm sorry it isn't much."

I can't see what the niece is doing, but they are both standing over by the shelves.

"Can I look?"

"Of course. Need some more light? I can turn on the desk lamp."

Hearing her step towards the desk makes me freeze. I stare at Tyler, helpless.

"It's fine," Madison says. "I can see here."

I release my breath slowly.

From the squeaking leather, I can hear that they've sat on the sofa.

"Now see," she says. "It's just a few pages. I found them in his diary from 1965."

"Could I see the diary entry?"

"Yes . . . there should be a copy of it here."

"Would it be possible for me to borrow these documents, to make photocopies?"

Her voice becomes smooth, almost patronizing. "D'you mind if I say no? The photocopying process can be pretty damaging to the manuscript. But I have a really nice digital camera somewhere. Terrific resolution. Just wait here."

We remain scrunched up under the desk, not daring to move a muscle. Tyler, I can tell, is doing a circular breathing capoeira technique to keep calm. His eyes are closed.

The niece returns a few minutes later; we hear her take a few photos and then she comes over to the desk. We tuck our legs in even tighter, so that our whole bodies are in shadow. Luckily she doesn't sit down, just plugs the camera in to a laptop, punches the keyboard. We hear the printer on the shelf nearby whirr into action.

"I did them at top resolution, so it'll take a while to print, I'm afraid. Let's go and find you some food while you wait."

We breathe a sigh of relief as they leave the room. I swing my legs out and wince at a sharp stab of muscle cramp.

"Come on, now's our chance!" Tyler says.

Over by the sofa, they've left a document wallet. "This is what they were looking at!" Tyler whispers. He grabs it and makes for the door.

"Wait!"

Tyler stops.

"I know that guy," I say. "I recognize the voice. It's Blue Nissan – the one who chased me, the one who tried to drown me."

"What? You're joking!"

"No. It's him all right. And he said his father's name was Martineau. That's one of the names he uses. And also 'Simon Madison'."

Tyler blows air softly through pursed lips. "Mate! We'd better get out of here fast."

"Yeah, except. . ."

I look at the printer and the camera.

"We have to take the printouts. We have to get rid of what's on that camera. Otherwise – whatever this stuff is, Madison will have it too."

I pick up the camera, fiddle around for a few seconds until I work out how to erase its memory chip. We wait impatiently at the printer and grab each page as glossy paper feeds out. It's agonizingly slow. I grab every page and stash each one in the document wallet with the originals.

There are footsteps on the creaky stairs.

"The window!" Tyler whispers.

I open the window, throw the document wallet clear of the house. We launch ourselves through the window, one by one. Tyler goes first, clinging to the timbers and ivy.

"Budge up!" I say, landing practically on top of him.

"Ow!" he hisses. I slide over him, grab the next timber and then a fistful of creeping ivy. It's not the most stylish stunt ever but we make it to the ground in seconds. Meanwhile back in the room, we can hear the door opening, and exclamations of surprise from the niece. By the time they've spotted the open window, I've picked up the document wallet from the gravel path and we're scooting around the back of the house. As I dip behind the corner, I turn and poke my head out just in time to see Madison leaning out of the window, his eyes hunting us out.

His face is silhouetted by the light in the room behind, but I can plainly see the shadow of a Batman mask pushed behind his head.

And for a split second we stare at each other, Batman to Batman.

I turn to Tyler. "The fields. Let's move!"

Between puffs for breath, Tyler asks, "Reckon he saw us?"

"Yep. No doubt."

The only question is – did he recognize me? A sinking feeling tells me that even if he didn't, he's smart enough to put two and two together.

We easily clear the low hedge at the back of the garden, and land in a soft, boggy field beyond. It's so dark we can't see more than about thirty metres ahead. Beyond that, the light from the Thompson house peters out.

We run flat out for five minutes, putting at least three fields between us and the house. Finally we collapse in a heap, totally spent. But the document wallet is safely clutched in my fist.

When I look back, I see and hear nothing. The darkness may have saved us – that's if Madison chased us at all. But a sneaking suspicion tells me that he didn't – for one really good reason.

Why bother – when he already knows where I live?

After running over those fields the costumes are muddy, so
we peel them off, bag them and leave them in front of the
shop, with a ten-quid note for the dry-cleaning. After the cost
of the return bus tickets, that's our last cash too. So we ride
the bus home, wishing we'd had time to eat at the party.

We don't care. We have Thompson's document wallet,
and Madison doesn't. It contains three sheets of paper on
which someone has copied a bunch of Mayan hieroglyphs
and two more pages as well – where I can see some writing in
English. In the dim lights of the bus, we pore over the pages.

The first page, I kind of recognize. The second two
are packed more densely with glyphs. The fourth page is
handwritten in English – a copy of a diary entry. The final
page in the wallet contains both English writing and Mayan
glyphs. It looks as though someone has tried to translate a
bunch of them.

Here's what the diary entry says:

12 May, 1965

Met this morning by appointment with a certain Señor Aureliano Garcia of the Yucatan, Mexico. Not a gentleman with whom I have any previous acquaintance; nonetheless, he supplied impeccable references from the National Institute of Anthropology in Mexico.

Our correspondence over the past few weeks concerned an object which came into my possession many years ago. The artefact in question was part of a consignment purchased at auction from the contents of a house in Vienna in 1951. There was an unfortunate incident involving its opening, and I have been reluctant to have any further dealings with the item.

Accordingly, I arranged for its safe storage. I tried to forget about the matter.

Now, almost fifteen years later, I find myself dredging up memories of an abominable nature. Señor Aureliano Garcia, most astonishingly, appeared to know about my possession of the artefact. Indeed, he wrote requesting that I agree to his purchase of same.

Naturally, I agreed. Anything to spare my heirs from having to deal with it.

It was therefore with considerable anxiety that I watched Señor Garcia remove the artefact from its place of storage. Unwilling to risk myself further, I hesitated even to watch. I was, however, assured that a gas mask would provide adequate protection. How I wish I had known this years ago when we first opened the artefact! Señor Garcia himself appeared oblivious to the perilous character of the relic.

He asked if I had read any part of the object. Wishing to be swiftly rid of Señor Garcia, I'm afraid I dissembled, replying in the negative.

In point of fact I did, years ago, attempt a transcription. Not touching the artefact presented a challenge. I turned a few pages with tweezers. What I read convinced me of the uselessness of proceeding further. I declined to share my findings with the world of fellow Mayan scholars. The artefact, I believe, has more in common with either an elaborate hoax, or perhaps more sinisterly, a supernatural nature of the most wicked kind. As such, it would hold no interest for me. I am an archaeologist, not a practitioner of the occult.

Señor Garcia, however, could scarce contain his delight. He claimed that before long the item would be displayed in Mexico City's spectacular new National Museum of Anthropology.

I await his findings with bated breath.

The language is a bit old-fashioned. We have to read it through a couple of times to get the gist. Tyler and I agree that basically, what is says is this:

Thompson got hold of a Mayan relic, which did something horrible to someone who touched it. When Aureliano Garcia (my grandfather) came asking for it in 1965, Thompson was only too happy to hand it over. Just like the *brujo* in Catemaco, he believed that the object was cursed.

I pretend to Tyler that I'm not sure what this "artefact" is, but even he guesses that it's the Ix Codex.

"So these must be copies of the first three pages!" he says in delight.

"I guess so."

"If that Madison bloke is bothering with them, that means he probably hasn't got the actual codex."

"Yep. Definitely."

"And now you've got these pages!"

"Uh huh."

"Mate, why aren't you excited?"

"Because," I reply, "I'm wondering why he didn't chase us."

"It was dark! We was out of there like lightning!"

I shake my head. "I know this guy. He wouldn't give up so easily. He's coming after me again."

Tyler gives me a long, curious look. "You know loads more about this than you're letting on."

"Yeah. It's true."

"But you're not gonna tell me. . .?"

"I will. One day, I promise. Right now it's too dangerous. You OK with that?"

He pulls a rueful grin. "Guess I have to be."

"There's a lot more to my father's death."

"Oh yeah?" he says, laughing. "Tell me something I *don't* know. . ."

"Madison and me . . . we've got unfinished business."

By the time we say goodnight and head for our houses, it's past midnight. The next day I decide I'm going to stay home. In fact, my plan is to stay in my bedroom with the pages until I can figure out what to do. I've pretty much decided that destroying the documents is the way to go. But first I scan the pages, set up a brand-new file storage account on a new website which claims to be super-secure, behind a password I've never used before.

And then I erase all traces of my activity from the computer's browser history. So even if Madison breaks in again, he won't be able to follow what I've done.

This is all very absorbing, so when Ollie turns up on my doorstep around lunch time, she takes me by surprise.

"Hey," she says, her voice all soft. "I was looking for you yesterday. Where did you get to?"

"Me and Tyler went on a trip."

"Fun?"

"To be honest, scary."

We go upstairs and I turn off the TV.

"Scary? How?"

I hesitate. But she's only going to hear the same from Tyler.

"We found something. Another clue to the Ix Codex."

She's blown away. "Wow! Amazing! What is it?"

I shake my head. "You know what, Ollie, it was great having you and Ty to help me last time, but this time . . . I dunno. I already got you both into trouble. So I'm going to finish this – destroy everything I have about that codex, forget about it and get on with my life."

"You really think it's that dangerous?"

"I *know* it is."

"And you're worried about me?" she says with a hint of a smile.

"What do you think? Of course!"

"That's really sweet."

She stares into my eyes then and I really don't know what to say.

"'Sweet' . . . come on, now," I say with a nervous grin. "No bloke wants to be 'sweet'."

She steps a little closer. "OK. You're not 'sweet'."

"Good."

She takes another step. I can smell her perfume – it's like flowers after rain.

"I stopped thinking of you as 'sweet' back in Mexico."

My mouth goes dry. "Uh huh. . ."

She takes both my hands in hers. "Yeah. And look . . . you're taller than me now."

"Just. It's only cos, well, you're quite. . ."

"Petite?"

"Yeah."

What are we doing? She can't be thinking what I'm thinking. . .

But she keeps going. "Think you'll get taller?"

"Hope so."

She shrugs, smiles. "A little taller couldn't hurt."

We're standing centimetres apart; she's holding my hands, breathing right against my mouth, and I somehow can't make myself move.

She's two years older than you, idiot! Whatever you think this is, you're wrong. One false move and it'll be a slap in the face for you.

And right then, she leans closer and kisses me. Right on the lips. I keep thinking she's going to stop but she doesn't and she doesn't push me away. Eventually it's *me* who pulls away . . . because I have no clue what to do next.

I hunt for something to say, which is tricky because I can hardly breathe.

She smiles. "That wasn't so bad, was it?"

I cough nervously. "No . . . no . . . it was like . . . wow!"

She leans a wrist on my shoulder and actually runs her fingers through my hair. "You're not weirded out that I'm older than you?"

I laugh. "Are you kidding. . .?" And emphatically add, "No way!"

"So you'd go out with me. . .?"

"Ollie, course I would!"

"How about right now . . . how about a film and then ice cream at G&D's?"

I could burble stuff about her making my dreams come true, but thankfully I don't. . .

My first date with Ollie and I can't even blog it. . . Mind you, the idea of anyone reading what I'd write about that is just too embarrassing.

Well, in fact, it's a false start. Ollie gets a text while we're in the queue for the cinema and she has to go home. Seems that she's forgotten that she has a big coursework deadline the next day. So I trudge home, a bit deflated.

How can she think of coursework at a time like this?

On Monday before school I manage to remember to grab the document wallet with the copied pages from Ix Codex before I set off. No way can I leave it around the house while I'm out. I stuff it into my backpack and carry it around all day. I don't take it out of my backpack again until I'm on the bus home that afternoon.

Seeing Madison again was a shock. Oxford used to feel so cosy and safe, especially compared with Mexico. But now that I know Madison's back in the UK, it makes me wonder.

Oxford, Beirut, Mexico; Madison sure gets around. Is he based here, though? When Madison burgled our house last year, stole our computers and that book by John Lloyd Stephens, I assumed he was a secret agent working for the CIA or something. Back then I'd never even heard of the National Reconnaissance Office.

But when I was actually interrogated by the secret agents who were on the case – agents from the NRO – they told me that Madison wasn't with them.

In fact, they reckoned he was on more than one Most Wanted list.

And anyway, the NRO were already on my case – ever since they captured and murdered my dad, they must have been monitoring my emails and Web searches. The NRO have been after the mysteries of Ek Naab ever since they found my grandfather's crashed Muwan, back in the 1960s.

So if Madison didn't tell the NRO about my involvement with the Ix Codex – who does he work for?

Or could I be wrong?

Could it all be a big ruse – Madison being a suspected terrorist, Madison being wanted by the FBI and CIA? What if he's actually one of their own, but working undercover? An undercover double agent, like Krycek from *The X-Files*.

Maybe only Madison knows who he really works for?

I turn these thoughts over and over, wondering. Who is

Simon Madison? Why did he steal that book by John Lloyd Stephens? Is it possible after all that he did kill my father?

And I'm so lost in this that it's only on the bus back home that I think to look at those pages one last time before I burn them. And that's when I notice.

The pages inside the document wallet have been switched.

The copied pages from the Ix Codex, the diary entry and the translation, and all the copies are gone. Instead, there are just a handful of blank pages.

I look around the bus. I'm suddenly paranoid. Is Madison following me even here?

But no. It's more serious than that. I've had these documents on me the whole time, except for last night. There's only one possibility, and it almost stops my heart to think it.

Ollie.

Is that why she came around last night? Is that what it was all about – getting me out of the house so that Madison could come over and steal the pages? I didn't lock the back door until I came home – Madison could have sneaked in, gone to my room. Mum might never have noticed.

The more I think about it, the worse I feel. I'm almost dizzy, totally distracted. When someone from school yells, "Josh, wasn't that your stop back there?" I realize that I'm on the way to Woodstock and way past my house.

Why, though? Why would she? That's what I can't figure out. Did Madison get to her somehow? Bribe or threaten her? Maybe he threatened me and she thought she was doing me a favour, getting rid of the last thing that put me in danger?

I'm about to call Tyler to talk it over with him.

But on the long walk home, my hands and face freezing in the cold December wind, I get to thinking. Tyler is the only other person who knew I was going to Saffron Walden. What if Madison's appearance there was no coincidence?

I remember now that Tyler was texting someone on his mobile while we sat on the bus. He said it was a girl, wouldn't show me the texts. But *that* was weird. He's always showing off about the girls who like him. Why not then?

Was Tyler giving Madison a tip-off that we knew there might be a clue to the Ix Codex in Saffron Walden?

Once I get started, it starts to look like it could be Tyler just as much as it could be Ollie. Now I think back, I remember I was with Tyler the night that Madison burgled my house.

Tyler came to me. He practically begged me to go to capoeira with him that evening.

It makes sense. Tyler hadn't been that much of a friend before that day. He was just another guy from capoeira. After that, somehow, he'd become involved with helping me solve the whole codex mystery. I haven't given it much thought before.

Why did he? Was Tyler working with Simon Madison?

Had Tyler betrayed me from the beginning, helped Simon Madison to get into my house and read files and emails from my computer, which led him to my half-sister in Mexico, which led to her death?

I reach my house, dazed. Mum takes one look at me.

"Goodness, Josh, what's wrong? You're as white as a sheet!"

I collapse on to the living-room sofa. I must look bad because Mum follows me.

"Seriously, Josh. You're worrying me. Are you ill?"

I look at her slowly. "I'm feeling a bit queasy, yeah. . ."

She touches my forehead with the back of her hand. "You don't feel feverish . . . but you're shaking."

"Huh . . . so I am. . ."

Mum wraps her arms around my shoulders and gives me a long hug. "My poor baby. Off to bed and I'll bring you a Lemsip."

My voice muffled against Mum's hair, I mutter, "I'm not a baby." But I don't stop her hugging me. Truth is I hardly notice, I'm so wrapped up in my thoughts. The implications are staggering.

I mean . . . everything that Tyler knows. It explains why he's so sceptical about my UFO-abduction cover story, why I've never felt able to fully trust him. The one thing I can't figure out is *how*?

I've known Tyler by sight for years. Did Madison recruit him? Is there some sort of organization?

Then something truly horrible occurs to me.

What if Tyler and Ollie are working together?

I feel physically sick.

What if he was texting Ollie? What if she's the link with Madison, not Tyler? Now I really think hard about it, both Tyler and Ollie came into my life around the time of the burglary. OK, I'd known Ollie as "TopShopPrincess" from my blog, but only for a few weeks. What if Tyler overheard me talking about my blog with someone at capoeira, and then contacted Ollie to tell her to start commenting on it? Did I ever talk about my blog, though? I start to panic, struggling to remember.

Dad had been interested in the Ix Codex for months before he went missing. The NRO knew about it, so whatever outfit Madison works for – if there is anyone else – they might have known about it too. Ollie and Tyler could *both* have known about the Ix Codex long before I did.

What if they've both been watching me from the start?

I try to think through everything they could know, everything that could put me in danger. My mind is racing, my heartbeat too.

I need to calm down. Be logical.

Abruptly, I pull away from my mother.

Mum strokes my frozen hands. "Would you like something to eat, too?"

"No," I say, feeling distant. "I mean, yes, a sandwich, please. A toastie. And tea."

"Well, you can't be all that sick. . ." Mum says with a smile, kissing my cheek.

I need food because I need to think. One of them betrayed me – Tyler or Ollie. Maybe even both.

I need to figure out which – and fast.

I lie spreadeagled on top of my duvet, staring at the ceiling until Mum arrives with my food and tea.

I kind of like getting this attention from Mum. I start concocting this little fantasy where Mum knows all about my secret life and waits at home for me with tea and home-made cakes and sympathy.

But that could never happen. If Mum knew . . . phew. There's no way she'd let me out of the house.

So, Ollie? Or Tyler? Or both?

I think about Ollie.

The way she kissed me.

That was acting? If it was, I don't know how I can ever trust a girl again. I could never, never pretend like that.

I can't tell whether I'm angry, upset or scared. It's some horrible combination of all three.

And I write down:

The Case Against Ollie:

1. She came from nowhere, just in time to get involved in the Ix Codex mystery.
2. She got me out of the house last night, the only time when someone could have stolen the pages from the document wallet.

I think *really* hard, then add:

3. In Mexico, after I'd been to Ek Naab, she kept asking me what was in the case I was carrying, and where I got it.
4. She heard me mention to Rodrigo that my dad might have been in Saffron Walden because of a famous archaeologist.

The Case Against Tyler:

1. He only properly started being my friend after my dad's disappearance.
2. He got me out of the house the night of the burglary earlier this year.
3. After Madison stole Mum's copy of the John Lloyd Stephens book from my house, I tried to replace it and found it in a second-hand bookstore in Jericho. How come Madison showed up at that shop? Only Tyler knew I was on my way there.
4. And how come Madison showed up in Saffron Walden?

Only Tyler knew I was on my way . . . and he wouldn't let me see who he was texting on the bus journey.

On paper it looks pretty balanced. One's as dodgy as the other.

My heart tells me it's Tyler . . . my gut tells me it's Ollie. And my head tells me that it really could be them both.

I get very close to calling Montoyo on my Ek Naab phone. Only the total dumbness of what I may have done stops me.

But then I get to thinking. What if the copied pages of the codex don't actually contain any important information – what if they only contain information that couldn't possibly be of any use? Stuff that could never harm Ek Naab?

Then all that running around in Batman costumes has been a wild goose chase – nothing more. And all that's really happened is that I've rumbled Tyler. Or Ollie. Or both.

For the first time, this idea gives me some hope. I even manage a grim smile, thinking of the NRO getting all excited, imagining they'd found the Ix Codex down in Saffron Walden. Only to find a big fat zero.

Maybe it's not such a disaster. Maybe I can decipher those pages myself and see what's written there. Then I'll know if I'm in big trouble – or not.

I munch the toastie, licking bean juice from my fingers as I bring up the scans of the codex on to my computer screen.

Thank God I scanned them. . .

I stare for ages at the page with a few glyphs translated into syllables. It takes me an hour struggling with a Mayan dictionary to work out that there's something wrong.

Each Mayan word is written as a glyph made up of a few symbols which represent syllables, all stuck together. Except when the glyph is one picture, one word – an ideogram.

If you can read the syllables, you should be able to put them together to make words that exist in the Mayan language. A syllable can be something like *ek* (meaning "black" or "dark") or *naab* (meaning "pool" or "water"). Stuck together, these become the glyph for "Ek Naab".

Well, I keep staring at the syllables on the pages I scanned – trying to work out the words they make. But all I get are words that I can't find anywhere in the Mayan dictionary.

It's not that I can't recognize the syllables. I know plenty – like *kan*, *ta, na*, *el*, *ek* and *to*.

But the words – gobbledegook!

Unless this is some older or different version of Mayan writing which used a different system of arranging the syllables in order to make words, then these are not Mayan words.

As in, the codex is not written in Classic Mayan.

And then I remember what they told me when I was in Ek Naab, meeting the other Bakabs, descendents of Itzamna who guard the four Books.

The Books of Itzamna are written in code.

Of course. Mayan glyphs, but not Mayan language. Like writing that uses letters from the English alphabet – but is in another language.

But how to crack the code?

From what I can tell, the "translation" page is nothing more than an incomplete syllabary – a translation of some of the syllables. As if someone, perhaps Eric Thompson himself, tried to decode the Mayan inscription.

My guess is that he got no further than me. And I'm sitting here with a Mayan dictionary – which Thompson couldn't have had. Because in his day, no one alive could read Mayan hieroglyphs. . .

And yet. I keep staring at the "translated" words I've written. There's something weirdly familiar about them. I just can't tell what.

kan-ta-na. el-ek-to mak-ne-ti-ka pul-sa.

Mum knocks softly at my door. "Finished . . . feeling better?"

I'm miles away, thinking about glyphs. "Hmm?"

Mum clears her throat, a little nervously. "Can we talk about Christmas again?"

I look up in silence.

"I've been thinking that I'd like us to go on a retreat."

I gulp down a mouthful of biscuit. "A retreat? Like, in a convent or something?"

"Yes."

"No way. No way *on earth*."

Mum presses her lips together tightly. In a very quiet voice she says, "Well, let's talk about it some other time, when you're feeling better."

"There's no way I'm spending Christmas at a convent!"

"Hmm," she says vaguely. "Oh, I almost forgot, there was a postcard for you today. From Mexico. There must be some kind of funny promotion on, because I've had a couple, too. You might have seen them lying around."

I stare at her, baffled. "Postcard?"

"They're in the kitchen. You didn't see?"

I follow Mum downstairs as she carries back the tray. In the kitchen she pulls a postcard from a pile of envelopes. Then she takes two postcards from the fridge door. One I recognize as a photo of Tikal, the famous Mayan city they used as the rebel base in the first *Star Wars* film.

How long have those postcards been on the fridge door? I've managed to blank them entirely.

She tosses all three on to the table. All are photographs of different Mayan cities. I turn them over, one by one.

The same capitalized writing. A few words on each card.

DEATH.UNDID.HARMONY.

WHAT.KEY.

Those are the messages on Mum's two cards.

77

My latest message reads – ZOMBIE.DOWNED.

"It must be some kind of game," she says. "We'll be on some mailing list after your trip in summer."

"I've got one of these postcards," I tell Mum. "You didn't say that there were others. . ."

I check the location stamps. All posted in Veracruz. I fetch my own first postcard and check the dates, then arrange the cards in order of arrival. Put together, the messages read like this:

WHAT.KEY.HOLDS.BLOOD.

DEATH.UNDID.HARMONY.

ZOMBIE.DOWNED.

"It's rather odd," Mum admits. I glance at her. Not a trace of irony – she totally means it! It's amazing what your brain will miss when you're completely in denial.

But me – I know better. To the untrained eye, it might look like gibberish, but somewhere, somehow, there's a message. It's meant for me.

And it almost certainly spells danger. . .

If there's going to be danger, then suddenly a retreat seems like a pretty safe place for my mum.

"So tell me more about this retreat. . ."

"We could stay with the Benedictines at Worth Abbey . . . they're really interesting and lovely people, and it's not all praying, you know. . ."

Warily I say, "Mum . . . you do know I don't even believe in God any more?"

She waves a hand, shrugs. "Oh, all teenagers go through that. The thing is to keep going to Mass, so that you're always open to the Holy Spirit."

"But . . . how can I believe in a God that let my dad be *murdered*?"

Mum sighs. "That's the sort of thing you can talk about on retreat. There'll be people around who can answer those questions better than I."

I shake my head. "I'm not going. But. . ."

"Go on. . ."

I take a deep breath. "I think *you* should go. It'd be good for you, over Christmas."

"But, Josh . . . without you?"

"You need something like this. And me . . . I need to be with my friends."

Although right now I can hardly imagine who. . .

Mum takes my hand. "I'm sorry. This has all been terrible for you, I see that now. I'm sorry if I was wrapped up with my own problems before. But don't you think we should be together – the first Christmas without your father?"

"I think that you need the praying and the talking and stuff . . . and I don't."

"And what do you need, Josh, to stay up late, hanging around with girls, drinking and listening to loud music?"

I grin and shrug. "Well, yeah. Mum, I'm fourteen!"

"You know you're not supposed to drink alcohol until you're eighteen? It's the law."

I roll my eyes. "Mum. . ."

"Who would you stay with? Tyler? Ollie?"

"Probably not, actually. I might stay with Emmy. From school."

"Emmy?" Mum eyes me suspiciously. "Is she your girlfriend now?"

"No! She's just a mate."

"Because I don't think you should stay over with a girlfriend."

I groan. "Mum!"

"Anyway," she continues, "in case you were wondering . . . Rodrigo called me back yesterday. About that whole business with him thinking he'd seen your father. Rodrigo checked his diary. Turns out he was also in Saffron Walden a couple of months before, in April. They made the recording then, in the same church. He's been wondering if he could have had the occasions confused. Seen your father the first time he was there, not in June."

I'm stunned. "He actually said that?"

"Well, he wasn't sure. To be honest, he still thought it could have been June. But the facts simply don't match with June, do they?"

I chew my lip. Now that I've actually been to Saffron Walden, I know that the facts show that it *was* June. But I can't let on.

"I suppose they don't."

Mum seems satisfied. "Well, Josh, I'm going on that retreat. I feel rather strongly that you should come too, but you're too old to be forced."

"Thanks, Mum," I say seriously. "Thanks for thinking I'm old enough to choose."

She sniffs. "It's a pity I don't agree with your choice. But I suppose that's how it is when your children grow up."

Mum settles more happily now. And I'm happy too . . . that I've found a way to keep Mum out of any danger while I investigate all the weird things that have started happening. I have this unexpected feeling of being Mum's protector, instead of the other way around. It doesn't feel bad, not at all.

We agree some dates for Mum's retreat and I promise to call Emmy to set up a week at hers. Then Mum leaves me alone in my room.

I lay the postcards on my desk, in order. Another puzzle.

What key holds blood – has to be a reference to my father and me.

Death undid harmony – too right it did.

Zombie downed – blatantly, the body in the airplane.

This is about my father's death. Someone, somewhere is trying to tell me something.

Well, to be precise, it's someone in the state of Veracruz. I don't know anyone who lives there, which makes that clue a bit of a blind alley.

I'm stumped. I look back at my Mayan codex puzzle. Nothing makes any sense. I can't think straight. There's just too much going on. My head actually starts to hurt.

I need to talk to someone – just get away from this for a while.

I look at the list of people on my instant messenger

program. Just like most days, Tyler's listed as "Away" and Ollie's not logged on. But "St_Emmy" is.

This is as good a time as any to ask about staying at her place for Christmas. . .

Hey, Emmy.
Wotcha, Josh. Sup?
Not much. You?
Mikey's party.
Mikey. . .?
You've seen my band, yeh? He's the bass player.
Party? On a school day?
Tis the season to be jolly. Last week of school. Plus it's his fifteenth today.
Cool.
I never see you at parties any more.
Yeaahhhh . . . I know. I've got lazy.
You should come to Mikey's.
Mikey . . . where does he live?
Old Marston.
He wouldn't mind?
He won't notice!
OK. Got his address?

I can't remember the last time I went to a party. Before my dad died, definitely. Right now, though, I'll do anything to be

83

out of the house and talking to someone else. And to be honest – if I'm going to ask for a week-long sleepover, it had better be in person.

Mikey lives in a big cottage in the old village of Marston. I take the bus and my skateboard. I manage to remember to change out of my school uniform, and wear an old black Nirvana T-shirt over jeans.

I arrive before Emmy, unfortunately. Mikey's friends are mostly kids who aren't particularly friendly with me.

"Oi, weirdo! Seen any UFOs lately?" one of them says to me, then laughs like he's made an award-winning joke. The crowd he's with doesn't seem to understand his comment, so he spends the next minute or two explaining the background to them.

Great.

I move away and stand by the punch bowl, sipping a disgusting mixture of red wine, vodka and fruit juice. Looking at the door, waiting for Emmy. Wishing I hadn't bothered.

With one ear, I listen to the conversation behind me. Garcia *this*, Garcia *that*.

Then one voice pipes up, "Josh Garcia, not the Josh Garcia with the, like, hilariously traumatized blog about UFOs and that. . .?"

There's a big laugh from the entire group.

I think about going over there and punching a couple of

them, but at that moment Emmy bursts through the door and is jumped on by Mikey and the rest of her band. Her latest hair-dye job is black with red; she's wearing bright red lipstick and black fingernail polish. She's wearing a matching "American Idiot" T-shirt. With this girl, it's all about Billie Joe Armstrong. Then she notices me.

"Hey, Josh," she says, grinning widely. "You made it! Cool."

From behind me, the voices continue.

"*The Joshua Files*, it was called."

"How d'you know, were you one of his readers?"

"Not me, idiot, my big sister. She lives to be a geek – I told her this loner from school was obsessed with UFOs and said they'd abducted his dad . . . and she started reading it. She used to leave comments on his blog . . . they were blog-buddies!"

Squeals of laughter. Emmy raises her eyebrows to say "What the heck?" but I put a finger to my lips, then point behind us. She gets the message right away.

"Let me try to remember her blog name . . . I know, it was TopShopPrincess."

"TopShopPrincess?"

"Something to do with the Arctic Monkeys. . ."

"They're *old*. . ."

"Nah, man, they're *nang*, idiot; shut up and listen. Then one day she left a comment – something so terrible that poor Joshey got all upset . . . and deleted the blog."

The guy's got a real audience now. Behind me, I sense them turning around to stare at me.

"Heya, Josh, what did she write?"

But I can't say anything, I'm just too stunned. Emmy picks up that I'm angry, furious. . . She puts an arm around my shoulder. "You OK?"

I can't tell if I'm OK.

TopShopPrincess was this guy's sister. Fact.

Not Ollie.

I can hardly take it in.

Emmy begins to sound properly concerned. "Ignore them. If you actually tried to collect the stupidest people in our school, you couldn't do better than that lot."

I manage to find my voice. "It's not that. . ."

"What's wrong?"

I'm thinking about the exact order of events. I met Ollie right after that comment of TopShopPrincess's – the one that made me delete the blog.

And then . . . my knees almost give way when I remember.

I met Ollie after the burglary. The one that happened when I was so conveniently out of the house with Tyler.

The burglar took my laptop computer, read my blog up to that date, found out about TopShopPrincess.

Ollie wasn't TopShopPrincess at all.

That was just the perfect way to sneak someone in under

my guard. A spy – a mole. Whoever "Ollie" is – if that's even her name – she knows what she's doing.

I stumble towards the kitchen. I need to get those taunting voices out of my head. Emmy follows me. She closes the door. For a second she leans against it, blowing her fringe out of dramatically made-up eyes that stare at me, sizing the situation up. And then she walks over and hugs me tight.

"Josh, mate, don't let it get to you. . ."

I'm so desperate to confide in her but I feel gagged, choked into silence.

Emmy asks softly, "Is this about when you ran away to Mexico? Everyone knows, you know. There was a big fuss about it, wasn't there?"

"A bit." I glance at Emmy. She stares sympathetically into my eyes. We look at each other for a moment. It gets a bit awkward.

To break the tension I say, "Thanks, Emmy. It's nice of you, you know. To listen."

Emmy laughs. She punches me softly in the chest. "Get lost."

And just like that, the tension vanishes.

"Let's get back to the party," Emmy suggests. "Put some music on nice and loud, dance. Forget the losers."

But how can I enjoy a party? My head is all over the place. At home there's a half-deciphered fragment of Mayan codex and a bizarre message coming through on mysterious postcards from Mexico. Not to mention what I've just learned about a girl I thought was becoming a really close friend.

Ollie wasn't TopShopPrincess. She's been lying to me from the beginning.

Whatever suspicions I had about Tyler, what I've discovered about Ollie pretty much blasts all that away. She's been lying, pretending to be someone she's not. And I fell for it – every word.

It's as though I've become entangled in jungle creepers, binding me more tightly every way I turn. I have to find my way out of this mess – sort the truth from the lies.

The truth is out there. . .?

You bet it is.

11

The next morning Emmy turns up at my house at seven, smartly dressed in her school uniform. I'd been thinking of pulling a sickie anyway, so I'm still in my PJs, clutching the three postcards from Mexico.

I've been staring at them for the past ten minutes. Getting nowhere.

"Thought I'd check that you're not going to go all emo on me, start cutting yourself or anything."

"As if," I smirk. "But I don't fancy school this morning. I've got stuff to do."

"'Stuff'," Emmy repeats, precisely. "Very mysterious. And you wonder why people think you're weird."

"My life . . ." I begin ". . . is not like everyone else's."

But instead of mocking, Emmy says, "Something happened to you in Mexico."

"Yes, it did."

"Something to do with UFOs. . .?"

I hesitate. "Emmy . . . I can't tell you. If I told you. . ."

"You'd have to kill me, I get it."

"No, no." I stare right into her eyes. "But someone else might."

"I can keep a secret," she whispers.

Then she looks at the postcards in my other hand.

"You got a new pen pal?"

I hesitate. Can I trust Emmy? I've known her since I was six, but the world's turned into a pretty suspicious place lately.

And my hesitation seems to make Emmy all the more interested.

"Oh, you have. . .? Is it a girlfriend? Is that it, Josh, you hiding some secret girlfriend?"

I hold the postcards behind my back. "I'm not."

Emmy pushes her way into the house. Now I'm starting to remember why we fell out. She always did come on a bit too strong.

"Go on, let me see."

"They're not from a girlfriend."

Emmy tugs at the cards, pulls one out of my hand. She's grinning, like she's sure she's on the brink of a hilarious discovery. And I can't resist it.

OK, Emmy, let's see how funny you really think this is.

"'Zombie downed'. . .?" She glances up at me with a puzzled look. "So you've got weird friends too."

"They're not from a friend," I admit.

Then I show her the others. After all, I tell myself, Mum's already seen them. It's not as if this is a complete secret.

When she's seen them all, Emmy just frowns.

"Now that's odd," she says, when I tell her that I don't know who's been sending them. "But if it's a message – it must be in code."

"Well, blatantly," I say, although it's the first time it's occurred to me. I guess I've been too distracted with the way the clues actually seemed to be saying something about my father's death.

"I'd actually been wondering whether it's a Caesar cipher," I say, thinking back to our Latin homework. "You know, the one Julius Caesar used to write coded messages to his generals."

Really I don't know what I'm saying. I'm just trying to impress Emmy.

Emmy looks at the postcards again. "Caesar cipher . . . where D means A and E means B and stuff? Where it's really the third letter along, or something?"

"Or something," I agree.

Emmy scrunches up her nose. "Course it's not that, muppet. Those messages all look like nonsense when they're in code. WTF and stuff like that."

"Not 'WTF'," I say, with a grin.

Emmy breaks into a laugh. "Not that, exactly. Cipher

91

words *never* read like proper words. Too many consonants. Your message has actual words – it can't be a Caesar cipher. I reckon it's a riddle. Like in computer games."

"Oh yeah, nonsensical riddles that bosses set for players, for no obvious reason," I say sardonically.

"Like that, yeah."

"Emmy, this is my *real life*, not *World of Warcraft*. In real life people don't waste time trying to get you to follow riddles."

Emmy stares at me, taken aback by my ominous tone. "Josh, man, it's just one of your relatives in Mexico having a giggle, yeah?"

I come to my senses.

What are you thinking? You can't involve her in this.

"You're probably right," I agree. "It's someone having a laugh."

"So . . . you really going to skip school?"

"Yeah. . ." I lie. "Coursework to catch up on. You know how it is."

"Totally. In fact, maybe during the school holidays, you could help me with the physics coursework," Emmy says as she leaves. "That stuff about electromagnetism. I just don't get it."

Electromagnetism. . .?

I'm nodding, smiling, whatever I need to get Emmy out of the house before I'm tempted to talk to her about my problems again. I don't really think about what she's just said until I get back upstairs.

When I do, I can hardly believe how blind I've been.

My translation of those glyphs from the Ix Codex: *el-ek-to mak-ne-ti-ka pul-sa*.

Or in English: *electromagnetic pulse*.

And *kan-ta-na*.

If you played around with the pronunciation . . . could be *container*.

It's not exact, but probably as close as you can get to make English words using Mayan syllables.

Except for the first page, the Ix Codex is written in English.

School is completely off the agenda now. The next few hours go by in a chocolate-and-fizzy-drink-induced blur. The next time I look up from my desk, it's almost three o'clock – and Mum will be home soon.

I have two of the three pages roughly decoded.

And now I know for sure just how bad it is that Madison and his people have this information.

It's worse than bad – it's a disaster.

And it's all my fault. By trusting Ollie – and Tyler too, maybe – I've fed Madison with all the juicy clues he needed to find the last few remaining scraps of the Ix Codex.

The first page, I can't translate. It's in another language, or there's a different reading order for the syllables – either way I can't figure it out. I get as far as reading the date (which uses the Mayan Long Count) and a fancy-looking glyph called the Initial Series Introductory Glyph – the ISIG – which tells me that the document is dedicated to Itzamna. Which comes as no big surprise, since the Ix Codex is one of the so-called Books of Itzamna.

On page one, after the ISIG come fifteen glyphs. Some are the same – I count only ten different glyphs. I try to translate the first two – get gobbledegook.

First glyph: *aj-la-ni-ne.*

Second glyph: *li-si-ne.*

The third one looks as though it isn't going to make any sense either. So I give up with page one, move on to the next page.

Where I have much more luck. Using my system of reading the Mayan syllables in each glyph to make a word which more or less sounds like an English word, I manage to get a pretty reasonable-looking translation.

The Fourth Book of Erinsi Inscriptions

To preserve technology under electromagnetic pulse from periodic galactic energy wave. Dates of galactic energy waves calculated.

Essential instructions on use of Revival Chambers. Three elements required. Key, Adaptor and Container. All protected by bio-defence.

First step shows how to make Key. In liquid form Key unstable. Use within sixty minutes. Crystal Key can be. . .
(And that's the end of the third page.)

All a bit mysterious . . . and it seems to be about the galactic superwave of 2012.

"To preserve technology under electromagnetic pulse. . ."

I'm guessing that these pages are saying that the Ix Codex is all about a way to preserve computer technology from being wiped out by the gigantic electromagnetic pulse that's coming with the superwave in 2012.

From what I can tell, they need three things – the "Adaptor", "Container" and the "Key".

The "Key", it seems, can be made. It looks like one of the missing pages gives some kind of formula – a recipe for the "Key".

So what about the "Adaptor" and the "Container"? Are they more ancient artefacts? Do the Mayans of Ek Naab have them – or know where they are? And what about these "Revival Chambers"?

If those pages from the document wallet have found their way to Madison, he might be able to figure out as much as I have. Will he be able to figure out how to make the Key?

Then from a forgotten little part of my memory, a tiny thought pops up. Madison stole an ancient artefact – from that collector in Lebanon.

Was it the Adaptor? Was it the Container?

What else do his people have; what else do they know?

We're in a race to get hold of and use this ancient technology – and now I have some idea of what to do next. But it won't be easy.

BLOG ENTRY: DEAR MUM

ΛᴖᴖᏇᴖᏗᏗᴖᏇᴖΛ

If you're reading this, it's because something happened to me; it's because I haven't come back. It means that you've been through my locker at school and found my letter, found the Web address of this blog and the password clue.

I've thought long and hard about this, and here's what I think.

I owe you an explanation. It's been really hard not to tell you what's been going on. At first, it was because I knew you wouldn't believe me. And then I began to worry about you.

I mean, people have died searching for this secret. They've been killed. Dad, and my sister, Camila. If I'd told you, I might have put you in danger. I couldn't handle that.

So why tell you now?

Well . . . if I haven't come back, it's because I'm in big, major trouble.

If I'm in major trouble, that could be the end for me.

If it is, well, that changes everything. This is what I've decided:

it's not fair to keep you in the dark any more. If I'm done for, you deserve to know why. I can't have you wondering what happened and why for the rest of your life. I've seen what that's done to you with Dad. I can't have that on my conscience.

To cut a very long story short – I haven't told you the complete truth about what happened in Mexico. Because when I met my sister, Camila, she died because of what she knew. I almost died too. The Ix Codex that Dad was searching for – it's real. I found it. I met the people Dad came from – his real family in Mexico. They live in a hidden city called Ek Naab and they're descendents of the ancient Mayans. They protect an ancient secret – a secret older than the Mayan civilization itself.

And, Mum, I'm one of them. There's some kind of genetic factor which is passed only through boys. It protects you from this mega-ancient technology that the Mayans have been guarding since, like, for ever. Their books of ancient knowledge can kill with a touch. Unless you have the genetic factor.

Which means they need me. Dad could have done the job too but he disappeared – captured by the NRO, a US agency that stole some of the ancient technology. Well, to be fair, the NRO found it when one of the Mayan aircraft crashed. But now they've had a taste of what that technology can do, the NRO wants more.

And then there's this guy called Simon Madison. Or Martineau – who knows what his real name is. I thought he worked with the NRO but they say he doesn't. Do I believe them? I dunno. Madison is the one who killed my sister. And maybe Dad, too.

Yes – I know. You think I'm making this up. But how could I? It's completely mad!

This blog starts the day you leave for your retreat at Worth Abbey. I said I was going to stay with Emmy, remember?

Well, I might, but I haven't quite got around to asking her. And anyway, I have something important to do.

I've messed up, see. Made a big mistake which allowed a certain document – part of the Ix Codex – to fall into Simon Madison's hands.

I don't know who Madison works for. I do know that he doesn't work alone. He's had an accomplice for months. You know her as "Ollie".

Who knows what her real name is.

You know how everyone comments on how grown-up she looks for a sixteen-year-old? Camila reckoned that she was at least twenty. I'd guess Camila is probably right.

Luckily, I haven't told Ollie everything. I didn't tell her about my secret blog. I didn't tell her what really happened in Mexico. What she already knows has already got me into trouble. Not just me, but the Mayans of Ek Naab.

What it comes down to is this: I let those pages of the Ix Codex fall into enemy hands, so it's down to me to get them back.

I'm going to do that. I'm the only one who can. Ollie doesn't know that I know. She won't suspect. The hunter will become the hunted.

I know it's dangerous – I'm not a complete idiot. Which is why you're reading this – the only record of this Web address is on the letter I left for you. I'll keep blogging here when I can. Right until the last minute, I promise.

Mum, I really hope you never read this.

It's the last day of term, so we finish school at midday. I
pick a random school computer on which to post the "Dear
Mum" entry to my new ultra-secret blog. I know it's going
against what I promised to Montoyo.

But this is for my mum. I mean, there's a line even I
won't cross. She deserves to know the truth about what's
happened to me, if anything goes wrong.

I write the Only To Be Opened If Something Bad Happens
letter to my mum and tuck it away at the back of my locker.
I walk to the bus stop. My plan is almost ready to hatch.
I've written the messages to Mum; all that's left is to say
goodbye. And to make one very difficult phone call to Ek
Naab.

When I arrive home, Mum's already packed for her retreat;
her coat is on and she's standing by her case, ready to go.

"You're sure you won't come?"

"Thanks, but no."

Mum looks sad, yet resigned. "I spoke to Tyler's mother. Everything's fine. She's expecting you for supper tonight."

I pull a disappointed look. "Oh . . . sorry, I should have said. Tyler and I aren't getting on too well. That's why I was kind of hoping to stay with Emmy. . ."

"Honestly, Josh." Mum makes an irritated clucking sound. "I haven't time to change things. Really not sure about you staying with a girl. . ."

"Couldn't you please just tell Tyler's mum for me?"

She pauses. "What about Emmy's mum?"

"I'll sort that."

I'm not sure whether Mum is going to agree, and I'm starting to get pretty worried. I can't just scooch off to Ek Naab if mothers all over Oxford are waiting for me with soup. Luckily, Mum seems in too much of a hurry to argue.

"OK, fine," she says reluctantly. "I'll take my mobile, but it's better if you don't call unless it's very urgent."

"OK."

"And send me a text first. That way I can arrange to take your call where I won't disturb anyone else."

"Will do."

"I'll be back for Christmas Eve. And we'll go to that hotel you like."

I manage a weak smile. "Great!"

With a last regretful look, Mum hugs me tightly, whispering, "I love you, Josh" into my ear. She marks a cross on my forehead and kisses me. For a couple of seconds I feel a gaping hole open up somewhere deep inside me, and it fills with fear and guilt. I hug her back, trying to ignore it.

"You won't do anything daft?"

I can't speak, so just shake my head and swallow. I watch her get into her car and drive away.

And then I'm alone.

I go upstairs, take a few deep breaths; then on my Ek Naab phone, I call Montoyo.

"Josh! It's great to hear from you!"

Montoyo's voice sounds warm and confident. He tells me that the transcription and translation of the Ix Codex is all finished. Blanco Vigores has worked solidly for months. "He's been looking very old lately," Montoyo admits. "And he seems lonely, like never before. Can't remember seeing so much of him."

"I have a bit of a confession to make," I begin. Then I explain about discovering that Dad might have been in Saffron Walden on 16 June, and about our escapade to the archaeologist's house the other night. When I come to the part where Simon Madison saw us, I sense Montoyo growing wary. When I admit that the pages of the Ix Codex were taken from my bedroom (I don't mention the kissing), there's a long silence that crackles with tension.

Finally, in a dry whisper, he says, "You're telling me that you let Madison get his hands on pages from the Ix Codex?"

I can't help cringing. "I tried to stop it. . ."

His voice sounds hollow with dismay. "Josh – how do you think he came to be at the Thompson house the same night as you? He must be having you observed. He could only know about it because of you."

Miserably, I tell Montoyo my theory about Ollie. He doesn't seem all that surprised. Instead, he breathes a long sigh.

"*Dios mio*. I was afraid of something like this."

"You knew someone was watching me?"

Montoyo practically growls. "Of course not, Josh! What I mean is this: it was perhaps inevitable that you'd try to get involved on your own account. As I suggested, we would have been wise to keep you in Ek Naab. The plans for the 2012 problem are well under way. This is the safest place for you. With what you know, you should not be in the outside world, meddling."

"I wasn't 'meddling'. I was trying to find out what happened to my dad!"

Montoyo lets rip with an impatient yell. "We don't know what happened to him! It's possible we never will! And look what you've done in the process!"

Now I'm angry. After all I did to help them, Montoyo has done nothing to help me find the one truth I really care about.

"I'm going to send someone to pick you up," he snaps. "Where is a good place?"

"I'm not going to live in Ek Naab."

"Josh, listen to me. Do you realize what's in those first three pages? Enough information for Madison's group to control part of the 2012 technology."

My heart sinks. It's true, then . . . Madison's stolen artefact is one of the things written about in the Ix Codex.

"They *have* the Adaptor," Montoyo continues, exasperated. "They can *make* the Key."

"The Adaptor is what he stole from that guy in Lebanon?"

Montoyo sighs. "We think so. We were negotiating with a private collector – Abdul-Quddus. He bought it from the Baghdad National Museum after the start of the Iraq War. But as you'll know from that news story, Madison took it."

"Damn. . ." I say. "That is *not* ideal."

"Not ideal?" Montoyo repeats, annoyed again. "Of course it's not! Listen, Josh. I'm looking at a map of Oxford. There's a big meadow near your home. Port Meadow. A river runs through it. Be by the river at four tomorrow morning. OK?"

I hesitate. "Where on the river?"

"Don't worry. When we get close enough, we can locate the phone. Just make sure it's on you . . . and switched on!"

"I'm not saying I'll be there. Let me think about it."

"*Hijo que te pasa* . . . what's wrong with you? I'm giving you an order! You *will* be there."

BLOG ENTRY: PLAN A

△⩛Λɱ3⪍⪎Ոⴴⵀ

So, Mum. I'm going to have one last go at sorting things out. I've made a right mess of everything, but it's not too late to fix it.

I'm going to Ollie's. All lovey-dovey-like. I'll work out a way to distract her, then I'll find the pages they stole from me and destroy them.

I know it's a risk. Ollie may have spied on me, betrayed me. But would she actually harm me? Somehow, I can't imagine that.

By the way, two more of those postcards arrived this morning. I picked them up on my way to school. One was addressed to you, one to me.

The one to you was a photo of some ruins at Ocosingo. The message was: WHEN.FLYING.

Mine was another photo of Tikal. You've had one from Tikal, haven't you? My message was: KINGDOM'S.LOSS.

Both posted in Veracruz. Again.

If I only had time to sit down and really think about those postcards, I bet I could figure it out.

But there's no time for that. It's just a matter of time before Ollie works out that I'm on to her. I need to strike while the iron is hot. . .

"Ollie" lives in a street off the Woodstock Road. I've only been there once before, when her father helped us buy the flights to Mexico. I want to catch her off guard, so I don't call first.

I change into a fresh pair of black jeans, an ironed charcoal-grey shirt with black stripes over a vest, and proper shoes, not trainers. I pack my two mobile phones into my front pockets, put twenty quid in the back jeans pocket. I fix my hair with a bit of gel, even splash on a bit of my Dad's aftershave.

When I arrive, however, the house is dark. There's no one home. I check my watch – it's just gone six. Maybe they've gone out to eat?

I'm standing there wondering when to come back when it hits me that this is a perfect opportunity. So long as I'm up to another bit of housebreaking.

This is the type of neighbourhood to have burglar alarms, so there's a good chance I'll set something off. On the other hand, I think of the number of times I've heard alarms going off, no sign of the police, people nearby going about their business as though nothing unusual was happening. No one cares enough to do anything apart from calling the police. Who might get here after an hour or so.

I'll have enough time to do what's needed.

I make sure I'm not being watched, then sneak around to the back garden. Motion-sensitive lights flicker alive, lighting the back garden as if for a party. The house backs on to a golf course, so there aren't even any overlooking neighbours to worry about. I try the downstairs windows – all closed. It's the same with the back door.

Nothing for it but breaking and entering.

I find a big, flat stone, wrap my sleeve around my hand and smash the rock into a window, near the latch. The sound of breaking glass seems deafening, as does the high-pitched whine of the burglar alarm. I try to shut both out of my mind and climb in, making straight for Ollie's room.

It's a largish house, but only two of the four upstairs rooms are made up as bedrooms. There's a double room, which is so spotlessly tidy that it looks totally unused. A second large bedroom, also with a double bed, is obviously Ollie's. She's messy – clothes are draped all over the floor. A pristine school uniform hangs against the wardrobe. The desk is totally devoid of any school books or anything that looks like it belongs to a schoolgirl.

The other two upstairs rooms are offices. One is packed with high-tech equipment – in a quick sweep my eyes take in computers, cameras, video machines. There's more, though – electronic equipment I don't recognize. The other room is stacked with books. More books about the Maya than even my father has, but also books about linguistics and ancient writing from all over the world.

And a grey metal filing cabinet.

I open the drawers and start going through the folders. The alarm is blaring, a massive distraction, but I try to ignore it and press on. Somewhere in the second drawer, I find the familiar copied pages of the Ix Codex. I check the rest of the drawers for any sign of photocopies, and when I'm sure there aren't any, I stuff the pages into my back pocket. My heart is pounding with a mixture of elation and fear.

Then I start on the computer in the other office. It's in standby mode, and flicks back into action when I touch the spacebar. My luck is in – no password protection on the screensaver.

I run a search for all files created in the last week. Then I look thoroughly through the image files. Four of them are scans, made two days ago – the same day the pages were taken from my house. I bring them up on screen. Bingo.

I delete all four images of the codex pages and leave the room. All I need to do now is to destroy the original hand-copied pages, and that's it – mission accomplished. No need to worry that Ollie and Madison's group will be able to use any information from the Ix Codex.

In the kitchen, I turn on the gas stove and set fire to the pages, watching them crumble to ash on the stove top. I can hardly believe I've got away with this so easily. I'm all set to leave the same way as I entered when I realize what an opportunity I'm missing. Her computer is totally accessible! This is my chance – maybe my only chance – to gather information about the enemy.

I can't pass it up. Even the NRO and Montoyo seem to know almost nothing about Madison.

I go back upstairs, the alarm shrieking like a banshee – but the world outside is still oblivious, as I predicted. Back on the computer, I go to her email.

The first thing I notice are emails from "Simon". I read a couple – they're short, telling Ollie where he is (Cambridge, Connecticut, Beirut), making comments about me – obviously responding to things she's been telling him.

But all I can see is the way they're signed.

Love ya baby, S

I feel my skin burning red, whilst the pit of my stomach turns to ice.

I push myself to look further. No other emails from anyone with familiar-sounding names. I read some of the emails to and from Tyler. It's pretty standard, friendly stuff. There's lots of speculation about what happened to me in Mexico, how "messed up" I am.

And that makes me wonder if Ollie had Tyler on the go,

too. Girls don't usually send a guy that many "hi there" emails. For a brief second I wonder what he'd make of it. Would he feel as bad as me? I could spend hours just on their emails, but I press on.

I look through her folders. No obviously suspicious names. I search for documents opened in the last week.

I find a Word document which was in the Temporary folder. It looks as though it was received as an email attachment.

It's a list of place names. They could be towns in Germany, Italy or Switzerland – Andermatt, Wengen, Morcote, Ticino. Beside each is a sum in euros. It could be a list of holiday homes and their prices for all I can tell.

The first page is followed by a long list of names, with nationalities. I punch the "Page Down" button a few times. There are pages and pages of these names; hundreds of names, from countries in every continent.

It's the letterhead design that really catches my eye. It's a Mayan symbol, or looks like one. Not a glyph made up of syllables, but a logogram – a whole word. I don't remember seeing it before, but then I'm hardly an expert. It looks something like the eye of a storm. I'm staring at it, when I hear the front door being opened. By someone in a hurry.

I freeze momentarily, staring in dumb horror at the staircase, waiting to hear someone walk upstairs. The burglar alarm stops; the downstairs lights go on. I hear someone pace towards the kitchen. Then I hear Ollie's voice: "Who's there?" In half a second I'm out of the office and into the unused double bedroom, hiding.

There's going to be no easy way to explain my being in her house, alone, window smashed and lights out. My only hope is to stay out of sight until she assumes I've already left, and then go. I glance around the room, hunting for a hiding place. I climb into a wardrobe, amongst a rack of suits. I breathe slowly, stay perfectly still.

Inside the wardrobe, I can't hear so well. I don't hear Ollie's movements until the bedroom door opens. She can't be taking more than a quick look around, because she closes the door a second later.

Time passes. I wait. In the calm of this moment, it sinks in; what seemed like a paranoid nightmare has come true.

It really was Ollie. But at least Tyler is in the clear.

The minutes tick by. It occurs to me that I've maybe done a stupid thing. In here, I've no idea where Ollie is. She could be anywhere. I can't leave until I know she's safely tucked away in the bathroom or her bedroom. Slowly, slowly, I open the wardrobe door, praying that it won't squeak.

It doesn't.

I step out, then stumble slightly and lose my balance. I manage to land on the bed with a quiet thud. I stay rigidly still, waiting for the inevitable sound of Ollie at the door. But it doesn't come. I stand, creep over to the door, where I stand listening. Faintly, I hear the sound of Ollie's voice. She's talking on the phone downstairs, quietly. With each passing second I'm getting more desperate to get out of this house, but I can't risk going downstairs while she's there.

Another hour goes by, at least. I check my watch – 8.30 p.m.

Then the front door goes again. I hear the sound of footsteps in the downstairs hallway and then Ollie's voice saying "Hi". There's no answer from the new person. A door closes and I hear the TV switch on.

I bite my lip, wondering what to do. I could risk leaving now, but they might suddenly leave the room. Or I could stay in this room until they go to bed. But that could be hours away. I still need to go home and pack a bag for Ek Naab.

I decide to risk it. I pry the door open, then tread down the carpeted staircase, keeping my step on the less creaky edges. I reach the front door, try to turn the handle.

Adrenaline spikes inside me and I gasp. The front door is locked from the inside. I turn around, expecting to see the living-room door open.

It doesn't. Cautiously, I pace across the hallway and into the kitchen, towards the back door. I reach it, almost leaping on to the handle.

It's also locked. A wave of absolute dread floods me. And just as I knew it would, the living-room door opens. Ollie saunters towards me, her expression somewhere between smug and disappointed.

"You didn't expect us to let you just leave?"

We stand facing each other, me frozen with horror, Ollie seemingly calm.

"Look at you, all dressed up," she remarks, casting her eye up and down. "What did you think you were coming round for, hey?"

I don't answer; instead I'm looking for a way past her. She's blocking the door, but I could take her down with a capoeira move. From there I'd have to make it to the broken window. I make ready to spring into action, when Madison appears behind Ollie. He pushes his way past her, stares at me for a second, his jaw clenched tightly, then throws a punch straight at my face. I drop out of the way and launch a spinning kick, the *armada*, aiming for his face. I feel my heel connect with his head and hear a yell of anger. But when I land, I stop short.

Ollie is aiming a pistol right at my heart.

My eyes go straight to hers. I can't help but look appalled.

"Ollie . . . I thought you were my friend. . ."

For just a second I catch the tiniest flash of regret. But as quick as she shows the emotion, she represses it.

"Chill out, Josh. And . . . the dance-fighting isn't going to get you out of this."

From behind, I feel a violent kick land hard against my ribs. The air rushes straight out of my lungs. I collapse to the floor. My arms sweep a container of cutlery to the floor as I crash. Knives and forks scatter. I try to grab one with my right hand, but Madison stamps on it, forcing a scream from me. Lying on the floor, I gasp uselessly, winded, trying to get my breathing going again.

This time Madison speaks. "Get up."

It begins to dawn on me, just how bad my predicament is. I stand up slowly, sucking in air. Still holding the gun, Ollie pats my pockets, removes both phones. She passes them to Madison. He switches off my UK mobile phone and places it on the stove top, amongst the ashes of the pages from Thompson's house. He doesn't take his eyes off me until he opens the Ek Naab phone.

"Who else knows about Ek Naab?" he asks, in a matter-of-fact way.

I say nothing. Madison smashes the phone down against the sideboard, snaps it in two, then proceeds to bring his heel down on the two halves, until it's reduced to fragments of metal and plastic, the internal chips exposed.

"This time, Josh, they won't find you," says Madison, with malice. "Now. Where's the new entrance to the city?"

I say nothing.

He shouts right into my face, "Where's the Ix Codex?"

That one, I answer. "It's in Ek Naab."

The answer earns me another hard kick, this time to my right shin. I double over, groaning.

"I know that, jerk. You think we don't know all about your little trip? *Where* in Ek Naab?"

Another blow, this time to my ribs, which by now feel as though they're on fire from the inside.

"You have any idea what you've cost me?"

Then Ollie's voice says calmly, "That's enough for now, Simon. Save it."

My mind is working overtime. I don't know exactly what they've got planned, but questions and more of Madison's kicks seem pretty high on the menu. Without weapons, I've no chance against the two of them.

I make a sudden lunge for Ollie's gun. She yanks the pistol out of the way, but fires it anyway. The sound is deafening, and chunks of ceiling plaster crash down over us. Madison sweeps my legs from under me and I land on my stomach, sprawled over the threshold between the kitchen and the hall.

The gunshot seems to have stunned them too. Madison recovers first. "Baby, you wanna give me the gun?"

"I'm fine," she snaps. "It's just . . . I forgot how loud these things are." Then she turns the gun on to me. "Get up. Hands above your head."

I do as she asks. Madison reaches into a kitchen drawer, grabs a fat roll of brown parcel tape. He twists my arms behind my back, wraps tape tightly around my wrists, over my shirt. He takes the gun from Ollie, turns me roughly around, opens a door that I'd assumed led to a pantry.

115

But it doesn't. This is serious. Behind the door are stone steps which lead to a dark cellar, smelling of damp. No one outside would hear anything from down there. They could kill me and no one would ever know.

The cellar is empty, except for a small side table against one wall. There is only a tiny window, right up against the ceiling, no more than two feet wide. Madison pulls a cord, turning on a single, uncovered dim light bulb. He pushes the nose of the pistol against my cheek, softly.

"On your knees."

I hesitate, then kneel on the concrete floor. He tapes my ankles together. I sit back on my haunches. Madison clicks his tongue.

"Not like that. Kneel up. Straight."

It's not easy to get up without my hands for leverage. I do it, slowly.

"Josh," he murmurs. "Look at me."

I stare at him in what I hope is defiance, but for all I know my face shows every bit of the terror I'm starting to feel.

"One thing I do know about torture . . . is you gotta give a little sample. Now maybe you and me, being old friends, can miss that bit out. So first we'll talk a little. If I like your answers, maybe I'll stop there. But if I don't like your answers, Josh . . . I may need to persuade you."

Madison places the gun slowly on the side table. His eyes turn cold, deadly, purposeful. I shut my eyes, steeling myself for the first blow, when I hear Ollie's voice.

"Let me try first. We should give reason a chance."

Madison stares at her. "He's a liar!"

"People lie under torture," she remarks.

"Soldiers lie . . . a kid like him isn't going to lie to me, not after I've broken a few of his bones."

What Madison is saying is so unimaginably horrible that I can't take it in. I blink, dazed.

Ollie says quietly, "Josh. Why do you think this is happening?"

My voice cracks slightly when I reply. "You want the codex . . . you want to get into Ek Naab? I don't know. . ."

"Well, let's try asking about you. Why are you involved with all this?"

I stare into her eyes. "The end of the Mayan Long Count . . . the galactic superwave. . . I don't want the world as we know it to end in 2012. Do you?"

Ollie sighs, as though this were an old, tired argument. "Hasn't it occurred to you that saving people is the last thing we should be thinking of? What the world needs is fewer humans using up resources. Fewer humans – just those who make sensible use of what the planet has to offer. Fewer humans so that other species on the planet can actually live instead of being driven to extinction."

I'm stunned. "So . . . you want to just let millions of people die. . .?"

She doesn't seem to have heard me and continues, "We've made a mess of life on Earth. Climate change, wars, religious fundamentalism. One way or another, civilization is doomed. Why wait for it to happen painfully over the next century? I say we let it finish now, while the planet still has a chance to recover. Our civilization doesn't need to be preserved – it needs to be *recreated*. By the right people." Ollie throws me a meaningful look. "That could include you, Josh."

I find my voice. "Me? Why?"

"You really don't know? That Bakab gene is just the tip of the iceberg. Have you any idea what you're capable of, if only we could unlock your potential?"

"What Bakab gene?"

"Don't play the idiot. The one that gives you immunity to the Erinsi bio-defence."

"*Erinsi?*" I scrub my memory for the reference. I've heard it before. But right now I can't remember where.

"Josh, you're forgetting how well I know you. Yes, the Erinsi – as in Books of Erinsi Inscriptions. The ancient people who actually wrote the writings in your precious Ix Codex –

the Erinsi, the ones who actually invented all that clever technology they're so proud of in Ek Naab."

"Itzamna wrote the Ix Codex. . ." I say, stalling.

"He copied them," snaps Ollie. "*As well you know.* Maybe *you* should stop underestimating *me.* I know that by now you've decoded the pages from the codex. You would never burn it to a crisp if you hadn't. We're not stupid either; we've decoded it too. I don't know how much you know about the Erinsi, but I'm certain that you've heard of them."

"Honestly, I don't know anything. I read the name, that's all."

"Well, it's not for me to tell you things that even your own people won't let you know."

I say nothing, thinking angrily of Montoyo.

"OK, here's what we're going to do. Simon and I will leave you down here for ten minutes, give you a good chance to think through your options. Then I'll come down, and Josh, you'd better start talking and fast. And I better like what I hear, or Simon is going to use his own methods."

I say quickly, "If I do talk, what then?"

A hollow silence descends. After a few uncomfortable seconds, Ollie says, "It's not my decision. It was your choice to come here. We were happy just to keep you under observation. Now, to be frank, I don't know."

My head swims just thinking of the possibilities. I'm almost overwhelmed.

"You've got five minutes to decide," says Madison, picking up the gun, "before we come back in here and get things moving."

"She said ten!"

Madison puts his foot against my chest and shoves me backwards. I manage to rock sideways, dampening the fall with my left shoulder.

"Ollie's too nice. Me, I prefer to get things done fast."

Shivering, my cheek clammy against the freezing cold floor, I watch them leave.

The second the door is shut, I twist my wrists, rub them together to get some give in the impossibly tight tape. After a minute I have just enough slack to grab the edge of my left sleeve between my finger and thumb. I tug hard, pulling at the cuff, working my hand back up into the sleeve. I throw my arm backwards, almost dislocate my shoulder as I try to push my left elbow through the shirt armhole. I have to grit my teeth to stop myself gasping with pain and frustration as I squirm around on the grime-encrusted floor.

But eventually, I do it. I pull my left arm round and rip the front of my shirt open. In another second I'm out of the shirt and the tape. And my hands are free.

I set to work on the tape around my legs. It's not easy – no time to find the edge and gently peel the tape; I'm way too panicked for that. I yank the tape with both hands and jimmy my legs to work the ankles apart until I can reach under the tape and pull hard enough to stretch it.

This all takes several minutes. Towards the end, I'm covered in a film of icy sweat. I've just managed to pull the last of the tape under my feet when I hear Ollie's voice at the top of the cellar stairs.

"OK, Josh, time's up."

I bolt up the stairs and throw myself at the door as hard as I can, hearing a scream as it connects with Ollie on the other side. I practically explode into the kitchen, almost trip over Ollie on the floor, the gun still clutched in her hand. Behind her Madison stands, momentarily paralysed.

We both stare at the gun.

I'm betting that he can reach it before me. I leap over Ollie, into the kitchen, knocking into the stove. I catch my UK mobile phone as it falls, then take another leap and land in the hallway. I duck into the back room and slam the door shut, grab a chair and jam it under the handle. No way out but the window. The broken window is closed, a curtain draped over part of it. Madison kicks the door; the chair shatters. I don't need any more incentive – I run at the window, clutching at the curtain as my body smashes through the glass. I fall for a second and land hard on the gravel path. The outside lights turn on. Shards of glass cling to the curtain. Madison shoots once as I'm climbing to my feet and running towards the back of the garden, towards the shadows. I vault over the hedge at the back, land on mossy grass at the edge of the golf course. It sounds like Madison is just metres behind.

I sprint, hearing rapid breath in the gloom as he chases me. But at least he's not shooting any more.

The places where Madison kicked me are beginning to throb painfully as bruising sets in. It's easy to ignore the pain; I concentrate on the need to survive. Madison will kill me now, if he has to – I don't doubt that. But given a choice, he'll probably capture me alive, take me back to the cellar and get down to the bone-breaking he promised.

And that thought just drives me to run harder – because I'm never going back in there. I increase my lead on Madison.

I cross the golf course, come to some railway tracks. I vault over them and sprint into a thicket. A partial moon hangs very low in a sky thick under high, orange-tinted clouds. Between the reflected city lights and the moon, there's enough light to navigate between the trees. Seconds later, I reach the canal. It's easy enough to cross, but I'd risk being an easy target with Madison so close behind. Instead I turn right and run across the waterlogged grounds of community allotments.

Now I recognize my surroundings – I'm on the edge of Wolvercote Village, near Port Meadow. I keep going. Somewhere ahead, I remember, there's a bridge, then a railway crossing.

I keep up the pressure, running hard until I come to the bridge. The soggy ground slows me down; the proper shoes don't help either. I can still hear Madison, now about thirty metres behind.

From the railway crossing, I pelt along the main path, splashing through puddles, crossing on to a meadow trail as I approach some houses near the road. I drag my thoughts away from my aching ribs and muscles, trying to think of a plan.

If I can find somewhere to hide, I can stay here until someone arrives from Ek Naab at four in the morning.

Although, in just a vest and soaked with sweat and possibly blood, I wonder how long I'll last in the open. . .

I desperately need to reach shelter. There's a pub in Godstow, on the river. I could probably reach it in a minute or two. I keep going, running past the car park, and reach the River Isis. I remember that there's a boathouse close by on the other side of the river, which is only a few metres wide and shallow at this point. By the time I jump into the water, the open run has helped Madison gain on me. He's now only twenty metres or so behind.

Nothing could prepare me for the icy shock of the water. It's like another blow to my chest. It takes only a few seconds to swim across. Already, I'm shaking. As I climb out on to a wooden jetty, Madison hits the water. I grab the end of a canoe with both hands and slam it into Madison as he approaches. He gasps, reeling; swears at me and falls back into the water. I turn and keep running. I can still hear him cursing in anger.

As I run through the boatyard, I realize that I can't see

any way out except via the locked buildings. The boatyard is on an outcropping where two rivers join into one. On one side is Port Meadow, where I've just come from. On the other is the village of Godstow. I reach the end of the yard, and run on to another jetty. For the first time, I'm out of Madison's line of sight.

The only way out seems to be Godstow. Which means crossing another river. It's narrow, like the first. I'm already soaked through, shivering from the wind chill. But the water will be deeper here, and freezing cold.

Dreading the cold, I slip quietly back into the water. It's horrible. I duck under the jetty and hold my breath, listening to Madison approach.

He runs into the yard and then stops.

I've lost him – so long as he doesn't figure out that I'm in the water.

I clamp my mouth shut to stop my teeth from chattering. My energy seeps away with every second.

Now that I've stopped moving and I'm up to my neck in icy water, I'm going into shock. My arms and legs begin to shake.

I have to keep going.

I take a deep breath and swim underwater. I move out from the jetty and into the river. When I come up for air, I can see trees and the nearby bank.

I drag myself out near the trees on the little island. And

then my muscles won't respond. I drop behind a tree, catch my breath, get the shakes. Downstream on the other side of the river, Madison is pacing around. There was a nearby garden with a house – maybe he thinks I've gone that way?

Then I hear him jump into the river. My heart sinks – he's worked it out. I stagger to my feet, keep moving through the trees. Metres later, I reach the other side of the island – the river again. Up ahead I see lights and hear the road.

I keep going, guided by the street lights. By the time I reach the road, I'm shattered. Madison must have bet on me hiding on the island because I hear him thrashing around in the interior. I stagger into the road. Maybe a car will pass by and stop? I must look a state – soaked from head to foot, wearing just a bloody vest on top. I make myself keep jogging, barely moving faster than a walk.

I turn around and peek through a gap in the hedge. I'm just in time to see Madison climbing out off the island, on to the road. He could catch up with me in two seconds.

I pull off the road and into the dark of the meadow. If I remember right from our compulsory family walks, there are some ruins close by – an old nunnery. If I can get behind the walls, I can hide for hours, always staying on the opposite side to Madison. The sombre silhouettes of the ruined walls stand out against the sky up ahead. I jog a little faster, cross the footpath and into the ruins. I lean against the wall, breathing deeply to recover.

I'm so weak, I seriously don't know whether I can keep going. But it's that or he catches me. I cross the grass to the opposite side of the ruins. I find what I'm looking for – a ruined chapel. There's just one entrance. Inside, I climb on to the ledge of an east window.

I keep very still, listening for Madison. After two or three minutes, I hear footsteps on the path. I duck back inside the chapel ruin, press myself tightly into the shadows. I hear someone take a running jump on to the window ledge and a head pokes through the bars on the window. I hold my breath. He almost certainly can't see me, but he hesitates. He knows I'm here – I sense it.

The only way into the chapel is the long way around, the way I came. After a minute on the ledge, he jumps down. I hear his footsteps recede, carrying on around the outer wall of the ruin.

I move to the chapel entrance, waiting.

This will be my only chance. I'm going to have to land a staggering blow first time. I doubt I'd last five seconds in a fight by now. I bounce lightly on my toes, waiting, shivering. My arms and chest are prickly with gooseflesh.

I hear Madison's breathing as he approaches. I try to visualize his hand holding the gun, to picture him walking into the chapel.

His gun will be in his right hand, about a foot in front of his body. He'll be stepping cautiously.

I don't even have to think about which move to use. This is it; time to prove myself worthy of my capoeira nickname – *Mariposa* – the butterfly twist.

I bounce into *ginga*, preparing: full concentration.

As Madison crosses the threshold, I lunge into the run-up, dip and flip myself into *mariposa* – a flying double scissor kick with a twist. As my torso whips through the air, my legs connect with his right arm, catch it between my ankles in a violent, rapid twisting movement.

Almost perfect.

Madison drops the gun, falls to his knees, yelling in agony. While he's on the ground, I aim a low kick to the back of his head. But he's too quick; he's already getting up. My kick lands in his back instead, knocks his head forward against the chapel wall. He slumps to the ground, grunting.

I struggle to hold my position, exhausted, wondering how long he'll be out of action. Probably not long – he's still moving groggily and moaning. I crawl on all fours, scrabbling in the damp grass for the gun. When I find it, I think seriously about shooting him in the leg.

But I've never used a gun. I'm pretty shaky – what if my aim wobbles and I kill him? Holding the gun already feels horrible, scary. Madison's right there, helpless. I could kill him, maim him – if I wanted to.

Except that *I can't*. I know in that instant – it's not who I am.

Instinct tells me to get out of there, and fast. So I'm

moving again, this time carrying the gun. Back through the looming shadows of the nunnery, across the footpath, deeper into Port Meadow, now with the river on my left.

I'm hoping that Madison will assume I'd head back to the road and the safety of Godstow Village, or the pub. But I need to find a place to hide until Benicio arrives from Ek Naab.

If he arrives from Ek Naab. With my Ek Naab phone lying in pieces back at Ollie's place, he can't trace me. Port Meadow is big; the river is long.

I stagger past a river lock. The warm lights of a brick cottage beckon. I find an old woodshed near the cottage. It's about the same height as me. There's a door on a latch, and I crawl inside. There are some rotting off-cuts from old carpet piled over the wood. I pull the chunks of carpet over me. They smell of mould, but they're mostly dry. I hold the gun between my knees, keep it pointed at the door.

I'm freezing cold, exhausted, terrified – but relieved. I can't risk letting anyone know I'm here. Daren't go home, daren't be seen. What if I'm handed in to the police and they call Mum?

Without my Ek Naab phone, my best bet is to stay near the river, in Port Meadow, until four in the morning. And hope Benicio has a way to find me.

The fight with Madison has drained all my strength. I have to make myself stay awake for the next few hours.

But I keep drifting in and out of consciousness. I'm shaking violently, on and off. Even my thoughts slow down. It's as though getting into the shed was the last thing my brain could force my body to do.

And now everything . . . everything is shutting down.

At some stage I become aware of a familiar yet eerily
displaced sound. . . It takes me a few minutes to work out
that it's the sound of a Muwan landing. I blink, push open
the door, lurch away from the woodshed. Beyond the house,
the meadow is thick with early-morning mist. Dawn is still
hours away. I can still hear the Muwan. But inside that mist, I
can't see anything.

I walk unsteadily to the riverbank, still wrapped in pieces
of carpet, holding the gun. Visibility is no better than ten
metres. I shuffle along the bank for several minutes.

A hand grabs my shoulder, spins me around.

"It's me, Benicio. What happened – where's your cell
phone?"

I don't answer, trembling with cold.

Benicio's eyes zero in on the gun in my hand. Alarmed, he
wrests it from my numbed fingers. "*No manches!* When it's a
real gun, don't even pretend! Where'd this come from?"

I still can't talk. Benicio looks carefully at the gun before he pockets it.

"I had to use the infrared scanner to find you. You're freezing! Hardly even a blip."

Benicio leads me towards the Muwan. He switches the lights on by remote as we approach it somewhere in the middle of the meadow. Then Benicio pushes me up the Muwan's ladder. I drop heavily into the passenger seat. My hands are too numb to get into the seat properly. In the interior lights of the Muwan, Benicio removes the rotten carpet and gets his first proper look at me. He inhales sharply. "Man . . . you're a mess."

I can't reply. My cracked lips move, but I can't make a sound. Benicio disappears briefly, reappears with blankets and a bottle of water. He throws the blankets around me and tucks me into one of the back seats. I begin to shake again. He tips water into my mouth and I drink the whole bottle, slowly. Then he follows up with another bottle. The contents taste sharp, rough, burning. I spit it out.

Benicio chuckles. "Take it easy, buddy. Is just tequila. Tequila! Drink. You need to get warm inside."

I take another mouthful and swallow. He's right. I don't much like the taste, but the heat goes straight into my chest. It's like a warm glow spreading through me – something I thought I'd never feel again.

Benicio takes off as soon as I'm safely in the Muwan.

The craft flies straight up into the sky for almost twenty seconds, then moves forward smoothly. Benicio must have hit autopilot because he twists around in the forward seat, looking at me.

"Man, you're beat up pretty bad," he says.

I nod, once.

"You think you can make it back to Ek Naab? I'm pretty sure there's blood on your shirt. And you're freezing, absolutely freezing."

I can barely answer without almost biting off my tongue.

Benicio sounds doubtful. "I don't know, Josh. It's gonna be around two hours. Maybe I should take you to a hospital."

I shake my head. "Hospital . . . will call Mum," I manage.

"Yeah, we should call her."

"No! No . . . can't."

"Ah . . . really . . . I don't know."

Benicio turns away and starts talking quietly into his headset, speaking in Yucatec. After a while, he says to me, "I'm going to land, take your pulse, blood pressure, temperature, and then we'll see. You have hypothermia, Josh. You can die from this."

We land ten minutes later, in Ireland. When Benicio tells me this, all I manage to mumble is, "I've never been to Ireland."

He takes all his readings, but I already know what the answer is going to be. I can feel myself warming up from the inside out and from the outside in.

Finally, he gives me a grin. "You're OK. I think!"

I breathe a long sigh of relief.

"You can tell me all about how this happened to you when we get home. But for now, you should sleep."

"Can't. . ." I say. "Tyler . . . danger."

"Your friend is in danger?"

I nod. I've been thinking through what Ollie will do next, and I've a nightmarish feeling that she and Madison will bring Tyler in.

What have they got to lose now? She's blown her cover with me. Tyler is their last chance to bargain.

"Have to warn him," I say.

My phone is soaked, so Benicio takes out his own phone. I dial Tyler's mobile number and wait.

"Who's this?" he answers, sounding sleepy and annoyed.

"It's me, Josh." I'm shocked at how much effort it takes to talk, even now. My lips are slow; my tongue feels thick.

"Josh! You know what time it is?"

"There's danger. Ollie – she's bad news. One of *them*. Stay away. Get out of Oxford."

"What. . .?"

"Tyler, I'm serious. Get up. Get out. You could be next."

"You OK? You sound awful."

"I will be OK. Can't talk much now. Keep your mobile on. Don't let Ollie know you know. Leave tomorrow. Promise me!"

"OK, OK! I'll do it. You gonna tell me why?"

"I will," I sigh. "But not now. Tired. Hurting."

"Where are you?"

"Safe."

"Who's with you?"

"A friend."

"You sure?"

"Yeah."

"OK. That's good."

"Tyler . . . one more thing. Listen, OK? Go to my house, soon as you can. Key is with neighbour, Jackie. Get postcards on my desk. There are six . . . keep them safe. Jackie can't let Ollie in. For *any* reason. Got that?"

I make him repeat the instructions and say we'll talk again tomorrow.

Benicio takes off again. The Muwan floats soundlessly through the sky. Flying west, we're headed away from the rising sun, backwards in time to the depths of night. Through the cockpit dome I can see stars gleaming in a velvety sky. The moon has set, but I can see a faint halo of its glow beyond the horizon. I have the strangest feeling of being wafted out to space, like a leaf caught in a pocket of warm air.

I must be dreaming, because just when I think I'm on the edge of sleep, I hear Stan Getz playing his sax over a chorus of violins. It's a slow tune with a deep, melancholy vibe.

Well, at least it isn't the "Blue in Green" dream again.

BLOG ENTRY: MOONLIGHT IN VERMONT

ΔӍХҼӠӍҼΛӍӠ

Remember that Stan Getz tune? I was listening to it last night, flying over the Atlantic. Dad left his iPod in the Mayan city when he was there. (My second cousin Benicio dropped that piece of information on me today.) Dad was expecting to go back to Ek Naab. He disappeared while making what he thought was a quick trip to look for the Ix Codex. Dad's iPod was still in the room where he slept in Ek Naab. Waiting.

I don't know why, but little things make me saddest of all.

I've got the iPod back now, just the way Dad left it. I'm going to keep it with me and I'm not going to change a thing.

About Ollie: Mum, how can you tell who to trust? I wish someone would tell me. Because I don't seem to be very good at spotting people who are out to deceive me.

I managed to find the stolen documents and destroy them. From what Ollie said later, though, I think it may have been too late. I think they'd already deciphered them. Then Ollie and lover-boy Madison came back and . . . let's just say I made it out of there with my life, OK?

I was hurt, but nothing too serious. Some nasty bruises and a few cuts from broken glass. A woman called Lorena here in Ek Naab patched me up. She gave me some pills and let me sleep in a nice comfy bed, not a hammock. I slept for most of the day, woke up, ate some food.

Then I found Benicio's computer and wrote this blog entry. Gonna have to finish soon. . . I can hardly keep my eyes open.

Ek Naab is just as bizarre as I remembered. I looked out of Benicio's window and saw the plaza, the lit-up church, the five-globed street lights and everywhere, the hibiscus flowers. And then looked up – straight into the meshed ceiling of Ek Naab.

I didn't dream it. So weird.

17

When I'm done writing the blog I lie down. It's only meant to be for a few minutes – the painkillers Lorena gave me are making me woozy. But I sleep the whole night through – my second in Ek Naab – and I don't wake until the next morning. I hear voices from the room next to the bedroom I'm in. I wander through to find Benicio with Montoyo. They're sipping coffee, talking quietly. When Montoyo sees me, he stands up, comes over to me and gives me a typical Mexican man-hug, with a slap on my back.

"Glad to have you with us again," he says. Montoyo hasn't changed his appearance at all – black shirt, black trousers and boots, grey-flecked ponytail. He's just as serious as ever. The only way I can tell he's happy to see me is because he says so.

On the table are two plates containing cinnamon buns and *molletes* – warm crusty rolls spread with refried beans, fresh white cheese and a tomato salsa. Benicio pours me a tall glass of orange juice. Benicio and Montoyo watch me eat, which can't be a pretty sight – I'm starving.

"So. Let's hear about this ill-fated excursion into the lair of the enemy," says Montoyo with a touch of sarcasm.

I tell them everything I remember, every detail, beginning with how I first met Ollie. They listen and occasionally nod. Montoyo's expression never changes. He's heard most of this before, from our last phone call. But when I come to my raid on Ollie's house, his interest picks up.

"This document you found on her computer," Montoyo says. "It's very important that you try to describe everything you remember. Even a detail could be crucial."

I remember all the town names I saw – Wengen, Andermatt, Morcote, Ticino – but none of the people's names.

"Hmmm. Switzerland. . .?" Montoyo thinks for a moment, then sighs. "It's a shame you weren't able to print this out."

"Hey, I burned the copied pages of the codex," I remind him.

"A good plan, but probably a waste of time. As you said, they'd already deciphered it."

"Yeah . . . about that. . ."

And then I ask the single question which has been troubling me since the minute I cracked the code of the Ix Codex.

"Why is the Ix Codex written in English?"

Montoyo and Benicio stare at me. Benicio's eyes become round and shiny. Montoyo sighs and turns to Benicio, who stands up.

"It's OK, I know, I know. I'm going," Benicio says and leaves the room. I just about hear him sigh as he goes out through the front door.

Montoyo turns a stern eye on me. "You don't talk about the codex to anyone outside the Executive. Never!"

"All right!" I say. "I'm sorry!"

"Benicio, as you've realized by now, did not know what you have just told us. For the sake of most of the citizens of Ek Naab, the Books of Itzamna are written in code – that's all they know."

"All right," I say. "But Benicio's OK, isn't he? I mean, we can tell *him*."

Montoyo pauses for a second. "Benicio is OK, yes, but the policy should not be changed."

I'm starting to feel defensive. "You could have warned me."

He nods. "Accepted. But from now on, you don't speak of the codex to anyone outside of the Executive, OK?"

We watch each other for a second. He's deadly earnest.

I say, "OK."

"I don't have a good answer to your question," he says. "It has been the subject of speculation for hundreds of years – the reason that we didn't decipher the codices for so long – but no citizen of Ek Naab knew English. And then in 1842, we had a visitor, the American explorer Mr John Lloyd Stephens."

Montoyo and I exchange a long, knowing look.

"John Lloyd Stephens. . .?" I blurt.

"Yes. . ."

"Who wrote the book. . .?"

Montoyo nods, calmly. "*Incidents of Travel in Central America, Chiapas and Yucatan*. . . The one Simon Madison took from your house, yes, that one."

I can hardly believe what I'm hearing. "John Lloyd Stephens came to Ek Naab? And kept it a secret?"

"It's a long and fascinating story," Montoyo says. "Remind me to tell you one day. Being economical, it is enough to say that from him, the members of the Executive learned enough English to deduce that the codices were written in English."

"But how is that possible?" I've been thinking it over for days and it just doesn't make sense. "I mean, I don't know much about British history, but I'm pretty sure that when the codices were written, Britain was part of the Roman Empire. Did English even exist then, as a language?"

Montoyo says drily, "You know even less British history than you imagine. Roman Britain dates from after 50 BC. The Books of Itzamna were written around 350 BC."

"But did anyone speak English then?"

Montoyo sighs. "What do they teach you at school? Of course not. In 350 BC, you'd find little trace of anything you'd recognize as English."

"So the codices are fakes?"

"Fakes . . . meaning what?"

"They weren't really written in 350 BC."

"As I just told you, they *were*."

"But how? If no one spoke English at the time?"

"Well, that's the question, isn't it?"

I hesitate. "Are you saying you don't know why they're in English?"

"I'm saying that in over fifteen-hundred years, with all the resources at our disposal, we have no conclusive answer to that question."

"But you have a theory."

"A theory, of course. We have several theories."

I pause, expectant. But he says nothing.

". . .and?"

"Well, Josh, let me ask you: what do you think is the answer?"

I think about it again.

"Itzamna definitely wrote them?"

"So it is claimed."

"Who claims it?"

"Itzamna himself. He claims to have copied them from

the walls of a temple he found. Where – as you'll know from reading the beginning of the Ix Codex – they were first written by the Erinsi."

"Right," I say. "Ollie mentioned that. The Erinsi – she knows all about them. So could you tell me: who are the Erinsi?"

Montoyo gives a tiny smile. "You don't by any chance know any ancient Sumerian, do you?"

"Actually, I don't."

"I was wondering. Maybe you learned it when you weren't learning British history."

"No, I learn modern stuff, you know, that is actually useful for modern life," I say, impatient. "What's Sumerian?"

"Sumerian was an ancient language of Mesopotamia – what you now call Iraq. In old Akkadian, a dialect of Sumerian, *Erinsi* translates as "people remember" – or perhaps "people of the memory".

"It took us a while to work that out. We came to recognize that our own poor linguistic skills proved something of an impediment. Since then we've started training a group of linguists and epigraphers. There are few ancient languages we don't know here – we've even cracked Linear A."

"And that's good?"

"It's *remarkable*. No one else on earth can read Linear A."

"So the Erinsi wrote in English?"

Montoyo sighs. "Be logical, Josh. If their own name for themselves uses words from ancient Sumerian, why would they speak English?"

"So . . . the Erinsi wrote the stuff in the codices . . . and Itzamna just copied it and translated it into English?"

"We believe so. With no evidence of the original inscriptions, we can't be sure."

"The original inscriptions on the temple walls – they're gone?"

"So far as we know, destroyed by a lava flow," Montoyo says.

"Where was the temple?"

"At Izapa. It's here in Mexico, near the volcano Tacana."

I think of the thrilling flight with Benicio, when we were chased by the NRO in their Mark I Muwans. "I've been there," I say.

Montoyo bows his head and actually smiles. "I know."

"So you're saying . . . there were some ancient inscriptions in a Mayan temple . . . written in Sumerian?"

"That's pure speculation. We've yet to find the remains of this temple of inscriptions. We believe it to be buried. Believe me, we're searched."

"So what are the Erinsi? 'People of Memory'? *What* do they remember? And they're the ones with all this technology, the Muwans, the poisonous gas on the Ix Codex, the genes that protect the Bakabs?"

Montoyo smiles again. "Yes, that's right. Now you know almost as much as us."

"And Itzamna is . . . what. . .?"

"What do you think. . .?"

I can't bring myself to say it. It sounds so ridiculous.

"If he wrote in English . . . and modern English wasn't spoken until the fifteenth century . . . then?"

"Yes?"

"Then . . . he must be a time-traveller. From the future."

"You got it."

"That's your theory?"

"That's our theory."

"That's just *mad*."

Montoyo shrugs. "You never heard that saying from your Sherlock Holmes? 'When you have eliminated the impossible, whatever remains, *however improbable*, must be the truth.'"

"But time travel is impossible."

"Is it? Can you prove that?"

"No . . . but . . . wouldn't we have seen people from the future?"

"And you can prove you haven't?"

"No . . . but . . . isn't it impossible, I mean, according to the laws of physics?"

"Depends which physicist you ask."

I think about it a little more. "You actually believe this?"

Montoyo shrugs. "We have no proof. And yet, the theory would appear to explain the facts."

"You've looked for his time machine?"

"We have."

"And?"

"Nothing so far. But as you know, the Depths under Ek Naab have mysterious qualities. We've never fully explored them. Too many people have disappeared in the attempt. It's fair to say that within the members of the Executive there's a belief that somewhere, there exists a time-travel device."

"And that's why you want that thing my father took, isn't it?"

Montoyo inhales sharply. "Smart boy." I guess he thinks I've forgotten that he all but accused my dad of stealing the Bracelet of Itzamna when he was in Ek Naab. Or that we made a deal; a personal secret mission to track down any news of what became of the Bracelet. Not a mission I took very seriously, to be honest, once my mysterious leaf-storm dream began to lead me to the Ix Codex.

"The Bracelet of Itzamna . . . it's part of the time machine?"

"We think so. The Bracelet itself has no function. We've run all manner of tests on it . . . nothing. We think that the Bracelet is incomplete."

"Broken, you mean?"

Montoyo considers. "No . . . *incomplete*; just one part of a more complex machine. We assume that it fits inside another device."

"The Container?" I say, remembering the text I translated from the Ix Codex.

"Could be. We can't be sure."

"And you think Madison's group have the other artefact – the Adaptor?"

"I'm afraid so."

"Do you know what *that* does?"

"Naturally, we know exactly what it does. Abdul-Quddus sent us digital images of the Adaptor, before Madison stole it. It matches the diagram from the Ix Codex."

I stare at him. "But you're not going to tell me?"

"That rather depends."

"On what?"

"On whether you insist on going back to your life in Oxford. If so, then I can't tell you anything else."

"But . . . I don't get it . . . you told me all that stuff about the Erinsi and Itzamna."

"Actually, I told you very little. You mostly worked it out for yourself. And most importantly, we discussed theories, not facts. The Ix Codex is an instructional document. It contains facts, not theories. In the wrong hands, a fact may prove fatal."

"Any mention of time travel?"

Montoyo hesitates just long enough for me to doubt his answer. "No."

"Do any of the other codices mention time travel?"

"We need to get back to this document you saw in Ollie's house, Josh. That interests me very much."

"Why?" (I don't miss the fact that he's sidestepped my last question.)

"It may be that you saw a membership list. For the organization that employs Madison and Ollie. And those places may be the towns where their bases are located."

"Oh. . ."

"You're sure you can't remember anything else? Even one name?"

Then it comes to me. "I remember one thing . . . the logo. It was a Mayan glyph. Looked something like a storm. Like a twister."

Montoyo stiffens. "Can you draw it?"

"I can try."

He rises, goes to the desk, grabs a pen and removes a pad of paper from a drawer. He hands them to me. For the first time I see something new in his eyes, something which, if I didn't think he was so much in control, I'd call fear.

I draw the glyph from memory. It's not particularly good, but looking at it, Montoyo visibly pales.

"You saw this? For sure?"

"Sure as I can be. What is it?"

He takes the pad from me and just stares at the glyph, transfixed.

"The symbol of the Sect of Huracan. They worshipped Huracan, the Mayan storm god – the bringer of the Great Flood."

He looks at me.

"We thought they'd been gone for centuries. They were expelled from Ek Naab in the seventh century. . ."

"Who were they?"

Montoyo answers reluctantly. "A death cult. The most dangerous death cult ever known."

He stares at me, his eyes sunken with dread.

Nervously I say, "So . . . this is bad. . ."

"This is very, very bad. They're back – the Sect of Huracan. They engineered the collapse of Mayan civilization. If they're back . . . they're probably the only people on the planet who might really enjoy witnessing the collapse of *all* civilization."

BLOG ENTRY: STUCK WITH ME

ﬞﬞﬞﬞﬞﬞﬞﬞﬞﬞﬞﬞ

Montoyo and I talked. It was pretty heavy. Stuff I could never write down, just in case.

Afterwards he left me with Benicio while he went to meet with the

150

Executive. I managed to soak my phone in a river again, so Benicio lent me his phone to call Tyler. And when he went out for bread and milk, I borrowed his computer again to update my blog. I'm not going to try to explain or justify to them that I'm blogging for you, Mum. Whatever I say, I know Montoyo will order me to stop.

Tyler persuaded his parents to let him go stay with some cousins in London. I asked him to send you a text so that you know I'm OK – hope you got it. Montoyo's going to get me another mobile phone and have it programmed so that I can make ordinary calls too.

I don't know what's going to happen. I think they might pile on the pressure to move to Ek Naab. That would mean you also.

To be honest, I can't see us fitting in here. It's odd. I'd miss Oxford too. A lot.

This latest thing has Montoyo pretty anxious. The people we're up against could be much more dangerous than they'd thought.

I didn't understand what Ollie said about wanting to let as many people as possible die after 2012. I couldn't see what's in it for anyone.

Unless, of course, you've actually found a way to benefit from the collapse of civilization.

What if they have? What if they've done it before?

A little while later there's a knock on the door. When I open it, Montoyo is standing there. For a few seconds, he actually looks quite awkward, like he can't quite get the words out.

"Blanco Vigores wants to meet with you," he says. "He's waiting."

"In the Garden?"

"No," he replies curtly. "Not the Garden. In the church. In Our Lady of the Hibiscus."

Montoyo escorts me there. Outside, bright sunlight streams through the meshed ceiling of Ek Naab. We meander through the narrow alleyways and across the water channels. I'd forgotten how claustrophobic the city feels. The streets I could handle – it's the meshed ceiling you see when you look up that freaks me out a bit.

When we reach the church, I see Vigores sitting on a bench in the tiny plaza outside. He's alone. The heavy wooden church door is shut.

Montoyo doesn't take me all the way to Vigores, but just nods at him.

"There he is. Just as you remember him, no doubt."

I stare at Vigores. He's wearing a cream-coloured linen suit again, not Ek Naab clothes. No hat this time. "Yeah," I say. "Pretty much the same."

"Benicio will pick you up in a little while," Montoyo says. He seems reluctant to leave, throws a final, suspicious glance at Vigores. Then he turns to me one last time. "I hope you remember our deal, Josh. If Vigores says one single word about the Bracelet of Itzamna that your father took, you tell me about it."

I nod. "Sure thing," and then add hesitantly, "but why would he? He didn't last time. Didn't mention it once."

Montoyo sets his mouth, hard. "He's either forgotten, doesn't know or else. . ."

But that sentence, he doesn't complete.

Then Montoyo leaves, and I join Vigores on the bench.

"Hello, sir," I say quietly, touching his arm.

His face suddenly beams, and he looks up. "Young Josh! No need to call me sir!"

"It's good to see you, Mr Vigores. You're looking well."

"I'm looking decrepit, with few years left to me," he says, brusquely. "A few critical years. Now, more importantly, how are you?"

I shrug, then remember that the old man can't see. "I'm OK, I guess."

"Family?"

"Mum – she's got into religion, big time. But yeah, she's OK."

"You? Girlfriends?"

I'm surprised to have Vigores spring that on me. I thought old geezers like him didn't even think of stuff like that any more.

"Uh, not right now."

"But you've been in love?"

"Not really. I'm only fourteen."

Vigores smiles sadly. "My memory can be most unreliable. However, I seem to remember that fourteen is quite old enough."

"Well, not me," I say. *Lying.* "I can't be bothered much with girls."

"That may be for the best," Vigores says in a grave voice. "And yet, not always possible."

"What do you mean?"

"Only that you can't always choose what happens, in matters of the heart."

I look at him, trying to fathom the expression in his watery blue eyes. "Sorry, Mr Vigores . . . I still don't get you."

He seems to consider my question, and then begins to talk. His storytelling voice – I recognize it right away.

"There was a young man named Kan'ek Balam. A boy, more or less, like you. Destined for life as a Bakab Muluc. Kan'ek would refuse to study; instead he used to just watch the construction of the temples. Or he would disappear into the Depths, alone, and emerge many days later, half-starved yet seemingly contented. And always clutching a handful of papers on which he'd written his poems. Meandering, lyrical poetry; words that touched the intellect as surely as the heart. Each poem was dedicated to the same person: Mariana K'awil, his betrothed. A young lady who, alas, was in love with another."

"He was 'betrothed'? How old was he?"

"He was betrothed almost from birth. As are all Bakabs, as are you. You know that the trait which protects against the curse of the codex is too precious, too rare, to allow chance to intervene. The *atanzahab* makes the match and thus the continuation of the Bakab line is ensured."

"Yeah," I say, slowly. I think of Ixchel and how she was so horrified by the idea of being fixed up with me that she took off. "To be honest, that's a bit of a bind. . ."

"Kan'ek was her intended, it's true. But from early childhood he was a strange one, an outsider. Hard to love, especially for a girl like Mariana. She was from a very practical family. Everyone thought Kan'ek was an odd one. And Mariana . . . she fell in love with someone else."

He stops, and looks hard at me. Or more accurately, at

155

a space about two centimetres left of my face. "She paid a high price for falling in love with the wrong boy, believe me."

"People here aren't allowed to fall in love?"

Vigores answers drily, "Romantic love can be dangerous. It can drive people to do . . . questionable things. And a good match doesn't require it."

"That is *harsh*, man!"

Vigores nods, sadly. There's a long pause. "It can be, yes."

"So what happened to them?"

"It happened that one day Kan'ek descended into the Depths. This time, he didn't reappear, even weeks later. Eventually a search party went out for him. They found Kan'ek deep within the labyrinth, sitting beside a phosphorescent pool. The minerals in the water glowed a faint pink; the only light Kan'ek had seen for weeks."

"I don't get it . . . how had he stayed alive?"

"No one 'got it'. He wasn't starving, not even thirsty. Nor had he written a single poem. No one had the faintest idea how he'd stayed sane – or alive, for that matter. He returned to the city quite happily, seemed pleased to be reunited with his friends and sisters. Upon his return, the difference was there for everyone to see. Well, to be more accurate, for the women to see."

"What happened to them?"

"Not to them. To Kan'ek. There was something about him that was instantly irresistible to women. The men noticed nothing. But the women – apart from his sisters – all swore he smelled different. Like gardenias on a hot summer's day. Young or old, they couldn't get enough of him. Mariana was the most affected of all. She was like a woman possessed. They had to be married within the week, despite their youth. And that other young man – the one she thought she loved – she dropped him like a stone."

I consider this. "So what became of Kan'ek and Mariana?"

"What else – they married, had children. Normality resumed. Kan'ek didn't only change his smell, he forgot about poetry, started working hard, like everyone else. Under the pressure of all that rock in the tunnels, the poems had seeped out of him, he claimed. Like apple juice pressed from the fruit. All that remained was the scent of gardenias. It continued to seep out of him for a few more years, and then that was that. He was ordinary again. No different to the rest of us."

Listening to Vigores, I recall the smell of gardenias – hot and sickly, how drowsy it makes you feel. His voice is almost hypnotic. It takes me back to the gardenia petals in the pool at the Hotel Delfin when I first met my sister, Camila. Tears well up in my eyes. I brush them away quickly, hoping that Vigores won't notice the change in my breathing.

So quietly that I can barely make it out, Vigores murmurs, "It gets easier, Josh."

I'm still wondering that he means when I notice Benicio out of the corner of my eye, hovering.

"It's all right, Benicio," Vigores murmurs. "You can take him back to Montoyo now. I just wanted to talk to the boy, before. . ."

And his voice trails off. We wait politely, but it doesn't look like he's going to say anything else.

Before what?

Benicio asks, "Do you need help getting back to your apartments, Blanco?"

"No thank you, Benicio," Vigores says, clearing his throat. "I have other plans today."

As we walk away, Benicio mutters to me, "He's the weirdest guy. But brilliant! I haven't seen him once since you were last here, you know that? He's sure taken a special interest in you. What did you talk about?"

"He told me some story about a guy called Kan'ek . . . who was lost in the Depths. . ."

Benicio frowns. "Oh yeah. Everyone knows that story. Those Depths are pretty strange. Some crazy stuff happens down there."

"So that's not the only bizarre thing?"

He rolls his eyes. "No way! Believe me, man, there is a *lot* more."

BLOG ENTRY: EK NAAB ... SO WEIRD.

⟨⋔◻⧫⬥⬧⬦⬥⋇

Did I mention yet how weird Ek Naab is? Well, it's the oddest. For a start, there's the way it looks.

Imagine you're in a room furnished by IKEA. Plain, minimalist furniture. A simple, modern kitchen. Sure, there are Mexican touches – sisal-weave bags, hammocks, colourful paintings on the walls. These are bits of flavour, though – no more.

You stick your head out of a window. You're still indoors. The apartment block across from yours is just a couple of metres from your window. You look down the alleyway and it's like being in an old medieval city. If medieval cities were built from concrete, glass and ceramic tiles. Buildings are packed tightly, teeming around narrow, winding lanes. Every now and again you come across a small plaza. There might be a little café, and at least a park bench or two. Flowers hang from baskets; trees sprout from pots which line the alleys and plazas. Then you might come to a little canal, or a fountain.

Because there's lots of water. Someone once told me that Ek Naab is the "city of a thousand wells". There's a great big cenote – like a wide, deep well – in the centre. The famous "dark water" for which Ek Naab is named.

Think Seville mixed with Venice mixed with – what's a really snazzy modern city? Like the "City" part of London that everyone goes on about with all the new skyscrapers and mad buildings. If half the buildings were inspired by Mayan temples. . . Like that.

And it's underground, did I mention? Apart from the surface bit of the city, which isn't – the "public" face of Ek Naab. That part looks like a posh jungle eco-resort. Swimming pools, cafés with thatched-roof palapas, all the fruit trees you can imagine.

The way it looks isn't the strangest part, though. It's what goes on. There's a busy, purposeful look on everyone's faces. It's a town where everyone's on a mission. And then . . . and then.

Then, without blinking, someone will tell you the strangest story. Hibiscus flowers that bloom overnight, in the dark. Mysterious underground tunnels with pools of glowing pink water. A boy who goes missing and reappears weeks later, smelling so amazing that all the girls fall for him.

I don't know what to make of it. Part of me wants to stay and find out everything about this place. And part of me is just a bit freaked out.

Because it's a world of bizarre dreams and spirits and miracles, things I don't understand. They aren't outside of me, I sense it; they're in me. I don't know if Ek Naab put them there, or where they came from.

And, Mum . . . truth is . . . I'm not sure I want this in my life. It's kind of scary.

I hear Benicio opening the door, so I finish typing quickly, press "Post" and then close the Web browser. By the time he knocks on my door, I'm stretched out on the bed.

"How's the invalid?" he asks.

Every muscle aches, every rib is throbbing, but. . .

"I'm fine."

"Let's take a tour of the city," he says. "We can go to the market, or for a swim."

I pull a face.

"You don't want to swim?"

"Not really . . . still pretty sore."

"Oh yeah, I'm sorry. That's OK. Would you like to see the Tec?"

"The 'Tec'?"

"The College of Technology. It has libraries, labs and a museum."

I try to sound enthusiastic. It's hard to get interested

161

in sightseeing when I suspect Montoyo is telling the Executive that mainly thanks to me, the scary guys out there now have a chance of ruining all the work they're doing to stop the galactic superwave of 2012. Worse still, it looks as though the Mayans of Ek Naab are about to face the rebirth of an ancient enemy – the Sect of Huracan.

"Sounds OK."

Benicio opens his phone. "I just have to get permission from Montoyo."

Montoyo won't give his permission. Benicio looks disappointed. There's no explanation, and he doesn't ask for one.

"I guess he wants to be real careful who you meet" is Benicio's cautious answer.

He doesn't say why, but it's obvious to me. Montoyo is making it clear that I'm back out of the loop. I might have the right to join the Executive when I'm sixteen, but until then, he's planning to make me toe the line, like a good little boy.

I settle for the offer of a walk around the city. The air is warm, the light muted as it filters through the lattice of the surface. Everything in Ek Naab is just as I remember. Just as calm, orderly, the trees clipped, the flowers groomed. People go about their business dressed in their linen trousers and overshirts. I notice the way people look at me, just like last time. A few of the kids even whisper and stare. Benicio smiles at everyone, says a polite hello.

And never introduces me to anyone. Montoyo's instructions?

We stop at a café and take a table on the mezzanine, overlooking the fenced underground *cenote*. Benicio buys drinks – ice-cold *agua frescas* made from dried hibiscus flowers. I sip mine and stare into the shiny black of the *cenote*. Like a perfect mirror, it reflects the overcast white of the sky, overlaid with a black criss-cross pattern: the silhouette of the artificial ceiling.

And then I chuckle. It's the first time I've felt my spirits lift for hours. "Hey, know what *Ek Naab* means in English?"

"'Dark Water'?"

"Yeah," I say, ". . . or . . . 'Black Pool'."

For some reason, this really makes me laugh.

"So?" Benicio shrugs. Guess he's never heard of sunny Blackpool or the Pleasure Beach.

I stop chuckling. "It's nothing. Look, why aren't I allowed to meet people?"

He looks uncomfortable. "I'm not supposed to say anything. There are some tensions in the city. Montoyo and the Executive need to be sure that you aren't approached."

"Tensions . . . what do you mean? Who's gonna be approaching me?"

Benicio grimaces and shrugs. He picks his next words with precision.

"There are people in Ek Naab who aren't happy with the way the Executive is running things. Who question the decision to keep what we know a secret."

"What you know . . . about 2012?"

"2012, yeah . . . what we call here the 'Baktun Problem'."

"Baktun, as in the final date of the Long Count Calendar?"

Patiently, Benicio says, "Baktun, yes, as in the twenty-second of December 2012, the date that the galactic superwave hits. The Baktun Problem is what we're calling the whole solution to that. Beginning with the contents of your codex, Josh, the Book of Ix."

I frown. "And some people aren't happy about what the Executive is doing . . . why?"

"There are a few people who think that we should be working with the top scientists in the world to solve this problem."

"What do you think?" I ask him.

"Well, I'm with Montoyo," Benicio says, facing me with a smile. "Of course! Montoyo – and the majority of the Executive – feel that unless we need help from outside, we should solve the Baktun Problem within Ek Naab. After all, that's what we have lived to do. From the beginning. That's the reason for the foundation of Ek Naab."

"The majority of the Executive . . . but not all six of them?"

He hestitates. "Not all."

I shake my head in wonder. Politics isn't something that really interests me. But I can see that if some people in Ek Naab are starting to question the whole basis of the secrecy, it could be a big problem.

"And that's not the only tension."

"What else?"

Benicio sips his drink and seems to think long and hard before he speaks again. "Maybe I shouldn't be saying this." His eyes almost glaze over as he stares into his glass, trying to hide the fact that his cheeks have gone red. "In fact," he adds with an embarrassed laugh, "this is more or less the kind of conversation that Montoyo wants to prevent. So, guess I'd better stop. . ."

"Wow," I say. "It's like a police state here!"

"These are difficult times," he admits.

"Is that why Ixchel left? Or was it just to avoid me?"

I notice that Benicio is tense too – he cracks a grin that seems almost forced. "Ixchel? Nah . . . it was pretty much the thought of having an arranged marriage to you."

I hardly know Ixchel – we only spent a couple of hours together walking through the jungle as she guided me to Becan. And I wasn't exactly at my best. In fact, I was in a state – it was just hours after Camila died. But hearing

165

Benicio say those words actually stings. Especially since I know he's her good pal. Jokes aside, that must be what she feels.

It's not nice to feel you've been judged and found wanting. But like Benicio, I force myself to smirk, like it's hilarious. "Thanks, pal. So . . . did you find her?" When I met Benicio in Oxford, I was so excited by the whole flying over Oxford thing that I forgot to ask that question. But now I remember that Benicio had been leaving to search for Ixchel, my last time in Ek Naab.

"Yeah, I did. I tracked her down to Veracruz."

Veracruz! My ears prick up. I try to sound casual.

"Which town?"

"I mean, the city of Veracruz itself."

The postcards. . . All posted in Veracruz state.

Things are starting to make sense.

Ixchel must have sent them – she's the only person I know in that state. What the heck is she playing at?

Benicio tells me that Ixchel is "working, would you believe it? All her life she's been this excellent student; now she wants to work tables for tourists in Veracruz."

"Why Veracruz? It's not exactly the ritziest part of Mexico."

"That's why," he replies. "She hates Cancun and all the Riviera Maya."

"But all that is really nice!"

"She prefers 'real Mexico'. Which is strange for a girl who never lived in 'real Mexico', but that's Ixchel."

"Great," I say with heavy sarcasm. "'Excellent student' . . . the type of girl who prefers 'real Mexico' to posh hotels and powdery beaches. And this is the girl you all want me to marry? She sounds ideal."

Benicio bursts out laughing. "Yeah, you're the ideal couple. . ."

There's something about his tone I don't like. It's as if he thinks she's too good for me. But I shrug it off. "Well, it's the twenty-first century; she can do what she likes."

"That's Ixchel all the way," Benicio says, with an emphatic nod. "She's gonna do *whatever* she likes."

Sourly, I ask, "I suppose she has a university degree already at fourteen?"

"No, she doesn't have a 'degree'. She finished high school, though. She was gonna study ancient writing."

I don't say anything else. No wonder she doesn't want anything to do with me – in educational terms, I'm years behind Ixchel.

"Would you like to go see her?"

"In Veracruz?"

"Sure, why not? You've told Montoyo everything you know and he's not so happy for you to chat to people here. Blanco Vigores had a chance to catch up with you. . . Montoyo seems kind of surprised that Vigores already knew you were here, by the way. Montoyo surprised by something – that's always nice to see. . ."

I interrupt, "Montoyo didn't set that up?"

"Nope. Blanco just turned up! Imagine that. He even *behaved* like it was all arranged with Carlos Montoyo."

"Why would it be?"

"Didn't Carlos tell you? Vigores left instructions that whenever you are in Ek Naab, he wants to know about it."

I reflect on that for a bit. "No, he didn't tell me. Wonder why not?"

"That's Carlos. Always likes to be in control." Benicio sighs contentedly. He seems to be relishing the chance to get out of Ek Naab. "Yup, I'd say you're all done in Ek Naab for now. And with a very good excuse for a little trip."

I think about the postcards. This is my chance to find out if Ixchel has been sending them . . . and if so, why.

"All right, you're on. Let's go to Veracruz."

Benicio parks the Muwan on an isolated spot on the beach a few miles north of the city. They call it the Emerald Coast of Mexico, maybe because the sea is green, not blue. The beaches at Veracruz aren't very crowded. On a clear day you can see the oil platforms in the Gulf of Mexico. Approaching Veracruz, we walk along the beach, sniffing the air, picking up a petrochemical stink from the sand.

I'm surprised when Benicio tells me that Montoyo not only gave permission for us to visit Ixchel; he thought it was a good idea.

Still trying to matchmake us, obviously. What a waste of time. Even if I was keen, Ixchel never would be. She's made that pretty clear.

In Veracruz, Benicio takes me to the central plaza, the *zocalo*. Colonnades line the square on two sides, in front of what I'm guessing is a town hall. There are tall, dense palm trees with thick, drooping fronds providing plenty of shade from the pale afternoon sun. A vendor calls: "Ices, ices, I've got mango, guanabana, coconut." On the shiny marble tiles of the square, old couples are dancing to piped music. We stop and watch for a moment. They dance slowly, with tiny yet stately movements. It's not a dance I've seen before. Benicio tells me it's called *danzon*.

At one corner, behind an arched colonnade, is the old-fashioned café where Ixchel works. Inside it's spacious, lots of old wood stained deep and dark, round wooden tables and a long wooden counter. Behind that there's some antique-looking coffee-making equipment, all polished copper and brass.

Benicio orders coffee at the bar and Ixchel brings us two glasses containing a couple of centimetres of dark-brown syrupy liquid. When she sees him she immediately grins, throws her arms around his neck and hugs him. With me, she looks suddenly frosty. Sullenly, we kiss each other on the cheek, saying hello.

In her waitress uniform, Ixchel looks older and prettier than when we met in the jungle that time. She's wearing a black miniskirt with a little white apron, a tight white blouse and flat black shoes. Her hair is longer and pinned back with a couple of chopsticks. She looks tired and flustered, but there's a bit of colour in her cheeks.

Benicio clinks his glass with a spoon. A waiter in a white jacket arrives with a huge silver pot of hot milk. He pours milk into our coffee from a height, frothing the milk as it falls. Benicio smacks his lips when he tastes the coffee. "Worth the trip just for the coffee!" Ixchel brings us club sandwiches, bottles of Orange Crush and glasses crammed with ice. She asks permission to take her afternoon break at our table.

Benicio's in a good mood, which I really don't understand. I feel miserable every time I think about Montoyo's face when he saw the symbol of the Sect of Huracan. I guess Benicio doesn't have any idea how bad it is that I let Madison's group get hold of pages of the codex.

He's obviously happy to see Ixchel, and she's happy to see him.

"You two should try to get to know each other," Benicio tells us.

I glance at Ixchel. She gives me a defiant stare.

"What do you think. . .?" I begin to ask.

"I think you're too easily influenced by Montoyo."

"I am not! And what's it to you, anyway?"

"You don't get it, do you? I've had it with the traditions of that place. Arranged marriages! As if we were some sort of animal to be bred. Think I want to have one of your little Bakab children? Guess again."

"Yeah . . . Benicio . . ." I say, "why do they care if any more Bakabs are born? 2012 is just around the corner. We've got the four Books of Itzamna, we can just take them out of their boxes and leave it at that."

Ixchel rolls her eyes. "You're so clueless!"

"Josh. . ." Benicio says carefully. "All the ancient technology is protected by a similar 'curse' – the bio-defence. Only the Bakabs can touch it and not die."

"Wear gas masks! Use gloves! There are ways around it, aren't there?"

Benicio nods. "In some cases, yes. But each bio-defence is unpredictable. In other cases, even those protections are not enough. And . . . the Bakabs have other abilities."

"Like what?"

"Well, it's not completely understood. My guess is that the answers are in the Ix Codex, but you know, I don't have the security clearance to know that, so. . ."

I think about what Ollie said: *That Bakab gene is just the tip of the iceberg. Have you any idea what you're capable of, if only we could unlock your potential?*

Is this what Ollie was talking about? Do I have other abilities that I'm not even aware of? I'd ask Benicio, but I'm pretty sure he'll just say he doesn't "have security clearance".

I turn to Ixchel, ask her straight out if she sent the postcards. She claims she didn't. Benicio seems interested.

"What's this? You never told me someone was sending you coded messages."

"I don't know who they're from. But they seem to be talking about my father's death."

Benicio suddenly gets a call on his mobile phone.

"It's the automatic defence system of the Muwan," he says after a few seconds. "They've detected someone getting nosy. I'd better go check it out."

He leaves me alone with Ixchel. She watches him go. Then a change comes over her. She leans forward, lowers her voice.

"Josh, there's something I need to tell you. About that guy in the blue Nissan."

"His name is Simon Madison," I tell her, "and he keeps turning up, trying to beat me up. Benicio didn't say?"

"You think we talk about you all the time?"

I glare at her. "Course not. But this is major!"

"Well . . . Benicio doesn't tell me everything . . . and I don't tell him everything."

"You're sneaky."

"I just want to be my own person. Not a trained monkey working for Montoyo."

I'm silent, but I'm starting to agree with her about Benicio. Why does he just do everything Montoyo says?

Ixchel polishes off her Orange Crush. "I did my last favour for Montoyo back when I rescued you, led you to Ek Naab. That includes marrying you, by the way, which *obviously* I'm never going to do."

She doesn't leave time for me to respond, and I'm actually a bit irritated at the cutting way she says that. I know what she means, but it still isn't very friendly.

"But later, I saw that blue Nissan in Becan, you know. It was in the car park from about four in the morning. I was waiting until the site opened so that I could take the bus. I watched him. He stayed in the car for about twenty minutes, then walked into the site. He came back about four hours later. He waited until the restaurant nearby opened, ate a plate of eggs, then he went back into the site with a few tourists. The second time, I followed him. Well, as usual, there were hardly any visitors to the site, and one section was completely empty, except for your blue Nissan guy. And, of course, me. When he thought no one was watching, he went into one of the ruined temples. He disappeared for *another* two hours. I almost fell asleep waiting for him to return. What was he doing in there? After he left, I followed him out and then to the Nissan. He drove away at around ten-thirty in the morning. I went back to take a closer look at that temple, but it looked ordinary. Until I noticed the ground near the back wall. It was really clean and smooth. No grass. Like it had been scraped often by a heavy rock."

I listen in amazement. "What do you think it is? A hiding place? Another secret passageway?"

Ixchel just shrugs and takes a couple of bites of Benicio's abandoned club sandwich. For a second, her eyes light up. "These are so good! The chef makes them with the most delicious bacon."

"Yeah, the bacon's amazing." Talking about bacon at a time like this?! "But what about this secret passage?"

"If there is one, then it might lead into the Depths, under the city."

"Have you told anyone this?"

She shakes her head, chewing. "Nope."

"Why not?"

"Because I don't trust anyone in Ek Naab."

"Why?"

"Something is going on. I don't know exactly what, because I'm a 'child' – that's how they see me, at least. And they don't tell me anything important. But I have eyes and ears."

"And. . .?"

"People have become secretive about who they talk to. My parents started talking quietly behind closed doors. Saying things like 'Don't tell so-and-so that such-and-such was here.'"

"Any particular names?"

"Montoyo – anyone linked to Montoyo, people are really cautious around."

"So – what – Montoyo's a bad guy now?"

Ixchel shrugs. "Benicio is a great guy. But he does whatever Montoyo asks."

"You really seem to have a problem with Montoyo . . . why?"

"He has a lot of power in Ek Naab. And when you turn

sixteen, you'll replace him on the Executive. He's going to
lose his position. That doesn't worry you?"

I shrug, wondering. "Never even thought about it."

"Maybe you should."

"What are you saying?"

"I don't know what's going on, Josh. But the atmosphere
has been weird for months. What if there's another way into
Ek Naab? What if there are spies in the city?"

"Spies, why would there be spies?"

"Josh, there are people in Ek Naab who want to sell our
secrets to the outside world."

"I thought Montoyo already did that . . . isn't that how
the city is so rich?"

"No – he sells technology that doesn't have to stay
secret. I'm talking about the secrets of the Baktun Problem.
The secrets in the Ix Codex."

It strikes me that this isn't quite the same story that Benicio
told me. He didn't mention anything about selling secrets.

"Look," Ixchel says slowly, as if I might be a bit thick. "If
there's another way into the city, then . . . secrets might be
leaving through that route."

I shake my head. "No way. Madison threatened to beat
me to a pulp unless I told him how to get into Ek Naab. He
doesn't know the way."

Ixchel seems genuinely surprised at this. "Hmm. Then
maybe it's nothing."

"It's *not* nothing. Madison's up to something. We should investigate. Then we can tell the Executive what we've found. The whole Executive – all at once."

"You're dreaming," she says. "Benicio told me you're in trouble with Montoyo. You think he's going to give you permission to investigate?"

"Hmm. Probably not. So let's not ask."

Ixchel stares at me with what looks like admiration. "You'd do that?"

"Yeah." I stand up. "You and me. Let's go, right now."

She shakes her head in disbelief. "I thought you were Montoyo's errand boy too."

"Hey, in two years I'm going to be on the Executive," I say. It's the first time I've heard respect in Ixchel's voice, so I go further, get bolder. "I don't take orders from Montoyo."

"That's tough talk, but what about me? You want me to walk off my shift – which will probably get me fired, by the way – and go all the way back to Becan with you . . . and use up all my money for the bus. . .?"

". . .and crawl into the temple and find the secret way in. . ." I say. "Yeah, all that. Come on. Please. This Madison guy, he's killed my sister; for all I know he may have been involved in the murder of my father. He beat me up, was going to kill me. . . And his *evil witch* girlfriend has been spying on me . . . pretending to be my friend. . ."

177

I almost spit that last sentence out, and Ixchel seems a bit startled. She looks at me for a long moment.

"What about Benicio?"

"Well . . . first thing he's going to do is call Montoyo and ask for permission. So that's out."

She nods. "OK. But we can't leave saying *nothing*."

"You've got your phone, haven't you?"

"I'd better turn it off." Ixchel gives a mischievous smile. "He can trace us."

We decide to leave a note.

Benicio. I want to show Josh this really interesting thing. Plus I think it would be good for us to spend some time alone. See you back here in a couple of days.

"'This really interesting thing' . . . are you joking?" I say, incredulous. "He's never going to believe that. And we should 'spend some time alone'?"

"I know," she replies, grinning. "Benicio had better keep this quiet. Because if Montoyo finds out, he's going to completely lose it."

"What Montoyo's gonna have to realize," I say as we stand up, "is that he can't have everything his own way. Not when it comes to you and me."

"OK, Josh," Ixchel says with a smile. "Now you're talking!"

She jabs my arm. It feels a lot like affection. . .

BLOG ENTRY: GRAN CAFÉ DEL PORTAL

ㄨㄖ◁ㄹつ)Ю◯◯ㄨ◲

A friend of mine called Ixchel has been working in a famous coffee shop in Veracruz. My cousin Benicio took me to visit her. When she started, they made her clean floors and wipe tables. They didn't know then that she spoke fluent English, French and Japanese. Even fancy rich Mexicans get impressed with that. You'd have thought they'd have offered her a bigger promotion. But no. They only moved her up to waitress.

Anyway . . . I'm still fine. I had to get out of Ek Naab. I thought maybe Ixchel had been sending us those postcards, the ones with the photos of Mayan cities, posted in Veracruz. I asked her right away. She said no. She'd never heard of them.

Then I thought – obviously she's telling the truth. I don't know why I didn't think of it first: how would she know your name and our address?

"Oh, I know all that," she said. "Josh Garcia, son of Eleanor and Andres."

And then she told me our address.

"You don't think I checked you out?" she told me. "You must be even dumber than you look."

Nice. They fixed me up with a girl who thinks I'm dumb.

I find an Internet café, where I persuade them to change the twenty-pound note that's stashed in my back pocket under my dad's iPod. They make me buy fifteen minutes online, so I do a quick update to the blog.

And that already seems like too much time . . . I don't even want to Ixchel to stop off at her room and change out of her waitress clothes, but she insists.

"You want to hitch-hike?" she says, more than a bit irritated as we trot through the streets of Veracruz. "No? Then, OK, I need to get my money."

Ixchel lodges in what used to be the maid's room at the top of a house. The room is completely separate and has its access on the roof. The walls are brick painted with thick, pale-pink paint, the floor a dirty marble tile. Ixchel's bed is low and narrow. Apart from that, all she has in her room is a small chest of drawers with a twelve-inch television on top. Behind me Ixchel changes as I stare at the wall, where she's taped postcards of Mexican film stars Gael Garcia Bernal and Diego Luna. It's the single personal touch, the only decoration in the room.

"Why are you living like this?" I ask, wondering. "I really don't understand."

Ixchel turns me around. She's dressed in blue jeans, sandals and a salmon-pink T-shirt and carries the little sisal-weave bag I remember from the jungle. The chopsticks have gone and she wears her hair in a high ponytail.

"Let me ask you this – you want to move to Ek Naab? Live your life there?"

"Not really, but . . ."

"You see?"

". . . but I wasn't born there. I'm not used to it."

"Ek Naab is a prison with golden bars, unless you are on the Executive or a pilot like Benicio."

"Everyone seems so happy."

"They are terrified of the real world outside. They believe someone's going to kill them or rob them the minute they step out of the place."

"And you don't?"

"I never believe things just because people tell me," she says with a little toss of her ponytail. "I like to see for myself."

We leave her room in a hurry, make straight for the bus station. She buys two tickets on the express to Villahermosa, in Tabasco. I remember my lonely bus trip last summer, and I'm relieved to think I'll have company this time.

Ixchel and I take two seats somewhere in the middle of the bus. She lets me have the window seat, "since you're the tourist here. . ."

Typical.

We decide to phone Benicio right away, whilst the bus is still in the streets of Veracruz. Ixchel tells him that she's abducting me to show me something of the "real" Mexico. When she passes her phone to me, I can hear the anxiety in his voice.

"Josh, I'm not kidding. Tell her you're coming back with me. Montoyo will kill me."

"Then don't tell him. We'll be back the day after tomorrow. Just tell him that everything's fine, that we're hanging out together."

Benicio goes silent. "If anything happens to you guys, I'm toast. You understand? I'm finished as a pilot."

Ixchel takes the phone. "Don't be ridiculous, Benicio. You're the best pilot we have. Just be calm. It'll be fine."

But Benicio doesn't seem to agree, and hangs up, cursing us both.

Ixchel giggles, embarrassed. "Gee. Now I feel really bad."

"Don't. We're only going to find out what Madison is up to. OK? When we find out, they'll thank us."

Ixchel glances at me, and seems to mull something over.

I also use her phone to call Tyler. It turns out he hasn't left Oxford after all.

"My mum drove me past Ollie's," Tyler tells me. "And her house has a 'To Let' sign. I looked through the windows – it's empty. The neighbours said she moved out yesterday. I called her on her mobile – it was turned off."

I ask him to check my house for any more of those postcards. He's already been to the house and found another two. I ask him to read out the messages.

They are:

KINGDOM'S.LOSS.
QUESTIONABLE.JUDGEMENT.

Ixchel copies this down, as well as the rest of the messages. All together, in date order, the message so far is:

WHAT.KEY.HOLDS.BLOOD.DEATH.UNDID.HARMONY.
ZOMBIE.DOWNED.WHEN.FLYING.KINGDOM'S.LOSS.
QUESTIONABLE.JUDGEMENT.

She asks, "You know what this means?"

I glumly fix my eyes on the message. "Not the faintest idea."

But the latest messages seem to tie in with my theory. *Zombie downed when flying*. Sounds like a nasty reference to my dad's corpse being in the plane. *Kingdom's loss, questionable judgement*. Could that be a reference to Ek Naab?

"Maybe you need the whole message to decipher the code," suggests Ixchel.

"That's not how deciphering works," I tell her.

"Oh, so you're the deciphering genius now, are you?"

"Hey, I worked out that the Ix Codex is written in English!" I say.

Oops.

"It's in English. . .? But how?"

"I'm having a laugh," I say. "Course it's not in English. As if!"

Ixchel says nothing more for a few seconds, instead looks at me closely. I try to look relaxed, but I can actually feel my cheeks burning. Time to change the subject.

I put the message aside and I tell Ixchel all about my adventure last summer, how I found the Ix Codex, and some of what's happened in the past few weeks. Every time I come to a bit about what I read in the pages from the Ix Codex, I have to stop.

"Gosh . . . sorry . . . I can't tell you about that. . ."

Eventually she tells me to shut up about the Ix Codex.

But of course she wants to know. And of course I want to talk about it. We can't . . . so we change the subject again.

She tells me about how she left Becan by bus the morning after she saw me. She headed out to Playa del Carmen, where she spent a few weeks waitressing in bars on the beach. From Playa she went to Merida, from Merida to Veracruz.

"I wanted to see Mexico. And not just from a beach. I want to see the whole world too, one day. Might as well start with here."

I'm full of admiration, but I can't really understand how she can stand to live that way. I think of my own comfortable life in Oxford. Not much would persuade me to abandon that.

We reach Villahermosa just in time to catch the overnight bus to Chetumal. I can't help thinking sadly of poor Saul there without Camila. I wonder if he stayed? Without her, he'd only have the avocados and their beautiful house. Still – it beats being in jail.

These thoughts turn over and over in my head. I clench my jaw, trying not to let bad memories get to me. I turn to Ixchel to see if I can get her talking again. But she's asleep, breathing quietly, leaning against the window. Outside it's pitch-black. The interior lights of the bus are switched off, the video screen blinks into action and a film begins to play.

It's one I've seen before – *Memento*. I plug in to my
dad's iPod. It's mostly classical music, jazz and prog rock.
Wondering if I'll have the dream about my dad, I select *Kind
of Blue* and try to sleep.

22

It's still dark when we arrive at Chetumal. We have to wait a few hours to catch one of the buses that take tourists to Becan, Chicanna, Xpujil and Calakmul.

At Becan, a group of six German tourists get out, as well as us. The minute we arrive, Ixchel strolls ahead of the other visitors, who move in that slow, bewildered touristy way. We quickly leave them behind near the thatched entrance hut. She takes me straight past the main plaza and to a set of buildings to the west in the central plaza, labelled on the map as Structure X.

Apart from the German guys, we have the whole site to ourselves. I turn away from Structure X for a moment and peer behind the curtain of spindly trees. There, looming above the plaza, is the enormous pyramid I climbed last summer: Structure IX. There's absolutely no sign of the secret entrance to the gateway of Ek Naab on the western wall of Structure IX. I'm still amazed that the entrance even exists.

The recently cleaned stones are a cool grey-white in the even light of morning sun. The air is still fresh, slightly misty and mercifully free of mosquitoes. The site is thick with skinny trees that shade everything but the temples.

I haven't even broken a sweat. It isn't like this in summer. My mum and dad and I used to visit Mayan ruins in August. In summer, you bake, and the mosquitoes eat you alive. Sweat pours off you, rolls down your face, stings your eyes and cracks your lips; bugs land on any part of you that isn't drenched in insect repellent.

We walk around Structure X, a broad temple with two towers and one main staircase, looking for an opening in the wall. We find a three-foot-wide opening in the middle of the eastern side. We climb inside, turn on Ixchel's torch and squirm through on hands and knees. We continue crawling straight ahead until the tunnel makes a left turn. Then quite suddenly, we emerge into a system of rooms and linking passageways, all inside the temple.

I turn to Ixchel. "Which room did Madison disappear into?"

She closes her eyes, concentrating.

I gasp. "You don't *know*?"

"Give me a minute . . . I'm visualizing it. . ."

"We came all this way and you're *guessing*?"

Ixchel snaps open her eyes. "Stop hissing at me and let me think!"

I'm silent, chewing on my lower lip. Ixchel pokes her head from room to room. She turns back to me.

"OK, I didn't exactly see which room he went into, obviously. . ."

I blurt, "Obviously?!"

"I didn't go inside at the same time as him – what are you thinking? He would have seen me. I'm trying to remember where I saw the scraped floor."

Ixchel decides that it's one of two rooms. We crawl into the first, a dank hole of a room, about eight by ten feet. There's no sign of scratching on the ground. In the second room, however, shining the torch into the corner, I immediately see what Ixchel means. Part of the floor has been worn away. The wall next to it even looks different to the others – it's much less crumbly.

We try leaning on the walls, pushing stones, pressing our fingers into any depression, but nothing happens. We're about to give up when we hear the unmistakable sound of someone else in the passageway.

We look at each other, eyes wide with astonishment. Ixchel flicks off the torch. We crawl into the adjacent room and hold our breath.

"You're just gonna have to build a better way in, Marius," drawls a woman's voice, her accent from somewhere in the American South. "Cos I sure don't see myself as an Indiana Jones."

"All in time, my dear professor," comes another voice – a man's. He has a lofty, distracted way of speaking, like he's got some better place to be. His accent sort of sounds like American trying to sound British. The next time he speaks, his voice comes from the other side of the wall we're leaning against. Ixchel and I stand as stiff as boards.

"You have no idea the favours I've had to pull in to keep this structure from being further excavated. And to keep the tourist traffic down."

The woman's laugh sounds like church bells.

"Oh, sure. I'm guessing you owe dinners to politicians in all the best parts of Mexico City."

He answers with a dry chuckle. "Indeed. . ."

"But I'm being serious now, Marius. We gotta have an entrance we can properly guard. Right now any dumb old tourist could just wander in."

"If they had the key, perhaps," the man replies drily. "Fortunately, dear lady, they do not."

"Well . . . we'll all need to suit up," says the woman, "with all that ancient Erinsi technology around – who knows what might be deadly to touch if you don't have the Bakab gene. Even the men, as a precaution."

"That makes sense. We can't be too careful."

"I've sent a team down to prepare."

We hear a sound like metal scraping heavily against rock. The couple's voices continue as they walk away from us, becoming fainter. Then we hear the rock beginning to scrape again.

I grab Ixchel's hand and whisper, "Let's go for it!"

We dash into the next room just in time to see the secret door closing. The entire back wall swings slowly. We just about have time to squeeze in before the door seals us inside.

Neither of us dares to breathe a word, but each knows what the other is thinking.

They've got their own way into Ek Naab. They've found another piece of ancient technology protected by the Bakab curse.

Have we stumbled across the Sect of Huracan? If so, then we're probably already too late. . .

The entrance in Structure X leads to a sloping tunnel. It's wide enough for two people to walk abreast, and meanders deeper and deeper underground. The first few metres of the tunnel seem to be recently cut. After that the walls look exactly like those of the limestone tunnels around Ek Naab. My guess is that the entrance is part of the same system.

We walk just far enough behind "Marius" and the woman he calls "Professor" to be able to benefit from the light of their torches. At times it's hard to believe that they don't hear us. But they don't stop yakking loudly for a second. The more I hear, the more uneasy I become.

Now I remember where I've heard the name "Martineau".

Marius Martineau – the Mayanist from the Peabody Museum in Connecticut. The guy who replied to my dad's email about the Ix Codex, telling him that he was too busy to get involved chasing what was probably a hoax.

Yeah, right.

The NRO told me that Simon Madison sometimes uses the name Martineau.

In the house in Saffron Walden, Madison talked to Thompson's niece about his father, and then *she* mentioned the Peabody. Coincidence? I doubt it.

Is Marius Martineau actually Simon Madison's father? If he is, then it looks even more certain that Martineau and this "Professor" lady are also part of the Sect.

I have my suspicions, but I don't have to wait long before the couple ahead of us confirm them.

"My son arrived last night. The boy, Josh, almost broke Simon's wrist. As it is, he's got a nasty sprain."

The woman sighs. "We're going to have to do something about the boy."

"But what? I've always warned Simon not to kill him. If the boy's death is traced back to me, it could be disastrous for the Sect."

"Simon probably shouldn't do it," she agrees. "For a job like that, we need a professional. Simon's never actually killed anyone intentionally."

"Well, that's partly the problem. Perhaps we should train him."

"He doesn't have the temperament, Marius. You ought to know!"

"You're right, of course," says Marius with a little sigh. "Now the girl, we *should* have trained to kill."

"No, she was right for the job she did. She's an excellent agent. I wonder how the boy broke her cover?"

They both take their time to ponder that one.

The woman says, "It's high time we started graduating some of the students at Ticino."

Ticino? Wasn't that one of the places on that document?

"They aren't ready. They've had barely half the time it takes the CIA to train an assassin."

"And they need to be a lot better than the CIA," she remarks.

"Hire someone from outside the Sect?"

"Never. We must stick to our own rules, Marius."

"Yes, my dear, you're right."

"We'll get Simon to bring the boy to us. Even if he really is there now, he won't stay in Ek Naab for ever."

"You read his blog – he has an open invitation to go back."

I close my eyes in dread. Ollie's betrayal went all the way. She must have snooped on me when I was using my computer.

They read my blog.

"What about the boy's mother?" says the woman.

"Well, it's all rather tragic. She'll lose her son as well as her husband."

"Who cares about that? The question is: do you think she knows anything? Is she a threat?"

My blood almost freezes when I hear these words, and I feel the sudden touch of Ixchel's fingertips on my arm.

Marius seems to think things over before responding. "I very much doubt it. It's clear from his blog that he doesn't confide in her."

"You believe what he writes in his blog?"

"So far, yes. It's been consistently accurate."

"So why has he stopped writing it? After he wrote the dream about his father, nothing. . ."

Marius gives a small sigh. "I very much doubt that he's stopped. He's simply moved it, as he did before."

"How will we find it again? Without our agent to spy on him?"

"My dear professor, we don't need to."

"Because he's no longer useful to us?" There's a touch of doubt in the woman's voice.

"Precisely so."

They're silent for the next few minutes. This does not sound good. I'm dying to say something, and even in the shadows I can see that Ixchel keeps turning to glance at me. But we have to progress even more quietly now that they've stopped talking.

And then the woman starts up again. "I'm not sure we should kill him, not yet, anyway. It would be a waste of a useful resource."

"How so?"

"I could use him as a test subject. For the gene therapy. It's almost ready to trial, but we need a human subject – one with the Bakab gene. And the experiments are illegal."

"Dangerous?"

"Potentially fatal – no way to predict side effects."

"And the benefits. . .?"

"If I can get the gene therapy to work, Marius, the Sect will be in a position to completely take over from Ek Naab. We won't need them or their Bakabs to handle the Erinsi technology. And that's just the beginning. The other abilities of the Bakabs – we may be able to enhance them."

"Enhance them?"

"Right now it's a weak ability at best. But in our hands, it could be turned into a weapon."

Marius pauses just for a second, gives a tiny sigh. "If the boy can be useful to you, my dear, you must use him while you can."

"So we agree?" the professor says. "Whoever captures the boy, he'll be taken alive?"

"Absolutely."

At this point, Ixchel stops in her tracks. I can't get her to move. Martineau and the professor's voices disappear into the gloomy depths as I silently try to persuade her.

When we can't hear their voices any more, Ixchel pulls away from me and whispers, "No! We have to go back – didn't you hear what they said? Do you want to become a genetic experiment?"

Help the Sect to take over from Ek Naab. . .? There's *no way* I can be part of that.

Ixchel turns around and starts walking back the way we came. She switches on the torch. I catch up and grab her wrist.

"How do you think you're going to get out? You think there's going to be a door handle?"

"Weren't you listening?"

"Course I was. But don't you see? We can't stop now. We have to find out what they're doing."

"Josh, we're walking into a trap."

"It's only a trap if they know we're here."

And then I get the most terrible idea. Slowly, I relax my grip on her arm.

"Is it a trap? Have you tricked me into coming here? And now that you know what they've planned, you've changed your mind?"

Ixchel stares at me in horror. "No! What? You're crazy . . . what's wrong with you. . .?"

I raise my voice. "Have you, Ixchel? Have you lied to me, too?"

Ixchel clamps her hand over my mouth and hisses, "Shut up; are you insane? Of course not! It was your idea to come here, idiot, *your idea*, not mine. I followed you."

I push her hand away and glare at her.

She shakes her head. "You're mad. I'm leaving. I'm sorry I ever met you."

With that, she turns, continues walking back to the entrance.

That's when I realize how paranoid I've become. I chase after her again.

"OK, maybe I'm wrong. . ."

"Maybe?!"

"OK, I'm definitely wrong. But it wouldn't be the first time someone tricked me."

"You're the one who let himself be tricked."

"No, Ixchel. Listen."

She stops.

"That girl they talked about, the one they reckoned was an 'excellent agent' . . . that's Ollie. I thought she liked me. You know, *liked me*."

"Oh." Ixchel taps her foot for a second. "I'm sorry. That's too bad."

"But she was a spy all along," I mutter, almost to myself. "A spy for the Sect of Huracan."

Ixchel stiffens. "The Sect? Tell me you're kidding."

I shake my head. "You've heard of them, then. . .?"

"The Sect of Huracan? Everyone in Ek Naab has heard of them. But they're supposed to have gone hundred of years ago – disappeared."

"Yeah, I'd say they're back. And in pretty good shape, too," I say grimly. "Training secret agents in Switzerland and doing . . . whatever's going on here."

I take the torch from Ixchel and offer my hand.

"Come on. We've got to finish this. We've got to find out what they're doing here. We don't even know how to open the outside door. We're already trapped."

We jog back through the tunnel. It always slopes down, heading deep under Becan. Long past the point where we last saw Martineau and the professor, we come to a fork in the tunnel. We pick the left tunnel and continue. Then, from somewhere up ahead we see light and hear voices. I switch off the torch. Behind a gap in the rock, several figures are moving.

There are more voices this time, not just the two we heard on the way down. This time, they sound muffled, as if coming through filters or a mask. I just about recognize Martineau and the professor. Then, unmistakably, I hear the higher voice of Simon Madison rising above them.

"No, no, no, that's not how it works. The codex says something like, 'In liquid form the Key is highly unstable . . . must be used within sixty minutes.'"

The professor says tartly, "Yeah . . . I remember the instructions, Simon."

"But if you're using the liquid form of the Key from frozen, it isn't fresh . . . it's not going to work."

The professor sounds smug and confident. "We've modelled the experiment with a bio-sensor. Fresh or freeze-thawed – there's hardly a difference."

"*Bio-sensor* – are you serious?!" Madison's voice rises to a shout. "A bio-sensor is fine for working things out in the nice, perfect environment of a lab. But things could be totally different here. We're working completely in the dark! We should stick to the damn instructions."

Now it's the professor's turn to shout. Except she doesn't just sound loud and angry when she shouts – she sounds dangerous. I don't quite understand what, but something is clearly going wrong with their experiment.

"Did y'all see a high-tech production facility anywhere around here? No, sir! If you want this to work, then it's gonna have to be frozen. Now, Simon, apply the Key to the Adaptor. Stop wasting my time."

Marius interrupts in a mild yet firm way. "Perhaps you'd explain *your* objection to Simon's objection, my dear professor? After all . . . it seems like he knows what he's talking about. . ."

She rips into him. "Oh, well, pardon me, suddenly I'm surrounded by experts. . ."

Madison is still angry. "A frozen Key is not gonna work!"

The woman remarks, "The codex does say that the Key should be fresh. But in the lab we've used the liquid form of the Key after freezing, then thawing. It still binds tightly."

Super-politely, Marius asks, "'Binds tightly'. . .?"

The Professor begins to speak very slowly, like a teacher talking to a class. "Well, this Key, see, it sticks to a chemical coating on the surface of the Adaptor. The Key changes the chemical coating in some way. Like magic! Yeah – imagine the Key is a magic potion, and we put some on to the Adaptor. When the magic potion is on the Adaptor, the Adaptor can do its job. . ."

This time Marius sounds frosty. "No need for quite such a patronizing tone, my dear lady."

The professor sighs, exasperated, but she keeps going. "We activate the Adaptor with a 'magic potion' – the Key. Then we place the Adaptor in the Container . . . it activates the Revival Chamber. We think."

Marius's lofty tone is back. "My dear, we all know what we're trying to achieve. I just don't see why you aren't taking Simon seriously."

"Right," Madison agrees.

With a tone of finality, she says, "Why waste more time arguing? Do the damn experiment."

Pressed back against the walls of the tunnel, we can

hardly see anything of what's going on. I lean forward for a second and catch a glimpse of six or seven people, all wearing protective suits made of a crumpled blue material and gas masks. Madison, as well as "Marius" and this "Professor", stand by the entrance of the room.

Ixchel pulls me back against the wall. "Did you understand *any* of that?" she whispers, baffled.

I'm pretty chuffed to be more clued in than Ixchel, for once. "Not everything . . . but this stuff is mentioned in the first pages of the Ix Codex. I think they're going to try to use the Adaptor in the Container. To activate the Revival Chamber – whatever that is. But for this to work, it needs some kind of chemical reaction. Madison thinks that one of the chemicals in their reaction might have gone off."

"The Adaptor?"

"No, the Key. Shhhh. I'll explain in a bit."

There's a long silence. Seconds turn to minutes.

Finally, the professor says in a strained voice, "Well. . .?"

Madison replies, "It's all in position."

"But nothing's happening."

"I told you! The Key must be fresh!"

The Professor snaps, "Listen, sonny, it's not the freshness that's the problem here. . ."

Martineau asks, "Then what?"

She sighs, sounding tired. "It could be a number of things. Bottom line – we need to do more research."

Their experiment hasn't worked. . .

"Or we could just try the crystal form of the Key, as it says in the codex," Martineau says, in a dry voice.

Irritably, the Professor replies, "Well, sure, that's a no-brainer. But it'll take months to make the crystal. All our attempts have failed so far – I reckon it needs to be made at zero gravity. Do y'all have *any* idea how hard it is to get time on the space station?"

Madison says nothing, but pushes past them both. He starts walking away from the bottleneck of suited observers near the room.

And straight towards us.

I'm paralysed with shock; Ixchel's just the same. We blow the fraction of a second that we have – our only chance to make an escape.

Amazingly, Madison walks right past us both. We're pressed right back against the wall, hidden in the shadows of the tunnel. But even so, I'm surprised. Then it hits me – with the protective suit and gas mask, his side vision is limited. His head is bowed when he approaches; he nurses one arm in a sling. The others walk past too; incredibly, within a foot of us.

Totally oblivious.

I've just begun to think we've got away with it when the last suited person passes us and then stops, turns around slowly. She must have caught something out of the corner of her eye, but she doesn't seem sure. She reaches for a torch on her tool belt. As the light goes on, I grab Ixchel and run towards the room they've just deserted.

The suited woman yells, "Hey!" and there's a panicked rush in the tunnel beyond, as the others turn around to see us. The second we're inside the room I press a large button in a panel against the door. We watch, our breath like a stone in our throats as the rock door slides closed. We're entombed for the second time today.

I can hear them behind the door; angry voices, mostly Madison's.

"He's mine," he orders. "No one touches him."

A wave of claustrophobia hits me. For the first few seconds it blots out everything else going on outside the stone door. I scarcely take in anything about the strange room. Ixchel's the same. We don't even talk. We run in opposite directions around the octagonal space, looking for any sign of a way out.

I manage to register that there's a tall lamp near the middle. It casts an acidic yellow light into the low corners of the room, but the ceiling is shadowed. Around the room, there's the eerie spectacle of stone sarcophagi; three against each wall except the closed entrance, twenty-one in total.

No way out.

Dominating the middle of the room is a small stone platform or altar, about waist high. The surface is covered with glyphs and wedge-shaped writing. Inserted into a groove on the platform is an object a little larger than a cell phone, with one end slightly fatter than the other. It is a sort of greyish salmon-pink. The surface looks as smooth as polished alabaster, except for some tightly packed, intricately patterned markings near the wider edge. The materials don't look much like what I've seen of Muwan technology, but the way everything is covered in inscriptions seems familiar.

I immediately guess what it is from Montoyo's description: *the Adaptor.*

Next to it there's a tiny plastic test tube. Ixchel is about to touch the platform when I shout out, "Don't!"

She pulls her hand back, as if it's been burned.

"We don't know if it's safe," I say. "For you, I mean. *They're* wearing suits."

Instead of making some sassy reply, she just nods and steps further back.

"Throw me the torch. I'm going to check the ceiling," I say. "Stand well back. And hold your breath."

I climb on to the platform, clutching Ixchel's torch and avoiding the Adaptor. I leap across from the central platform to the sarcophagi, grasp the upper edge of one and crawl on to the top. I walk all the way around the room on the surfaces of the sarcophagi in their rows. I peer closely at the ceiling.

It's impossible to ignore the sounds of Madison and the others working on opening the door. For some reason they can't get their passkey to work. Madison is shouting in frustration, threatening all types of violence. I can just make out Martineau's voice, sounding angry, as well as the professor's. She still sounds smug, repeating, "What did I tell you about the security in this place?"

Above the rows of sarcophagi, the cave ceiling is rough. I find a single narrow opening, like a chimney flue. I stick my head into it and flash the torch upwards. The opening continues for as far as I can see – more or less at the same width. I try to get my shoulders in. I can just about do it. The limestone surface of the tunnel doesn't have many footholds, but it's narrow enough to squirm up by balancing your weight against the sides.

We hear the sound of the limestone door being slowly prised open. I call to Ixchel, "Come on, jump up, the way I did!"

"But . . . the curse. . ."

"Just jump! Stay clear of the Adaptor."

Ixchel does as I say. When she arrives next to me on top of the sarcophagi, I hand her the torch. I cup my hands to give her a leg up the chimney flue.

"It's narrow," she says. "You OK with that?"

"Course. You?"

"I have to be, don't I?"

"All right, go!"

Ixchel disappears into the chimney flue. I glance down to see that the stone door has moved apart enough for me to see the face of one of Martineau's team.

An idea strikes me – a beautiful idea.

I jump down, land near the door, reach through the

opening. Before he realizes what's happened, I've yanked off the guy's gas mask. He bellows with anger and thrusts an arm through the widening gap, trying to grab me. I jump down on to the central platform, grab the Adaptor, make a final dive across and climb on to the sarcophagus directly under the chimney.

Standing beneath it, I call out to Ixchel and toss the gas mask upwards. I give her three seconds to put it on. Then I stuff the Adaptor into my back pocket. I watch Madison groan as he slides into the room, easing his arm sling through a narrow gap in the door.

He's two seconds away from catching me.

I scramble into the chimney, feeling around desperately for a decent handhold. Without someone to give me a hand getting in, I begin to wonder whether I'm going to make it. I only just manage to lever my whole body into the chimney.

Madison is almost directly beneath me. I hear him jump on to the central platform. In another swift leap, he's on top of the sarcophagus. Ixchel's ahead of me, climbing steadily with the torch in her mouth. The space is incredibly tight. I can't imagine how Madison will fit. Ixchel's smaller, more slightly built than I am; I have to squirm through every centimetre. Madison's hand grabs my foot. I kick viciously until he shouts in pain and lets go.

Underneath us, the commotion continues. With only one

thing to concentrate on – moving upwards – I can actually hear what they're saying.

People shout at Madison to move aside, to let someone else in – a specialist they called "Priya". I sense Priya filling the gap underneath me. The chimney darkens. She's blocking the faint echo of the lamp. Now we're all three climbing in a determined manner. It's horrible. I don't suffer from claustrophobia normally, but this is almost too much. I manage only by thinking just one thought.

Keep moving up.

I want to ask Ixchel, how much further? Or anything about what lies ahead. Is it going to be a dead end? But even that thought is too distracting. The second I take my mind off the grim task of wriggling up the nightmarish tube, I stop climbing.

And I mustn't stop.

Being squashed by surrounding rock starts to feel more like pain. Or maybe it's just my muscles complaining about the work of inching up the chimney flue. Above me, Ixchel yells out in frustration. "How much further can it possibly be?!"

"Dunno," I shout back. Ixchel is only a foot or so above me now. I can't see past her into the tunnel beyond. I keep hoping that she can see the exit. But no. She's as desperate as me.

Priya says nothing, no complaining. I hear the steady

breathing in her gas mask. She keeps moving upwards. I daren't stop for a second, or she'll gain on me.

"Just keep going, Ixchel," I shout. "You're doing great, you're doing amazing. Just don't stop. I've got one of them on my tail. Can't shake her off."

Priya laughs, but says nothing.

There's a cry from Ixchel. She stumbles. The next thing I know, her right foot has landed on my shoulder. She's fallen. "Get off me!" I shout. Panic kicks in. Trapped between a non-moving Ixchel and a moving Priya, I'm almost crazy with claustrophobia. I yell louder. "Move! Keep moving!"

And then Ixchel makes the sound I've been waiting to hear: she yells in triumph. "I'm at the top! There's a way out. . .!"

The light ahead disappears for a second. There's a short scream. Then silence. It sounds like shock and fear rather than pain.

Ixchel's scream stops me in my tracks. I can't help it; neither can Priya. There's something terrifying about hearing a scream from a dark hole ahead of you; a dark hole into which you know you've got to crawl.

"Ixchel . . . you OK? Ixchel, answer me!"

There's no answer. I hear Priya pick up the pace again. She's less than a metre away from me now. I keep moving up, steeling myself for something nasty. A few seconds later I reach an opening in the wall. It's not exactly a way out –

more an alternative route. I'd rather keep going up – at least we're bound to run out of ground to be under.

But with Ixchel gone, disappeared into the gap in the side of the chimney, I can't see any choice. I can't just abandon her. So I step into the darkness.

Then I scream too.

It's the unexpectedness of it. Just when you expect your foot to touch ground, there's nothing. The fall isn't entirely vertical – more of a wickedly steep slope. This time the limestone is smooth, bowl-shaped, as though worn away by a huge bubble. I land and start rummaging for openings in the wall. I can't see my hands on the ground – it's that dark. A hand grabs my shoulder. I hear Ixchel's voice as she pulls me to my feet. "Don't speak!"

She pulls me next to her. We stand, rigid, trying to hold our breath: tough, given how scared we are.

We hear Priya land just centimetres away. She gets to her feet instantly, grabs her torch from where it's fallen. She stands with her back to us and flashes it into a tunnel that leads away from the "bubble" chamber.

I push myself off the wall and crouch, preparing a high kick. Then I hear it – the last sound I wanted to hear. The sound of another guard sliding down the side of the bubble chamber.

Priya wasn't the only guard slim enough to fit into that chimney.

This guard lands almost gracefully, right next to me. Priya swings around. She shines the torch on to my face. With her light in my eyes, I can't see their faces.

Yet I recognize the voice. Hearing it stuns me like an electric shock.

"Hello, Josh. I do hope you're not thinking of trying any of your martial art thingies. Priya here is a sixth *dan* in tae kwon do."

Ollie.

Behind me, Ixchel tenses. I don't know how far she's looked down the tunnel. I reckon that for a split second, she thinks of running. I wouldn't be far behind her. But with Priya and Ollie right on top of us, I doubt the chase would last long.

There's something else, too. What do Ollie and Priya think they can do with us? They don't seem to be armed. Are they going to physically force us to go back down that chimney?

Or maybe they know another way out of here.

Priya lobs her torch to Ollie and takes up a martial arts stance. She's slim, slightly shorter than I am. I glance at her feet – she's wearing some kind of suede trainer. I can just see large, dark eyes behind her gas mask.

I've never had tae kwon do used against me. Unlike capoeira, it's actually designed to be a combat sport. I've no idea how I'll match up against a sixth *dan*.

But Priya has a disadvantage – the mask. If I can take that, the bio-defence on the Adaptor will do the rest. Priya will die horribly, just like the NRO agents who touched the Ix Codex.

It would be brutal. Even thinking about it makes me queasy. Until Priya launches her first attacking kick. I hardly even see it coming.

She's so fast.

She lands a hefty blow to my shoulder, then rains kicks and punches down on me. I parry and dodge as well as I can but she gets most of them in. I've never done capoeira at such speed. The first few seconds of our fight belong entirely to her.

How can a girl hit so hard. . .?

And then I start to get the hang of it. Instead of thinking about which move to use, I just let things flow. I react instinctively. Without the music, it's tough, so I let myself hear the music in my head. A fast song, with a pounding rhythm.

I'm amazed at my own memory for defensive moves, and at how well they work against Priya's tae kwon do. I'm flipping, rolling, spinning, blocking, bouncing into handsprings. Once in a while I even get an attack in. I only make good contact once, when I land a *tesoura de frente* – a scissors take-down.

Every so often one of her blows lands on a fresh bruise. Each time, I lurch in pain.

Priya steps back for a second, guarding herself.

Then, for the first time, she speaks. And I hear a posh Indian voice. She sounds young, like Ollie.

"You've got no chance, OK? Obviously you're talented. But no match for me. I'm not allowed to kill you, boy, but I can hurt you pretty bad. Save yourself the pain – give up now."

Ollie joins in. "Priya's right, Josh. Give up. It's fascinating to see you being put through your paces. But I'm sure your little girlfriend won't enjoy watching you being properly beaten."

I can't help losing my cool. "You lying cow."

"Don't take it so personally. I had a job to do."

"'Don't take it personally?'"

I hurl the statement at Ollie. I'm flushed with a violent anger. In a flash I realize it's Ollie I want to hurt, not Priya. I don't even think about it. Out of the blue I launch an attack on Ollie.

Before my kick reaches Ollie, Priya takes me down with a forceful slam to my back.

I lie on the floor, gasping. The wind's knocked out of me. I decide not to move; wonder if they'll believe I've passed out.

Ollie stoops to check me out. Priya warns, "Take care!" That's when I grab Ollie's head, go for the mask. She drops the torch. Priya swoops to defend Ollie, but it's too late. I have a solid grip on Ollie's mask. Struggling against the two of them in the dark, I manage to pull it away from her face. Ollie shouts in protest. When the mask comes off, her jaw is clamped tightly shut.

I fling the mask across the cave, into the gloom. Priya's torn between retrieving the mask and guarding Ollie.

Priya and I race for the mask. I grab it. We struggle, but when we hear Ollie's voice, we stop.

Smugly, she says, "Too bad, Josh. Looks like your magic weapon just wore off."

I'm amazed to see that nothing's happened to Ollie. While I'm distracted, Priya grabs me in an agonizing arm-lock. Behind my back, I try to stretch my fingers to touch the Adaptor. Each time I budge, Priya gives a sadistic twist to my arm, bringing tears to my eyes.

I just stare back at Ollie, my cheeks blazing.

"You're weak, yah?" Priya mutters against my ear. "No killer instinct. You'll never get anywhere as a fighter."

Her patronizing comment makes me angrier. I kick backwards, feeling my ankle connect with her shin. I'm astonished – Priya hardly even reacts. Out of the corner of my eye, I notice Ixchel in the shadows, watching. Ollie and Priya seem to completely ignore her. To them, she's irrelevant.

To me, Ollie says, "You're wondering why I'm not bleeding to death? The poisonous gas eventually runs out." She turns to Priya. "Simon told me. If the surface coating of the Adaptor is in permanent contact with something –

like your pocket, Josh – it keeps releasing the gas. Until eventually, the gas fizzles out. And after a while it isn't dangerous."

"So I can remove my mask?" Priya asks.

"The effect isn't permanent. It's like a car battery – it can recharge. We'll be safe now for a few minutes, maybe twenty. But to be on the safe side, we'll get him to put the Adaptor in a nice, safe, airtight bag."

Ollie takes a Ziploc bag from her pocket. She fetches her mask from the other side of the room and picks up the torch. In the tunnel, I notice a blur of movement.

Ollie opens the bag. "Come on, then, Bakab boy. Use your special powers, pop the Adaptor in here for me, there's a good lad."

"No."

Ollie's voice hardens to steel. "Do it. Now."

"Make me."

"Or the little girl gets it."

Softly, I ask, "Which 'little girl'?"

Ollie flashes the torch into the mouth of the tunnel, where Ixchel was standing.

Ixchel has vanished.

"Oh, how sad, she left you. Didn't even try to help. What kind of friend is she?"

I don't answer.

"Is she one of them, Josh? From Ek Naab? I bet she is. Is

she your betrothed? Have they matched you up like a pair of racehorses?"

Ollie's taunts are almost more than I can bear.

I find my voice. "You can't make me get the Adaptor out of my pocket. And you can't touch it yourself, can you? Maybe there isn't enough to kill you, Ollie, but even a whiff of that gas will make you pretty sick. I know; I've seen what it can do."

Neither Priya nor Ollie says anything. There's tension in the air, like a class waiting for the school bell.

I continue. "If you think I'm getting back into that chimney, you're out of your mind. You're not getting the Adaptor back. You'll have to kill me first."

Priya tightens her hold, twisting so hard that a bolt of pure agony zaps through my shoulder. I bite my tongue, trying not to let them see how much it hurts.

"He's got a point," Priya says to Ollie. "What are we going to do? I don't even think we could climb back up to the chimney. Not without gear – the walls of this chamber are too smooth. Seriously, Ollie, I don't know how to get out of here – do you?"

I look at Ollie. "So 'Ollie Dotrice' *is* your real name?"

She gazes back, impassive. "The 'Ollie' part is."

"Who are you? All of you, I mean. Are you really the Sect of Huracan?"

"Well, aren't you the clever one?"

"What's all this about? What's down there? What were those sarcophagus things?"

"Oh, please. You surely don't think I'm going to fill in the gaps for you. . .?"

I keep going. "What have you got against the people in Ek Naab?"

This time, Ollie seems irritated enough to answer. "Those people in Ek Naab are not just some charming, Yucatec-speaking Mexicans. They're not the remains of the Mayan civilization. And they're not your friends. Stop thinking of them that way. If you had any idea what they've done in their history. . . Why do you think there are so few Bakabs in the city?"

I gape, speechless. How can Ollie know so much about Ek Naab?

"Do the sums, Josh. Every male born to a Bakab is a Bakab since Ek Naab was founded. They should be ten-a-penny. *Where are they?*"

"I don't know what you're on about."

"Of course you don't. You haven't a clue."

Everything Ollie is saying confuses me further. I struggle to understand, but the truth is that I can't even grasp the most basic part of this.

Why?

"Why, Ollie? Why are you doing this?"

"I already told you; don't you ever listen? It's a mistake to save the world from the effects of the superwave."

"Things like this come along," Priya says. "And it's survival of the fittest."

"I just don't understand you. How can you say that?"

Ollie gives a scornful laugh. "Oh, what do you know? You've wasted most of your life being brainwashed by TV and computer games."

"What, then?" I yell. "We should just all shut up, wait for 2012 and just stand by while civilization crumbles, while billions of people die?"

"What's the alternative? You think we can go on like this indefinitely . . . everyone on the planet living to consume? Using up all the natural resources, poisoning the planet, driving every other species to extinction?"

I hardly even know what to say to her. "I thought you were the most amazing girl I'd ever met. But you're not. You're *insane*."

Priya rewards that remark with a vicious twist of my arm. I can't help yelling.

Ollie sighs. "See how confused you are? We love the planet, not just the human part of it."

"How did you get so two-faced?"

"You belong with *us*, Josh. Not with them."

"Are you trying to persuade me?" I ask. "Cos you're not doing a very good job."

"*All* the Bakabs belong with us. But stop all this stuff about 2012."

"We'll never stop. That's what Ek Naab is for!"

Ollie shouts, "And it's wrong!"

Our last two statements echo around the cave, jolting my nerves even further.

Ollie sighs. It sounds as though it comes from the depths of her soul. Her voice softens. "Josh. Please come with us."

"Who is that 'Professor' woman? She your mother?"

"What?" Ollie seems puzzled, suddenly thrown. "No . . . she's. . ."

I interrupt. "She wants to use me for some kind of medical experiment. That's the kind of thing you do out of 'love of the planet', is it? Using innocent people for lethal experiments?"

For the first time, I see that Ollie is surprised. Astonished, definitely. Even dismayed.

"She . . . she must know you'll probably survive. . ."

"No, she doesn't. She doesn't care. Listen. I'm not sure what this 'Revival Chamber' is or what it does," I tell her. I pronounce my words slowly, spelling it out. "But I know you need the Adaptor to activate it. Well, you're not getting it. Ever."

In the distance, there begins a faint sound, from deep within one of the tunnels. We're silent, tense. Listening.

Something's coming towards us – something huge, disturbing all the air around us. Something fast.

At first it's just a tremor in the stillness. A second later, I can put a name to the sound. *Fluttering*. Like hundreds of birds with delicate wings. A dark cloud belches up from inside the tunnel. The cave fills with shadows. Caught in the edges of the torchlight, I see the flicker of hundreds of wings. The air is thick with the creatures, flapping in our faces, against our skin, tangling in our hair.

Not birds – moths. Huge, each wing the size of my hand. And pink. Like strawberries in cream.

Priya's grip loosens the second a moth lands on her mask. She must have a thing about bugs because she shrieks like a smoke alarm, batting the things away with her fists.

I wriggle free and drop to the ground, crawling on my stomach. Most of the moths flap at least a foot above me. I glance up to see Ollie completely engulfed in the creatures. She's calmer than Priya; no screaming from Ollie. Her energy goes into getting the moths off her face and hair.

The Ziploc bag falls on the floor next to Ollie's feet. As I reach out to grab it, a huge moth lands on the back of my head. Hook-like insect feet settle into my hair, getting a nice grip.

It's kind of gross, but I'm not too freaked out.

I ignore it and hunt for the opening of Ixchel's tunnel. There's just enough torchlight, even if the beam is erratic, darting around from Ollie's flailing hand.

Once I'm in the tunnel, I stand up, kicking the last few moths away. My moth-hat is more stubborn – I have to rip it off. I don't stop to look back. Priya and Ollie sound more vexed by the second. I stumble onward, in the fading light, deeper into the tunnel. In a few more seconds the tunnel turns away from the cave. I have to walk almost totally blind. My left hand fumbles against the wall; my right hand is outstretched. I pause to delve for the Adaptor in my back pocket, and plant it inside Ollie's plastic bag. The bag seals with a satisfying click. I bury it deep in my jeans pocket and pull my shirt down over it.

I keep walking, as fast as I can. The sounds of Priya and Ollie battling giant moths fades. In the blackness, I close my eyes. It's actually less scary than walking along with eyes wide open, filled with *nothing*.

I wonder how far Ixchel's got by now. Will I ever get out of here? People have got lost in cave systems and never been seen again.

I turn a few more corners, and then stop. About twenty metres ahead, there's a light, pointing down.

Ixchel. She beams the light straight at me.

I yell, "Not like that! It's in my eyes!"

Ixchel directs the beam on to the ceiling. I sprint towards her.

"You waited!"

She gives a rushed smile. "Of course, dummy. There's a fork in the tunnel. Which way?"

Remembering Blanco Vigores's words, I tell her, "Left, of course. And you can take off the mask. I've wrapped up that Adaptor thing. It's safe now."

Ixchel insists that I show her. Then she removes the mask and puts it into her sisal backpack.

We jog ahead for what seems like several hundred metres. To save energy, we don't talk. The tunnel twists and turns so much that it's easy to lose track, but I have the sensation that we're going downhill again.

There's no sign of anyone in pursuit. We come to another fork, and again we take the left. It's another fifty metres before the next fork.

"Left again?" she says, slightly breathless.

"Why not?"

Travelling this way, we spend another ten minutes getting nowhere. Or maybe it's somewhere, but the surroundings don't change. Our jogging slows to a stroll. Neither of us says a thing. I have the strange sensation that we're burrowing into the rock, as though it were opening before us, like the Red Sea with Moses.

Eventually we both stop.

"This is no good," she says.

"It isn't," I agree.

"You want to go back?"

"Where, to that last turning?"

"Yes."

"And take the other tunnel?"

"Yes."

"Not a good plan."

"Why?"

"Because we'll get lost."

"We are lost."

I shake my head. "No. We don't know where we are right now, but we *do* know how to get back. The second we start taking anything but left turns, we'll be lost."

"Why *left*?"

I sigh. "Just because."

"I think you could be wrong, always with left."

"I could be, yeah. But a wrong turn in a labyrinth only leads to a dead end. We haven't come to one of those yet."

"What makes you think we're in a maze?"

"I didn't say we were."

Ixchel sounds irritated. "Yes, you did."

226

"I said *labyrinth*. There's only one path through a labyrinth. It's the maze that has more than one way through."

"Oh, I get it – you're showing off. Great timing, by the way."

"Hey, I've played a lot of computer games. I know how to do labyrinths, OK?"

Except that this isn't quite like a game: no secret doors, hidden weapons or monsters. Just tunnel, tunnel and more tunnel.

My bruises begin to throb. I lean against the wall for a second, wincing.

"What's wrong?"

"Nothing. I just got beaten up by that woman, in case you missed that."

"You didn't get totally beaten. You were doing OK there. For a minute or so."

I try to ease out the ache. "Yeah, right."

"Are you OK?"

I stand up slowly, flex muscles in my back and neck. "I will be. Let's keep going."

Ixchel is quiet for a several minutes. Then she pipes up. "I've been meaning to ask you. . . Back in Veracruz, you said that the Ix Codex is written in English. You pretended you were joking, but . . . I don't think you really were."

I'm silent for a while. "Guess you've been doing some thinking."

"Yes, I have. I've worked out that you know a lot, *lot* more than you're letting on. I bet you even know what that room is for, the one with the sarcophagi. It's the Revival Chamber, isn't it – the Professor mentioned it . . . and you said something about it to that Ollie girl."

Truthfully, I say, "I don't know what the Revival Chamber does."

Because having a theory isn't the same as knowing the answer. . .

"But, Josh, how do you even know about it?"

I breathe a heavy sigh. "If I told you. . ."

"What? Don't you trust me?"

I stop, and so does she. For a second, we look straight into each other's eyes.

"I do trust you," I admit. "But there are things I'm not allowed to talk about."

"Like the codex?"

"That's one of them."

Ixchel rolls her eyes. "I think you like being all mysterious."

"I don't."

She picks up her pace. "Sooner or later, you're gonna tell me."

We walk in silence for another ten minutes, then another ten, and another, and another. We come to an opening. As we step through, Ixchel's torch picks out the most incredible sight.

For as far as we can see in the low cave, rock drips from the ceiling, frozen in time, hundreds upon hundreds of delicate stalactites, some no thicker than a pencil, coiled like corkscrews, twisted and torn, some vertical, beaded, glistening in the light beam, pearl-white, like coral. It's like a fairy kingdom: an upside-down, fantasy vision of a miniature New York.

"What the heck is this. . .?"

Ixchel touches what looks like a giant hydra with her finger. "Amazing . . . helictites. I've read about them. I didn't know there were any so near to Ek Naab."

"You still think we're near Ek Naab?"

She turns to me. "Isn't it obvious?"

"What?"

"We're in the Depths. Under Ek Naab."

"You're sure?"

Ixchel nods. "Those giant moths, they came flying right past me. Just like bats out of hell. Did you see their colour? Pink!"

"So. . .?"

"The stories about the Depths always mention pools of pink water. It has some kind of red algae."

"You think the moths drink that water?"

Ixchel shrugs. "What else? That stuff must turn their wings pink. Like with flamingos."

I stare at the ceiling of the cave. It's astonishing. As well as helictites, there are also stalagmites, rising from the ground like miniature Leaning Towers of Pisa. There's something almost organic about their texture. They glisten with moisture, like the rippling muscles of a bodybuilder.

They take some navigating; we make slow progress through the cave. There's only one way out. A dark hole gapes ahead of us. Amongst the stalagmites and helictites, the torch doesn't reveal much of what's ahead. We don't see the blockage in the tunnel until I almost trip over it. I glance down just as my foot thuds against it.

A body. A human skeleton – wrapped in the ragged remnants of clothes.

Instinctively, we both leap backwards. I don't know what's stronger, the shock or the revulsion.

The instant I recover, I'm fascinated. It's the first real skeleton I've seen. The tattered clothes look like a shirt tied loosely at the waist, and trousers.

They look horribly familiar.

Ixchel crouches down, touches the hem of the shirt. She lifts it, examines the torso.

"This person was from Ek Naab. Look at the fabric – linen. We still use this weave, too."

I look closely at Ixchel's face. She's thoughtful, not disgusted. "There's no sign of injury," she says. "This person might have died of hunger, for all we know."

I ask, "Has anyone gone missing recently?"

Ixchel doesn't reply. She steps over the body and looks at it from the other side.

"You still want to keep going left?" Ixchel says.

"You want to go back?"

"I think maybe we should."

I pause. Ixchel actually sounds nervous. I say, "If we go back, *they* might be there."

Ixchel nods. "Yeah. But if we go deeper, who knows what we'll find?"

"Maybe we'll find the other way into Ek Naab. We know there is one."

"You're so sure?" Ixchel says.

I point to the skeleton. "How else do you explain him?"

"Chances are we'll never find it."

"No, we should keep going," I insist. "Until we come to a dead end; then we go back. That's the rule of the labyrinth."

Ixchel sighs. "All right."

"We have to have a system."

"OK."

But she's obviously unhappy.

Somewhere along the trail I notice that the ground becomes moist, then damp, then soaked. Pretty soon we're sloshing through a couple of centimetres of water. Ixchel's sandals are soaked; my trainers start to squeak. The sound of water echoes all around.

"There was no water before," Ixchel points out.

"I know, I know."

"This isn't the way we came."

"Think I don't know that?" I shout.

"Nice going, Josh," she says bitterly.

I clench my jaw. I'm sick with worry about getting out, feeling bad that I can't tell Ixchel what I know about what might be going on with the Sect. I can tell she's completely bewildered by what we saw and heard. It doesn't seem fair.

"Look, for what it's worth, Ixchel," I begin, "I think you're on to something. But I still don't understand how it all fits together. How come no one in Ek Naab knows about the room with sarcophagi, if it's so close to the city? Who else is in this Sect of Huracan? Back in Oxford, I found a list with names on it. There were hundreds of them! Ollie told me that they want all the civilizations of the world to collapse. Leaving just them! Can you even imagine that? Why? Why would anyone want that?"

"That's how it sometimes feels in Ek Naab," Ixchel says. "Like we're the only people on earth. Like no one else really matters. Maybe the Sect wants to feel like that. Maybe they want the whole planet to themselves."

"They reckon they're some kind of superior race," I agree, thinking of how Ollie had tried to persuade me. "And it's something to do with the Bakab gene."

"But the Bakab gene doesn't give you any special powers, does it? Just the ability to resist the toxin from the codex."

"And from the Adaptor," I add.

"Yes, that too."

"And from whatever other . . . ancient . . . technology we might find," I say, taking care not to break my promise to Montoyo and mention any secrets of the Ix Codex.

"You think there's more?"

"There has to be," I say. "The NRO has some of it – we know they have Muwans. The Sect has some of it. Both groups know there's more out there. And you know what? I think it's a race between us all, to get control of the pieces we need to stop the galactic superwave in 2012."

"But the NRO . . . they must want to save civilization. They work for the American people, after all."

"You'd think! But what if they're just clueless? Maybe for

them, it's just about grabbing useful technology. Stuff that they can sell or use for themselves."

"And where do you fit into all this, Josh?"

"Me?" I pause. "Honestly, I just want the truth about my dad."

After another four hours in the tunnels, trying to keep track of the options we've tried, losing count of dead ends, the tunnel opens into another cave with smooth walls about ten metres by five. Ixchel shines her torch into every nook and cranny of the cave. There's no visible way out.

By now we're tired, hungry and parched. And obviously lost.

The floor of the cave is uneven, with occasional lumps of rock raised above the water. Ixchel sits, arranges her body on three dry bits, and manages to lie down.

She whispers, "I'm so tired. . ."

Aching for rest, I cast my eye around for some other bits of dry land. My jeans feel uncomfortable now, stuffed with my dad's iPod and the Adaptor in its plastic wrapper.

Ixchel and I end up about a metre apart, facing each other, two bodies contorted across the dry land, little human islands in a vast puddle.

"These caves are filled with echoes," she murmurs. Her eyes are closing. "Don't you hear them? Footsteps ahead of us, behind us. Faint voices, like a radio in far-off room. Air that feels used up."

She sighs almost contentedly . . . like she's giving in to sleep.

Hardly louder than a whisper, Ixchel says, "I think someone else is here too."

I lie absolutely still, listening. Drops fall steadily into the puddle from water trickling through the cave walls. Ixchel's jeans scrub against rock as she tries to get comfortable. But no echoes, no footsteps, no voices. As far as I can tell, we're all alone down here.

"Think this water's safe to drink?" I ask. "Cos ours is all gone. If you really listen, you can hear it gurgling. I think it's flowing, you know. That means it could be all right."

She barely manages a sleepy shrug. I cup my fingers and scoop up a handful.

"Seems OK. . ."

"Good," mutters Ixchel. "Better not drink too much.".

But once I've got the taste for it, I don't want to stop. I slurp handful after handful. It tastes fine: a little warm, very slightly salty. I lean across to Ixchel and take the torch from her fingers. She's fast asleep.

The beam of light is much weaker than it was. There may

not be enough to get us back to the first cave, the one with the chimney. I try not to think about that possibility, or about how deep under the ground we are. I try not to think about the phrase "buried alive". And I especially try not to think about that skeleton.

I switch off the torch. Above us, the ceiling of the cave glows faintly, with luminescent pink and white. Ixchel's drifted into sleep.

I don't want to be awake in the dark. Not alone, not here.

The phosphorescent light dies out slowly. Finally, I give in and let my eyelids fall. Just before I drop off to sleep, I hear the distant buzz of quivering wings. Behind my eyes, colours flash inside my head.

I know almost from the beginning that I'm dreaming. In fact, from the instant I look down and see I'm wearing those linen trousers and a matching white shirt. Or maybe it's when I glance to my right and see the girl next to me. We're holding hands. It doesn't feel wrong. Just the opposite – it feels perfect.

OK, so this is a dream.

I've become another person, Chan. I'm with this girl, Albita. Somehow I just know this stuff.

"We're going to get out of here," I tell her.

She nods. "I know."

She trusts me. And I trust her. We've been lost in these

237

caves for hours. Somewhere down the line we became separated from the others. In the dream, I know all of this. In the dream, this is what I think about as we slosh through tunnels filled with centimetres of water. It shimmers with a fiery orange, reflecting the weak flames of my fading torch. I think about all the tunnels we've already been down, making a mental map. In that map, there's only one place left to try. If that doesn't lead us out of here, then I know we're lost.

And if we're lost, it's just a matter of time.

My best friend has been lost here in the Depths for many days. Somehow six days passed before anyone noticed that he was missing. That's the way it is with Kan'ek sometimes. He can be strange.

Kan'ek is the firstborn of the Bakab Muluc. He has no brothers. That's why our search is so urgent. He's an *heir*, but I'm only a *spare*. My older brother will turn sixteen in two months. He'll begin his training with the Bakab Ix. If I go missing in these tunnels, will anyone come to rescue me?

We find the cave again, the one with the incredible ceiling of translucent, twisting helictites. This is it now; we're not far. We go back through the cave, then take the next left turn. We follow the tunnels deeper underground, walking through water that gets deeper by the minute.

Until we come to a solid wall. I look up, see that there's a ledge. The ledge is narrow, but leads to another tunnel. It's high, though. Not possible to climb up without help.

"You can climb up there," Albita says, "if you get up on my shoulders."

I stare at her, amused. "And how will you climb up?"

"You'll pull me."

"What if I can't reach? You think I'm going to climb on *your* shoulders, and then risk leaving you behind?"

"And you think I'm going to climb on your shoulders and then risk leaving you behind?" she replies with a wide grin. "Listen, you have to do it my way. You're taller than me. More chance you'll be able to pull me up than the other way around."

"Always telling me what to do . . . is this how it's going to be when we're married?"

Albita's grin widens. "It works so well for us! Anyway, you shouldn't worry so much about me. I'm not as delicate as you think."

I begin by throwing the torch up on to the ledge. The first few times, it just rolls off. On the fourth attempt, it stays. It hardly matters anyway. I'm estimating we have less than thirty minutes of light remaining.

Albita braces herself against the wall, wedging her small feet in to form a triangle with the wall and the ground. I place a foot on her hip, another on the wall, and then land as lightly as I can get away with on her shoulder. It gives me just enough height to reach the edge of the ridge with my hands. I pull myself up and lie on the narrow ledge. It's too narrow to lie on properly, so I'm sideways on. I jam myself in as safely as I can, and reach down with my right hand. She stretches up. We both gasp with the effort of it. Our fingers keep missing each other by the narrowest margin.

Eventually, she gives up.

"It's no good. I'll stay. You go ahead and bring help."

For a long moment our eyes lock.

I say quietly, "No."

I swing back down, suspend myself from the ledge. Through gritted teeth I say, "Climb up along me."

Albita hesitates for a second. Then, without a word, she grabs hold of my ankles, and I feel my fingers take her weight. She's not heavy, but on top of carrying my own weight, I think my fingers are going to pop out of their knuckles. The tendons in my wrist feel as though they're stretched to snapping point. Albita moves quickly, clambering up my back and shoulders. It's over in a matter of seconds. Then I have to find the strength to pull my own weight up all over again.

A few seconds later we sit side by side on the ledge. I look at Albita, watching her brush strands of long, straight hair out of her eyes.

"I don't want to leave you behind again," I tell her.

Albita leans across and kisses my cheek.

"Of course," she whispers.

We get to our feet and edge along the rock. Further along, we reach another opening.

I hear water. It's unmistakable. The sound of loud, steady dripping echoes from a cave not far from our position. We rush ahead, reaching the cave within the minute.

The ceiling is so low in places that we have to stoop. The torch illuminates enough for us to see that the cave is filled mostly by an underground lake. The surface is opaque and reflects ribbons of flame-coloured light. It mirrors the overhanging limestone rock. When I lower the torch to just above the surface of the water, I can see that it's clear, all the way to the rocky floor of the lake.

There is only one way into the cave by foot. Any other exit must be through water.

"This water comes from somewhere," I say. "We'll wade through it."

I pass Albita the torch and lower myself into the water. This deep, the temperature is quite a bit lower than the puddles we've walked through. My teeth begin to chatter almost right away. The cold seeps into my bones. Very rapidly, the lake becomes deep. It becomes obvious that wading isn't going to be an option for long.

I clutch the torch as we swim, holding it above our heads. The water tastes salty, not like the water in the tunnel streams. We reach the other end of the lake, where there's a rock wall.

I turn to Albita, both of us treading water.

"I'll have to swim for it. Wait here a minute. I'll come back for you."

Albita can't keep the tremor out of her voice when she replies. "No, don't. Stay. It's too dangerous. It's dark. You won't be able to see."

"If you hold the torch here, I might."

"If you go too far you won't be able to get back."

"I'll find a way out. And come back for you."

She hesitates. "I don't want you to go."

"I have to, Albita. I'm the stronger swimmer. You know it's true."

Without warning, she begins to cry. I can hardly bear to watch. I hate myself for letting Albita join us on this search. I promise myself there and then that I'll never put her in danger again, never.

I place the torch in her hand and hold it close to the water. "Hold it like this, yes?"

Albita nods, still crying.

"Wait as long as you can. Then get out of the water and dry off."

"Don't go."

This last time, she whispers. It almost breaks my heart.

"Here I go."

I take a few deep breaths, preparing my lungs. Then I plunge into the water, diving low under the rock. I can just about make out the outline of the tunnel. It's about as wide as three people. It veers to the left, where there's a tiny gap.

I squeeze through the gap. Ahead I can see two routes,

openings, left and right. The right-hand tunnel narrows quickly, becoming very dark. The left-hand tunnel seems wider, and lighter. I keep swimming hard. By the time I reach the left-hand tunnel, I need to exhale. I release some air as tiny bubbles. I know I'll only last a few more seconds. If I'm going to turn back, it would have to be now.

I poke my head into the left-hand tunnel. There's definitely some light coming from somewhere.

Then everything goes black. The torch must have died out. The darkness and feeling of being trapped are terrifying.

I make my decision. There's no choice. Without light, I might not make it back through the tiny gap in the first tunnel. I don't know if I've enough air to make it all the way through, but it's my only hope.

I dive into the left-hand tunnel, using my hands to pull myself along. I ignore the burning sensation in my lungs. I can see a light. It seems impossible to reach. I can hardly bear another second of the pain in my chest. The light – it's so close. I can't give up now. I brace my legs against the walls of the tunnel, give a final push through the channel.

I emerge into the light. I'm opening my mouth to gulp in fresh air when I realize, to my horror, that what I assumed is air is actually another layer of water. On the verge of panicking, I float upwards. I have the sensation of flying above the water.

Finally, my head breaks the surface.

I gasp deeply, sucking in chunks of air. I float to the surface. I'm in an underground *cenote*, but no longer buried. Natural sunlight streams like gold dust from an entrance in the cavern. It falls into the water around me, which is a deep turquoise blue.

The feeling of relief is unbelievable. I'm on the verge of tears. I think of Albita on the other side, trapped in the dark, not knowing whether I've made it or not. More than anything I want to go back for her. But alone, in the dark, I wouldn't stand a chance. I need to return with people to help me, and ropes.

I drag myself out of the water, out of the cavern and begin to run. I don't know how far I am from home. Time may be short. I can't afford to rest.

I wake with a jolt, rolling into the puddle. I jump to my feet, confused. Then I remember where I am. Ixchel lies opposite. She wakes too, startled by me.

I switch on the torch and check my watch. It feels as though I've slept for days, but it's only been a couple of hours. My watch says it's five in the afternoon. We've been in the Depths for almost seven hours. Ixchel's right – there's something very odd about the sounds down here. Surrounded by all this geology, we should only hear water dripping, the infinitesimal growth of ancient rock. But the air seems to carry the distant whispers of life.

"What a dream. . ." I say.

"Me too," she says. "Horrible. A nightmare."

"I dreamt I was swimming through an underground tunnel," I tell Ixchel. "It was terrible. Thought I'd never get out of there. Thought I was going to drown."

"Huh," says Ixchel, only vaguely surprised. "I had the

same dream." She's suddenly thoughtful. "In fact, I think I did drown."

I stare at her. "You did?"

"Yes. Good thing you woke me up. They say that if you die in a dream, you die in real life."

"You were really about to die?"

"Uh huh. You can't imagine how nasty it was. Stuck in that tunnel, desperate to breathe, unable to see anything."

I'm confused. Ixchel had the same dream . . . but in her version she didn't get out? "But *you*, you made it out?"

Ixchel shook her head. "I don't think so. I was about to pass out from lack of oxygen. And I was still stuck down there. Lost. Just *horrible*."

I don't understand why, but I'm almost overcome with grief. Ixchel looks shocked.

"Hey, what's wrong? You look like you saw a ghost."

It's ridiculous, but I want to grab Ixchel and hold her close, just to check she's still here.

But it's not really Ixchel I want to hold. It's Albita.

Ixchel muses, "You know, I think it was Chan and Albita."

"In the dream . . . I was called Chan."

"Lucky you! I was Albita. Not so fun, when you think about how she ended up."

I'm staggered. "Chan and Albita were *real*?"

"They were part of the search party that went looking for this boy – a Bakab heir called Kan'ek – years ago."

"I know the story," I say. "It ends with them finding Kan'ek, and he smells of gardenias."

"Well, that's the nice side of the story. What's not so nice is that Albita didn't return. She must have given up waiting for Chan to come back and tried to swim for it by herself."

"She drowned. . .?"

Ixchel looks grim. "Pretty nasty, yes? Poor Albita; her spirit must still be down here, poor thing."

I say nothing, staring into the water.

"Not the nicest experience to share with me; thanks, Albita," says Ixchel to no one in particular. "You couldn't have chosen something better?"

"That Chan guy," I say. "He really liked her, right?"

"They were crazy in love. I felt that, you know – I actually felt what she felt. He risked his life to save her, but she died anyway. No wonder he never recovered."

I don't really want to know, but I can't help myself. "What happened to him?"

"Some say Chan left his soul down here, with Albita. He got out OK, but couldn't forgive himself for her death."

"Why not?" I say, my voice rising. "It was her decision to swim. He told her to stay! He told her to wait for him! Why didn't she just do what we agreed?"

I realize suddenly that I'm pounding the ground, splashing both of us with water. A feeling of almost overwhelming desperation grips me.

Ixchel seems deep in thought. "How amazing. . . You and me, visited by Chan and Albita."

"You've got to be kidding," I say, but it's a half-hearted objection.

I know what I felt.

Ixchel doesn't seem remotely thrown by the experience. She actually seems pleased. I'm still reeling from feelings of grief that aren't even really mine.

Or maybe they are. Because I keep thinking back to Camila, and how I couldn't save her.

"You know, Josh . . . what this could mean. . ." Ixchel grips my arm urgently. "You know the way out of here! Chan found another way, through the underground river. Can you remember how?"

Ixchel is right. I can see it all clearly in my memory. The cave with the lake. The tunnel. The narrow gap, the left fork in the underground river, the journey to the *cenote*.

I turn to Ixchel. "We have to go back to the cave with the helictites. There's a tricky climb – you'll have to climb up over me. And – it's not an easy swim. Long. Dark. Scary."

"But you know the way?" Ixchel says, hopeful.

I nod. "Yeah. Think I do."

We make our way back to the helictite cave. Beyond that, we find the second tunnel. We don't even need to discuss it – we both recognize the route.

"This is going to work," Ixchel says, almost to herself.

I'm silent, thinking about the underground swim. Without light, I can't see how I would find that narrow opening in the rock. But I won't do what Chan, my dream-self, did: I won't leave Ixchel behind.

And then the solution comes to me. My pace quickens.

"You're right, you know," I tell Ixchel. "It really is."

We reach the wall with the ledge. Just as in the dream, I use Ixchel's shoulders to give me the lift, then hang from my fingers as she climbs up my legs and over my back. It's not so easy for me as it is in the dream – the first couple of times I can't take her weight and we both fall to the ground. The mistake we're making is that I lose it the second that Ixchel grabs my ankles and puts all of her weight on me. The third time, I don't just hold on by my hands, but brace my shoulders and arms into the ledge too. Ixchel takes a running jump to reach my ankles. Once she's grabbed hold, I groan loudly, straining with the sensation of stretching in my knee joints. I breathe in staccato, shallow gasps, holding my shoulders firmly in position as Ixchel climbs along my back.

Just like Chan and Albita, we turn and sit on the ledge for a few minutes, to recover. I recognize suddenly that this is real. I'm visiting a place I only know from a dream – and *it's real*.

Ixchel and I steal a glance at each other. I can't help wondering – is she thinking what I'm thinking? Is she remembering the dream? It's confusing. In that moment, dream and reality collide.

And Ixchel *doesn't* kiss my cheek.

The torch light is down to a feeble point, no better than a match.

"Why didn't I pack batteries?" mutters Ixchel.

I've worked this one out. From my jeans pocket, I bring out my dad's iPod. Ixchel watches, at first bemused and then impressed as I switch it on, choose a playlist and change the "Backlight" setting so that the backlight on the LCD screen stays on.

"What d'you reckon?" I say. "Now it's a torch."

I take the Ziploc bag with the Adaptor from my other pocket. I make Ixchel use her gas mask while I open the Ziploc bag for just a second and place the iPod and my UK mobile phone inside the clear plastic.

"And now," I say, smiling, "it's a *waterproof* torch."

Ixchel gazes at me. Behind her eyes, something is different. "Well. That's actually pretty good."

I want to reply with a flip comment, but my mouth is suddenly dry. I can't say a word. Instead, I turn away, feeling my cheeks flush. I place Ixchel's Ek Naab phone in the Ziploc bag too, after which nothing else fits.

The cave with the underground lake is close by. We arrive within the minute, guided by the steady beam of milky light from my dad's iPod. The plastic bag crackles in my hand as we approach the water. We jump in, gasp at the shocking cold, and swim fast to the other end of the lake.

We reach the end, where the channel through the rocks begins.

"This is it," I tell Ixchel. "It's a long swim. But don't be afraid . . . I know the spirits wouldn't deceive us."

I'm risking my life for a belief in spirits. . .?

The dream of the leaf storm that led me to the lost Ix Codex was one thing . . . but at least that was some kind of a connection with a living Mexican shaman – a *brujo*. It's a whole other level to imagine that I've been communicating with someone long dead.

"Take deep breaths," I say. "Stretch your lungs."

We breathe deeply. If I think about it even for a second, my mind screams with fear. Fear of the dark, of being trapped, or drowning. So I don't let myself. Just going by instinct – that seems to work best for me.

And then we're in. With the iPod light to guide us, I spot the letter-box gap almost immediately. I have a very clear memory of the way in the dream I'd posted myself through it, like a letter. I swim through without hesitating, and then slow my pace until Ixchel catches up. Then I head for the left-hand tunnel, swimming as fast as I can. I sense Ixchel is close behind.

I keep having flashbacks to the dream. The moment

where the light went out is a terrifying memory. I don't let myself think what I'd do if that happened right now.

But it doesn't. My chest hammers with the ache of holding my breath. The iPod lights up the narrow channel to the *cenote*. Up ahead I see the most incredible blue colours in the water. The water is frothing, disturbed. When we emerge into the *cenote*, I understand why.

It's crowded. Filled with swimmers jumping, diving, playing around.

As I surface, one swimmer, a blond guy in his twenties, looks at me with a puzzled smile.

"Hey, man," he says with a laugh. "You didn't even bother to get out of your clothes?"

Ixchel breaks the surface behind me.

"That's so cool," says another, who looks almost identical – tanned and blond. "They just got off the bus and hurled themselves in. Awesome!"

Outside, an old Mexican woman in a multicoloured shawl and her son sell *tortas* and cold drinks from a cooler. My eyes go straight to the *tortas de jamon* – ham, tomato and avocado in rolls of chewy white bread. I buy four, and four cans of lemon soda. The old woman looks from the sopping wet fifty-peso note with which I pay her, then back to me. She blinks at my soaking clothes, saying nothing.

"I'm not a *gringo*, you know," I tell her in Spanish.

"Whatever you say," she replies in a thin, high voice, shrugging. "But you look just as daft."

Ixchel and I sit on stony ground behind the bus, in the hottest part of the sun, and we gobble the *tortas*, biting off huge chunks. We're famished – it seems like more than a day since we ate.

"I should borrow your backpack," I say. "Can't carry the Adaptor around like this."

I take her dripping backpack and open it up. Ixchel
snatches it back.

"Who said you could open my bag?"

We stare at each other.

"I just need to borrow it!"

"OK," she says. "But at least ask first!"

I take it back from her reluctant hand, a bit astonished at
her outburst.

"You really don't know much about girls, do you?"
she muses. "You don't open a girl's bag without asking.
Ever!"

"It's cos I don't think of you as a girl," I say, through
a mouthful of bread and ham. "You're more like a mate.
'Mate' just means a friend," I tell her hurriedly, furious that I
can't do anything to stop a blush. "Like saying *wey*."

"You better not call me *wey*," she warns. "I hate it! I
can't believe people in Mexico call each other 'ox'."

"OK, *wey*," I say, grinning. It's a word that always makes
me laugh. "Promise not to call you *wey*, *wey*."

"Stop it," she says. "I'm serious."

"You are *very* serious," I say. "Too serious."

Ixchel's eyes widen. "Listen to who's talking!"

"I'm not so serious."

"Yes, you are."

"It's just the situations we've been in," I explain.

"So really you're, what, a funny guy?"

"Maybe not funny, but fun. Yeah. I think I was pretty fun, once."

"What happened?"

I put my *torta* down with a heavy sigh. "Just . . . everything."

I get back to searching through the backpack. My fingers land on the napkin where Ixchel wrote my mysterious postcard messages. The napkin is soaked through, on the point of turning to mulch, but I notice the biro writing. It's fuzzy, but I can still read what she wrote. As I look at it upside down, the positions of the full stops suddenly grab my attention.

```
WHAT.KEY.HOLDS.BLOOD.
DEATH.UNDID.HARMONY.
ZOMBIE.DOWNED.WHEN.FLYING.
KINGDOM'S.LOSS.QUESTIONABLE.JUDGEMENT.
```

"What if. . ." I whisper.

Ixchel puts her bottle down. "What?"

"What if the full stops actually mean something?"

"You mean, like part of the code?"

I point to the letters at the start of each word.

"What if this message is an acrostic? Where you just use the first or last letters of each word? *What key holds blood* – W-K-H-B."

Ixchel shrugs. "It's meaningless."

"Yeah, but now," I tell her breathlessly, "now that *does* look like a Caesar cipher word."

"Caesar cipher? Like Julius Caesar?"

I nod. "He used it to encrypt messages to his troops. It's one of the simplest, earliest codes. You shift each letter along three places to get the cipher letter. So an A becomes a D, a B becomes E."

Ixchel's eyes widen, impressed. She looks down at the writing.

I continue, pointing. "W in the cipher message . . . go back three in the alphabet . . . that's T. Then K . . . that's an H. H is code for E . . . and B is code for. . ."

I stop, momentarily stumped.

"It would have to be Y," Ixchel points out. "Going back to the end of the alphabet."

"That spells . . . *THEY*."

We stare at each other.

"What's the second word?"

We work it out together.

ARE.

We continue, until we've deciphered the message so far.

THEY ARE WATCHING.

I jump up, run over to the woman selling *tortas* and beg her for a napkin. Ixchel digs around inside her backpack and finds her pencil. I scribble the decoded message. And we just stare at it in wonder.

"Josh," Ixchel says, her voice hushed, "how long have you had this message?"

"Days. . ."

I think suddenly of Tyler. If we want to call him before he goes to bed, we have to hurry. I check my watch – almost six in the evening. That's eleven o'clock in England. I walk to the other end of the field, far from anyone, and open the plastic bag containing the Adaptor. I have no idea if it's still giving off the poisonous gas, but better to be safe. I remove the iPod and both phones. I seal up the Adaptor again, stuff it into my back pocket and return to Ixchel. Then I try my UK mobile phone. It turns on OK – finally! But the battery is almost flat, so I use Ixchel's phone.

We call Benicio, who almost has a fit when he hears my voice. He's furious. I can't say I blame him. But he'll feel differently when he sees the prize we've captured – the Adaptor.

We assure Benicio that we'll be back by morning. Montoyo won't know that we ever separated; Benicio won't get into trouble.

I'm feeling my confidence return. This is working out. We've had everything thrown at us. But we're still in the game.

We call Tyler. He sounds tired and grumpy. When we ask if he went to my neighbour Jackie's and picked up today's post, he perks up.

"Yeah, there were two more."

He reads aloud the latest two messages, in date order.

FINESSE.REQUIRES.PROPER.HEED.

Just before I put the phone down, Ixchel whispers, "Ask him what the photos are. . ."

I'm a bit puzzled, but ask anyway. He tells me that they're photos of Labna and Palenque, two more Mayan ruins.

"You think that's important?" I ask Ixchel.

"Could be. Another way to give more information, maybe?"

"You mean there's a clue on the photos?"

"Maybe."

I'm suddenly angry with myself for not going back to my house for the postcards.

That's the first place Ollie and Madison would have looked for me, but. . .

Without the actual postcards, it seems that I won't be able to solve the coded message.

Ixchel and I concentrate on deciphering the next few words. In cipher-text they spell F-R-P-H. In English: *COME*.

THEY ARE WATCHING. COME.

It's definitely a message – with an instruction. But where?

"The clue to where could be in some more messages," Ixchel comments. "Or it could be right here, in what you already have."

258

"That would be the smart way to send a message," I agree. "Give as much information as possible in each piece."

"If 'they are watching', then the message has to be as subtle as possible. Hidden in plain view. So anyone could see one or two postcards and not get the whole message."

What do we have? Photos of Mayan ruins: Tikal, Labna, Calakmul, Altun Ha . . . I can't remember them all.

And then I realize. I've been thick. Blind as a bat.

It's another acrostic.

I call up Tyler again. This time he sounds really cross.

"Man, what? I'd just gone to sleep!"

"Tyler . . . this is really, really important. Can you read out the names of the ruins in the photos? In order of dates!"

I hear Tyler grumbling as he crawls out of bed and gropes around his desk. Papers rustle. "They're here somewhere. . ."

"Tyler . . . just get them!"

"Chill, man. You're so weird lately. Telling me to get out of Oxford! I dunno . . . what are you like, eh?"

I grit my teeth. Finally he seems to find the postcards.

"OK. Here we go. First one is – Tikal. Next is Labna. Next, Altun Ha, Calakmul, Ocosingo, Tikal again, Altun Ha again, Labna again, Palenque."

I scribble the names down.

"You done?"

"Brilliant, thanks."

"OK. Can I go to sleep now?"

"Uhhh . . . listen, think you could go round tomorrow and check if there are any more postcards?"

Tyler lets off a stream of swear words.

"So that's a 'no'. . .?"

"Yeah, Josh, it's a 'no'. I'm off to London tomorrow for the day. Where *are* you? You know your mum rang here yesterday? Emmy's mum told her you were with me. I had to tell her you'd gone out to the cinema."

"Thanks, Tyler, you're a pal."

I snap the phone closed and hand it back to Ixchel. My hands are actually trembling with excitement.

I can already see a pattern.

T-L-A-C-O-T-A-L-P.

"That's a Mexican place name," I say, breathless with the rush of discovery. "Has to be."

"Close enough," Ixchel says, frowning. "It could mean 'Tlacotalpan'."

"Where's that? I've never heard of it."

"It's a small town, not too close," she admits, "on the way back to Veracruz."

"That's it, then. We're going. We'll sneak aboard the bus with these Americans. How's the driver to know we're not with them? He's bound to be going somewhere handy."

Ixchel hesitates, looks doubtful. "I don't know. Maybe. . ."

"What. . .?"

There's real anxiety on Ixchel's face. "We really should take the Adaptor straight to Ek Naab."

I can hardly believe what she's saying. "You mean . . . you and me go straight back to Ek Naab? Not to Tlacotalpan?"

Ixchel nods slowly, gazes directly into my eyes. Something about her expression irritates me. A feeling of frustration wells up inside, and I step away from her. "No way! Montoyo will flip his lid if he finds out I ran off again. And he'll blame Benicio! I'm not doing that to Benicio, not again."

"But, Josh. We're close to Ek Naab here. We have to tell the Executive what we found about the Sect, about that Revival Chamber, what we saw them trying with the Key and the Adaptor . . . we need to do that right away. When they hear what we know, they won't care that we sneaked away from Benicio."

I glance away, avoiding her eye. I take a deep breath. "All right. I admit it – this isn't just about going back with Benicio. This is about me. I need to know who's sending these postcards. I need to go to that place."

"Yes, but later! We should get back now," she insists. "No more adventures."

"No!"

Ixchel stops in her tracks.

"This is a message about my father," I say. "I know it. Someone knows the truth! Maybe someone in the NRO who's afraid to talk. Don't you get it? I *have* to go."

BLOG ENTRY: WAITING

⚠☝ↄ☖⚠Ϟↄ⚔☝ↄ

Hey, Mum. I thought about calling you. It's four a.m. here, ten in the morning in England, so you should be finished with breakfast. I didn't want to have to lie to you, though. You still think I'm staying with Emmy's family, and I'm feeling a bit bad about that. So I texted you again. Just to let you know I'm OK, and ask how you are. But of course, you won't be able to reply – this number will just come up as "Anonymous".

I'm waiting in yet another bus station, this time for a bus to Tlacotalpan. Not a fancy tourist-style bus this time – just a regular rickety one full of ordinary Mexican workers and farmers carrying chickens and goats.

Tlacotalpan is a small town in the state of Veracruz, in case you didn't know. (I've never heard you mention it, so I don't know if you do. . .) It's on the banks of a big river, the Papaloapan. Someone there has been sending us the postcards. They have a message for me. Or maybe it's for both of us – you and me?

I don't really feel like blogging any more. I'm too nervous.

262

I wake up on the bus to Tlacotalpan to find Ixchel asleep and slumped against my chest, with my arm around her. I don't want to move her away, because that might wake her up. On the other hand, it's hard to get back to sleep now that I know we're practically cuddling.

How weird is that?

So I stay exactly where I am, trying not to move my hand too much. I try to breathe like I'm asleep. And I try to ignore how nice and cosy this feels – which is the hardest job of all.

It doesn't last long. Ixchel stirs against me. For about one second she squeezes me tightly. Then she sits bolt upright, staring at me like she's seen a ghost.

"What's going on?"

"Nothing!"

"Are you trying to. . .?"

I gasp. "No way – are you kidding?"

"So what. . .?"

"*You* leaned on *me*! I just woke up a few seconds ago."

".You didn't think to get your hands off me?"

"Hey! I didn't want to wake you up!"

Ixchel fumes. "Sure. Of course you didn't."

She shuffles into the corner of her seat. I sigh. Clearly, I can't win.

I pull the plastic grocery-store bag from under my seat. It's stuffed with cake bars and drinks that we bought in the bus station at Villahermosa. We each take two Gansitos. I open up a carton of pineapple juice. For the next few minutes we munch on squidgy cream-and-jam-filled chocolate-covered cakes.

"What's the plan when we get to Tlacotalpan?" asks Ixchel, sucking juice through a straw.

I've tried not to think about this all night long. It hasn't been too hard – there have been other things to distract me. The biggest one being: time travel? Did Montoyo actually say that? It was only a couple of days ago, but already the memory feels foggy, distant.

He couldn't be serious. Could he?

I've been trying to think of any other explanation for why the codices are written in English. But I guess anything I come up with, the Mayans in Ek Naab will have thought of.

Itzamna was a time traveller. . .?

It sounds too ludicrous. But then I ask myself – what is the Revival Chamber? Is it the time-travel device?

Is Itzamna still floating around somewhere in time?

Ixchel's voice interrupts my thoughts. "You know what I'm thinking about?" she says.

"Nope."

"I'm wondering about Chan and Albita. Why do you think they appeared to us in our dream?"

"How should I know? I don't even really know if that's what happened."

"What? You know it did."

"If they did, then it must have been to show us the way out of there."

"So we didn't finish trapped down there, like Albita?"

I nod slowly. "Yeah."

"And you don't think there's maybe another reason?"

I shrug, clueless. What's she getting at?

Ixchel yawns, begins to speak in a dreamy, faraway voice. "I've never been in a haunted place before, you know. We bury the dead of Ek Naab far from the city, in a cemetery on a hill surrounded by an orange grove. They don't come anywhere near us. We visit them on the Day of the Dead, and that's it. It seems to keep them happy. They spend all their time in the sun, after all."

I don't really know what to say to that. Somehow, telling her that I don't believe in ghosts seems like a dumb thing to say.

"Are your parents still alive?"

265

"My father is."

"But not your mum?"

Ixchel lowers her eyes for a second, and with a tiny movement, shakes her head.

"Oh," I say, struggling for words. "I'm sorry. I didn't know. Is . . . is that why you ran away? You don't get on with your dad?"

"It's more complicated. My mother died years ago. My father has a new wife and we don't get along so well."

I think about my own mother. I haven't ever really considered that she might marry again.

"I think I'd like it if my mum got married again," I say. "She gets pretty sad sometimes. It would be good if there was someone else around for her."

"Sure. That's how it seems. Until it actually happens to you. Until they marry an evil witch."

"You think your stepmother is an evil witch?"

"Yup."

"Like in fairy stories?"

"What do you mean?"

"Snow White . . . stuff like that."

"I haven't read it."

"Well, neither have I, not actually read it. But you've seen the Disney film, right?"

"What's 'Disney'?"

"Unreal."

"What is?"

"That you've never heard of Disney. What did you do for fun, growing up?"

"Play, swim, learn to cook, and read and study . . . play piano and . . . I don't know, the usual things. What's 'Disney'?"

I shake my head in wonder. "Man! We really don't have much in common, do we?"

She gives me a sad smile. "That's right. You see my problem with this whole arranged marriage thing?"

"Can I ask you . . . is there a boy you like in Ek Naab?"

"You think I'd leave Ek Naab if there was some boy I liked?"

"I dunno. If you weren't allowed to go out with him, maybe."

"I don't like having my life controlled, OK? That's it. This Disney film, for example. Maybe I'd have liked to see it, you know? Maybe it's good, maybe not. But I'd like the choice. I'd like to live in the real world. Not locked away – like in a convent."

"You know what a convent is, though?"

"Of course! They made me learn all about the history of Mexico. Didn't they think that one day I'd want to see all these places for myself? It's a crazy way to live."

"You should definitely see a Disney film," I tell her. "At least, you've got to see *Toy Story 2*."

"*Toy Story 2*," she repeats, thoughtfully. "I'll add that to my list."

I turn away and look through the bus window. The road is narrow, with sugar cane growing right to the edge of the tarmac. A faint morning mist floats above the surface of the road, barely a metre thick. The sky is grey, but the clouds look wispy, as if the sun could burn them away by lunch time. I watch as a falcon – or some other bird of prey – hovers high above the reeds for a moment and then plummets into the cane field.

Ixchel may be pretty different to me, but we have at least one thing in common.

We've both lost a parent.

Like me, Ixchel goes quiet. She finishes off the crumbs from her Gansito, licks melted chocolate from her fingers.

Not long afterwards, we arrive in Tlacotalpan. I've been trying to avoid Ixchel's question, but she has a point.

We've followed the instructions in the postcard message.

So – what now?

33

Ixchel, me and the other dozen passengers empty out at the bus station. Everyone else seems to know where they're going, with their chickens in cages, but Ixchel and I just mill around.

"Where do you want to go?"

"Give me a few minutes," I say, staring hard at a street map on the wall of the bus station. The truth is that I've got no idea.

I squint as I gaze around, use my hand to shade my eyes against the sharp white light. I've never seen a Mexican town that looks quite like this. Wide, potholed avenues, no cars; neat grass verges and old buildings with colonnades. The walls are brightly coloured – ice-cream pink, butter yellow, peppermint green, redcurrant red.

But where are the shops, the traffic, the bustling tourists, the townsfolk? It's only noon, yet it feels like everyone's gone home for a siesta. It's like a ghost town – if ghosts lived in ramshackle, quaint-old-town splendour.

We turn into the fanciest town plaza I've ever seen. Apart from us, there are a couple of backpackers taking photos of the oriental-looking gazebo in the middle of tall palms, hibiscus bushes and smaller trees. Behind the central garden is a church, painted in gleaming white and grey, with a picture-book bell tower. A Dominican priest wearing sunglasses and a white habit with a black cloak makes his way, head bowed, towards the church.

A middle-aged guy in an apron opens up a café on one corner of the square. He drags white plastic tables on to the marble tiles outside. He must turn on some music, because out of the blue, the square echoes with the tinny noise of an old-fashioned bolero, a romantic singer crooning over woodwind, scratchy brass and bongo drums. It's like we've stepped back in time – I don't even know how long – fifty years?

"So. . ." Ixchel says, turning to me.

I keep my eyes on the café, trying to ignore her. She's dying to hear me admit that I haven't a clue what to do. I don't want to give her the satisfaction.

"Any smart ideas?"

"Let's ask at the café."

"Yes, but . . . ask *what*?"

"I dunno . . . let's ask about the postcards. See if they know someone who's interested in Mayan sites."

Ixchel ponders. "I guess it's a place to start."

It's obvious she's not impressed.

"Look," I say, "whoever sent those postcards wanted me to come here. *They are watching* – which means it may not be safe to come up to us out of the blue."

"Who's *they*?"

"The NRO," I reply, a bit surprised.

"Really? Not the Sect?"

"Outside of Ek Naab, only the NRO have Muwans. My dad was captured by people flying Muwans – the NRO."

"And you're sure the Sect don't have them?"

I'm exasperated. "Why would Madison bother chasing me in a car if he had a Muwan?"

Ixchel shrugs. "Hey, I'm just asking. You seem to make many assumptions. . ."

As we're walking over to the tiny café, a fair-haired, elderly lady emerges from around the corner. She's heading for the café too, and beats us to it. She takes a seat at one of the two outside tables under the arches, and calls out in Spanish, "Some *manzanilla* tea with my *quesadilla*, could you, Victor?"

We sit at the opposite table. I can't help glancing at the lady. From her accent, I'd guess that she's not Mexican – probably American. I think she's in her sixties. She's about the same height as my mum, with very short blonde hair that's obviously been coloured. She's dressed in a light floral dress with a knitted shawl. Her skin is very pale, arms slightly

271

freckled, her face soft, with peachy cheeks. She wears just a hint of make-up, and lipstick. After staring out at the plaza for a minute, she takes a paperback book from her shoulder bag and starts to read.

Victor the waiter comes out with his notepad and pencil stub, asking for our order. We order *sincronizados* – ham and grilled cheese in tortillas – and bottles of fizzy apple. I count my money. I have enough for one more round of restaurant snacks, bus-ticket money and that's it. When Victor's gone, I look across at the woman.

And then she looks up from her book, straight into my eyes. I've never had a complete stranger stare at me that way before. Her gaze bores deep into me. She tilts her head to one side, as if considering.

"Excuse me," I say in English, "are you American?"

She pauses for a long time, pursing her lips. "That I am, young man. And I'm betting that you're British – am I right?"

"Yeah," I say. "And Mexican too."

"Well, congratulations. Lived here most of my life; wish I could say that. But I guess I'll always be a *gringo* round here."

That gets a smile out of us. The American lady puts down her book, and gives Ixchel and me a long, thoughtful glance.

"Now," she says, in neatly clipped tones, "if I were to ask you a rather surprising question, you think you could stay calm?"

I say, "I could try."

Ixchel looks from the lady back to me.

The American seems to think about our responses for a minute, then gives a short nod. "All right, that seems fair enough to me."

We watch her expectantly.

"Now. If I were to ask you," she says slowly, "if your name were 'Josh', what in heaven's name would you say to that?"

Ixchel grows very still next to me. I swallow. "I'd say . . . that yeah, it is."

The lady gives another quick nod, as if mentally ticking something off a checklist. "And if I were to say that your second name is 'Garcia', now: what then?"

I stare. For ages. Then I say, "You sent the postcards."

Slowly, she closes her eyes, nodding. "That I did."

"Why?"

"Because he asked me to."

I'm completely confused. "Who did. . .?"

"A certain Mr Arcadio Garcia, young man. He was most insistent that I wait at this table for you, every day in this month, until you arrived. I promised him I would, not that I knew what I was promising, and so I have."

"You have . . . what?"

"Waited for you," she says, simply. "Because he asked me to. And here we all are."

273

"Who's Arcadio Garcia?"

"I'd guess he was your grandfather," she says. "Going by age and looks."

"My grandfather was *Aureliano* Garcia. And he's been dead for forty years."

The lady's face drops. "Forty years? Are you sure?"

"It's about that long. . ."

"Forty years ago . . . well, heavens be, that explains most everything."

I think for a second, dredging up a faint memory. "Is Arcadio a common name in Mexico?"

She frowns. "Not really. . . Why?"

It strikes me as odd that "Arcadio" is the name signed in that book by John Lloyd Stephens, the one Tyler and I found in that Jericho bookshop – the one that Simon Madison stole. But I don't say any more – things are weird enough as it is. . .

I'm feeling more exasperated by the second. I don't know exactly what I expected to find in Tlacotalpan – something on the lines of a disguised NRO agent who'd decided to go rogue and leak the secret of what really happened to my dad. Definitely not a sweet old American lady, ordering tea and discussing my ancestors.

"You said 'that explains everything'. *What* does it explain?"

"For that, my darlings, you'll have to come to my home."

After lunch, the lady, who says her name is Susannah St John, leads us through the deserted streets of Tlacotalpan to her house. We walk at her pace: nice and slow. And she tells us the story of her and Arcadio.

"I met Arcadio here in Tlacotalpan. Right there in the *refresceria* where we all met, just now. He ordered a beer. I was with my friend from the hospital, Veronica, another nurse like me. We'd been at a nursing convention near Veracruz, and were enjoying a day trip on the last day." She smiles at the memory. "We were eating ice cream. I couldn't help looking at him, and so of course, he looked back at me."

I interrupt. "Why couldn't you help it?"

A blush appears in her cheeks. "Well, he was a handsome young fella in his thirties, of course. With a definite family resemblance to Josh. Except that Arcadio had the most compelling blue eyes. And he leaned over to me and said, in the most perfect English, 'Excuse me, ladies; I'd be delighted to invite you both to a cup of tea.'"

Her eyes sparkle. "My, what a charmer he was. He said he was a historian, educated in England and the United States. He was visiting Tlacotalpan as part of his research into the decline in influence of the state of Veracruz."

"What do you mean?"

"Well, look around you. Where do you think the money came from to build such a fine town? This place used to receive all the goods from Europe; from Cadiz, via Cuba. And from here they'd be taken down the river, to towns in the south of Mexico. It was a thriving port. But all that ended when the railroad came. By the 1960s – when I met Arcadio – it was much as you see now. Not as pretty – they cleaned the town up around ten years ago. No; back then we didn't even have the daily coach of tourists. It really was little more than a ghost town.

"Anyhow, Arcadio and I became friends. It's because of him that I decided to settle here, much later. Because not long after we met, he did something rather extraordinary."

She stops talking as we reach the door of her house. It's about five blocks from the centre: a powder-blue-painted house with white pillars at the front. The entire street backs on to the river.

Inside, the house is furnished entirely with heavy oak furniture, carved and varnished in the old colonial style.

276

There are plants everywhere – hanging in baskets from the ceiling, on raised metal stands, in chunky glazed pots.

This is too easy. It doesn't make sense. How can this sweet old lady be the secret informer behind the postcards?

On the wall are paintings of fruit, of deserted cobbled streets, baking in the afternoon heat, and of the fishing boats at the edge of the River Papaloapan. When Susannah sees Ixchel looking closely at them, she smiles.

"You like art, my dear?"

Ixchel turns to face her, expressionless. "You painted these?"

"Yes, I did. That's what I do now – I'm a painter."

"Did you ever paint him?" I say. "Arcadio?"

"I tried. He never would let me. He hated to have his photo taken, too. I used to laugh at him, tell him that he was just like those Native Americans who believe that the camera captures your spirit. He'd come along all grumpy and say that there was a good deal more at stake than his spirit."

I touch the cool whitewashed plaster of the walls, thinking.

What if this has nothing to do with my father? What if it's a trap?

Susannah perches on the long sofa in front of a glass coffee table. We do the same. I guess Susannah's about to launch into her tale of this extraordinary thing that Arcadio did when Ixchel says, abruptly, "So, why did he tell you to send those postcards?" Susannah turns to her in surprise, as if she's a little put out.

"Well, my dear, *I don't know why*. I didn't even know who Josh and Eleanor Garcia were until I met you both today."

"I'm not Eleanor," Ixchel says. It's the second time I notice a sharp edge to her voice.

Susannah raises an eyebrow. "Well, I didn't want to mention it. But you don't really look like brother and sister."

"Eleanor is my mother," I say. "And I've never heard her mention a relative called Arcadio. My grandfather was Aureliano."

"You already said that, dear," Susannah says mildly. "But Arcadio's instructions were pretty mysterious from the beginning. To start with, there was just a parcel. It said – *To be opened on April fifth, 1968*. Now, can you imagine? To be given a parcel like that, in 1965? I thought it a wonderful joke. Until the day rolled along, of course."

Her expression becomes solemn. "The date doesn't mean anything to you?"

We both shrug, which earns a disappointed sigh from Susannah.

"It's the day after Martin Luther King, Jr was assassinated, of course. So, imagine my astonishment when I opened the letter to discover two more envelopes. And a letter."

She opens a drawer in the coffee table, takes out a

yellowed sheet of paper and begins to read from it. The letter is covered with scratchy handwriting, barely legible to me, at least. I can't help but notice that there's another sheet of the same paper still in the drawer, also covered in the same handwriting.

"Dearest Susannah,

Yesterday, Dr Martin Luther King died after being shot on the balcony of the Lorraine Motel in Memphis, Tennessee.

I chose this date because it was necessary for me to prove to you that I have a way of knowing about events in the future. I often cannot use this knowledge to prevent events as terrible as this.

But there are a very few in which I am able to intervene. It's crucial that you believe me. Because I'm going to ask you to do something which could be important to the whole world.

I beg you to follow my instructions precisely. In the envelope labelled 'Postcards', you will find eight postcards. Each card is written, addressed and dated. All you need do is to buy stamps and send the postcards on the dates written on each card.

Please deliver the second envelope directly into the hands of a British teenager, Josh Garcia, aged fourteen, whom you will meet in the corner café in Plaza Hidalgo, Tlacotalpan, in which you and I first met.

Josh will be accompanied by a young lady of similar age. They will meet you around midday one day in the month when you start sending the postcards. They will not know you, nor be expecting to meet you.

Please be kind enough to explain to them how you have followed my instructions, and then present Josh with the second envelope. Please be sure to see that he DOES NOT open the envelope in your house, but instead folds it and places it in his front trouser pocket."

Susannah puts the letter down on her lap and looks from me to Ixchel.

"So, youngsters. Does this mean anything to you?"

Ixchel shrugs, eyes wide with wonder. I watch her closely – she seems genuinely to have no idea. Susannah notices that I don't look quite as baffled.

"Josh. What do you say about all this? I'm getting the feeling that you're not altogether surprised."

"It's not that. . ." I begin, but Ixchel's already eyeing me with suspicion. "It's more that – I have some idea who Arcadio might be."

Susannah says, "Like I said – your grandfather?"

"When did you last see Arcadio?"

"1967."

"Then . . . I dunno . . . maybe. It could be. I don't know why he'd change his name. He died forty years ago, round about, but I don't know exactly what year. It could be him."

But I'm thinking of another possibility. Just the idea that I may have found proof for Montoyo's crazy-sounding theory makes my skin jangle with electricity.

Arcadio had to be someone who would know about the future and the past. Someone who could write in English. The kind of guy who could easily pass himself off as a historian.

The more I think of it, the more excited I get. It would explain the mysterious note from "Arcadio" to John Lloyd Stephens in the book we found in that shop. The shopkeeper said that "Arcadio" couldn't possibly have heard of Tikal in 1843, because the Mayan city hadn't been discovered.

But if Arcadio was a time traveller from the future. . .

Ixchel points at the other sheet of paper in the drawer. "Is that the next page?"

Susannah shuts the drawer with a snap. Her eyes register annoyance, but she keeps her voice soft. "The second page, my dears, is of no concern to either of you. It's a private message from Arcadio to me."

"And the second envelope?"

"The second envelope, of course, I keep in the safe. Now, I'll ask you both to excuse me while I go upstairs to fetch it."

As Susannah disappears up the marble staircase, I turn to

Ixchel. Her hair, swept back in that neat ponytail, gives her an air of smugness that I'm only now noticing.

"What's up with you?"

Ixchel frowns.

"You're being weird," I continue. "Don't you like her?"

"It's not that," Ixchel says. "But this is all so . . . bizarre. Being *here*. Her. The way she seems to think she knows your family. Is this what you expected?"

I have to admit honestly that it isn't.

Susannah returns with a long white envelope. On the front, in capital letters, is written:

FOR JOSH GARCIA – DO NOT OPEN UNTIL YOU LEAVE TOWN.

She hands it to me with just a hint of hesitation.

"This is yours, I believe." I take it from her hands, watching as her eyes glaze over with sadness, glistening with tears. She sniffs, pulls out a Kleenex from a pocket in her dress and presses the tissue to her eyes. "Mercy, I didn't expect this." She tries to smile, which seems quite an effort. "Kids, I'm sorry. Guess it's been a long wait. It's just a little sad to let go of this famous message; this message I've waited most of my life to deliver."

My fingers play with the envelope, resisting the urge to tear it open.

"Now fold it," Susannah says with a nod, blowing her nose. "And into your front pocket with it. That's it."

There's a knock at the door. Susannah looks surprised.

"Seems a little early for the bridge club." She walks towards the door.

Ixchel and I stare at each other. Ixchel whispers, "How did 'Arcadio' know you would even exist? How can he predict the future? Is he some sort of prophet?"

It's tough not to be able to talk about what Montoyo and I discussed about the Ix Codex. I feel like it's getting to be too much to ask of Ixchel, to keep her so much in the dark. But how can I even suggest time travel without talking about the Ix Codex?

From the entrance hall, we hear Susannah talking softly in Spanish. She keeps saying "Yes, Father", and "Well, of course, Father, I'd be delighted to help." And in between, there's a man speaking Spanish in a low, rapid voice. I put a finger to my lips, signalling to Ixchel to be quiet. I grab her hand and sidle cautiously towards the opposite end of the room, where French windows open on to a tiny walled garden, walls of deep blue lined with pink bougainvillea. The garden is no more than two metres across. Opposite is a carved oak door.

"What is it?" Ixchel whispers.

"I'm not sure," I say. "Something feels wrong."

I try the handle of the French window. It's open, sliding smoothly on oiled runners.

Susannah and the man at the door are coming into the

283

main part of the house. At first glance, I'm relieved – it's only the Dominican priest we saw in the central plaza. But the second he yanks his sunglasses off, I stop being distracted by the white-and-black habit.

Facing me, with a hard gaze of triumph, is Simon Madison.

I don't stop to return Madison's stare, or to answer
Susannah's astonished cry of "Hey! What's going on?!" I
don't think for a millisecond about fighting him. Grabbing
Ixchel, I'm through the open windows, across the patio and
through the oak door in the garden wall.

Susannah tries to stop him, but Madison grabs her
arm and flings her aside. But she delays him for a few,
crucial seconds. We spill out into the street, another
cobbled alleyway just as empty as the last. Running, I hunt
desperately for anywhere we could hide. There's nothing in
this street, so I make a sharp turn into a crossing alleyway.
Ahead I see a handwritten sign outside one of the houses:
Mini-Zoologico de Tlacotalpan.

And more importantly – an open door. We dive in.
There's no way Madison could have seen us yet – he hasn't
caught up to the turn-off in Susannah's street.

Ixchel and I bolt into the house. We dash through

corridors lined with faded photos, handicrafts, rifles, old military uniforms; the tiny museum all passes in a blur.

And then we're in a huge patio crammed with low palm trees. Creeping plants cut out the sunlight, casting a forest gloom. On the right-hand side are a collection of cages, like you'd find at a zoo. From somewhere in the dense foliage of the trees, parrots squawk. An enormous golden eagle peers down at us from the perch on the roof, where it looms, wings tightly folded. A stork wanders right up to me, looks me up and down. For a second I think it's about to peck at my hands.

Ixchel and I cast glances around. Looking for another way out.

A white-haired old man comes ambling in. He's dressed in a loose white *guayabera* shirt and wears a tatty straw hat. He stops next to the stork, staring at the two of us as he puffs on a cigar.

"Enjoying the mini-zoo?" he asks, in lilting Spanish.

"We just got here," I tell him. I'm still a little out of breath.

The old gent shakes his head regretfully. "Doesn't seem like a good idea to me. There's a young fella in the house, just got here. A priest. Looks innocent enough, oh yes. But he's no priest – he's a bad 'un; I can tell. I can sniff 'em out, see. Trapping animals gives you a nose for the wrong 'uns. I'd sooner tackle one of my crocodiles than one like him. And crocodiles can be mighty tricky."

My hand unconsciously goes to my jeans, where I've stashed the Adaptor. The old man's beady eyes don't miss a thing. He glances down at my hand and says, "You've got what he's come for? Or is it you he's after?"

Then he leans forward and whispers, "The back door is open." He nods his head. Barely visible behind a tangle of vines is a white door. "It leads on to the riverbank. A few houses to the right, there's a boat. Now go!"

We bolt towards the door. But it's too late.

"OK, far enough," comes Madison's voice. In cold horror, I gaze over the old man's shoulder to see Madison emerging from the house.

Pointing a gun.

"Move aside, Pops. You don't want to take a bullet for this loser, I guarantee it."

The old man doesn't budge. Instead he whispers, "He's right behind me, yes?" I nod. Then, without warning, the old man gives a loud cry like a bird's caw.

"Justiiiiiicio!"

Madison is too astounded to react when the monstrous golden eagle swoops down on to him. Wings beating wildly, it pecks at his face. Madison has no time to shoot; not when he needs both arms to protect his eyes.

We're through the door within seconds, and on to the decking outside. And we're running along decks between the houses and the river, leaping fences and gates, eyes scouring the backs of the houses for the only thing that can save us – the boat.

A few houses ahead, I spot an elegant mansion, modern, all glass and grey brick, with a magnificent green lawn. Bobbing on the river next to it is a small speedboat. To even get to the house, we'll have to jump across a channel of water between the mansion and the neighbouring house.

And then I hear him. Madison smashes through the white picket fencing near the mini-zoo. He's yelling with rage. If running in a flowing habit slows him down, it's hard to tell. As we get closer to the gap between the houses I shout to Ixchel, "Jump!" I leap into the air, sail across the gap. Ixchel follows. She lands square on the lawn.

"Start up the boat!" I yell, panting.

She moves swiftly. I limber up as Madison hurtles towards me, preparing his jump. I'm getting ready to spill him into the water the second he lands on my side. Then he makes a movement which roots me to the spot.

Still running, he reaches under his cloak and pulls a pistol from a shoulder holster.

I throw a glance over my shoulder at Ixchel – she's sitting in the speedboat but I don't hear a peep from the engine.

Madison trundles to a stop on the opposite bank. He's grinning, shaking his head and waving the gun.

"Jeez, man, you should learn when to quit. Now throw the Adaptor over here."

It strikes me for a second that Madison doesn't know that the Adaptor is safely wrapped in plastic.

Yet he shows no sign of being afraid of touching the Adaptor or breathing in the gas.

"You can touch it," I blurt.

"Way to go, dumbass."

"You have the Bakab gene?"

Madison gives a slow nod. "You got it, kid. Not so special now, hey?"

I'm completely thrown. "But . . . back in the jungle . . . you wouldn't touch the codex. . ."

"First-time nerves."

"It was the same for me – but I did it."

Madison pulls himself up straight. His eyes grow cold. "You calling me a coward?"

"Me? I'm the one with a gun pointed at me."

Livid with rage, he spits his words. "Throw. Me. The. Adaptor."

"Or what?"

Madison cocks the gun, slips off the safety. Lightly, he says, "Or this."

"They want me alive, though, don't they? Your bosses – I heard them say so."

This confuses him, for just a second. Behind me, I hear the engine explode into action. I give the pistol one more glance, and then spin on my heel, make a dash down the jetty for the boat. Shots ring out from Madison's gun; bullets whizz past my ankles.

Then one of them hits me in the left thigh.

The pain is surprising. It doesn't feel anything like I've imagined. At first, it's like a good, solid kick, like you might get in a football game from someone wearing studs. I keep going until I reach the boat, and I jump in. Ixchel grabs the rudder and revs up the engine. The boat springs away from the moorings, cuts a deep swathe into the murky water.

I collapse on to the boat's deck, groaning loudly in agony. Within seconds the pain is deeper and fiercer than anything I've known. It feels like my thigh muscle has been sliced open and a hot poker stuffed inside. Desperately I clutch at the wound. My hands come away covered in hot, sticky blood.

When I see that, I practically faint.

"Don't look at it!" warns Ixchel. I close my eyes, leaning my head on the deck, on the verge of tears.

Ixchel's voice is firm, calm. "Take deep breaths. Into your nose, out through your mouth. As slowly as you can."

I grit my teeth. My whole body begins to shake violently.

"Hold on, Josh. You'll be OK."

Eyes screwed shut, I concentrate on breathing for a few minutes, on the high-pitched roar of the boat's motor, on the rush of water streaming past us. A few seconds later, I'm a tiny bit calmer. I open my eyes to look at Ixchel. She's gazing over the river, towards the town's main dock.

"Don't get up to look," she says in an even voice, "but he's hitching a lift from one of the tourist boats. It's going in to pick him up right now. They can't catch up with us. But when we get to the dock, you need to be able to walk. At least to a taxi."

I give a loud groan. "I can't bloody walk!"

"I'm sorry, Josh. You must."

I stare into the gathering clouds high above the river. It takes all my self-control not to whimper in pain. If I were alone I'd be a blubbering wreck by now. In front of Ixchel, there's no way I can let that happen.

The boat begins to swerve towards the left bank.

"Get ready, Josh. You need to get up in ten seconds."

I take a few quick, deep breaths, and then pull myself into a sitting position, roaring from the bolt of pure agony that surges through my left leg. Ixchel's waving at someone on the bank, and she shouts, "Help! Emergency!"

I can't turn around without hurting, so I can't see what's going on. The engine slows and Ixchel steers the boat into the moorings. As soon as it comes to a standstill, she steps over to me. She offers me a hand, helping me to my unsteady feet.

On the deck, two young guys hold out their arms, saying, "Come on, grab hold, grab hold!"

My blood is everywhere. My left jean leg is soaked, dark and rusty. Both my hands, and now Ixchel's too, are coated with blood. But that doesn't put the young guys off. They yank us both out of the boat, then the two of them support my weight, practically frog-marching me to a waiting silver VW Beetle.

They help me into the back seat, where I lie moaning and writhing. The pain gets worse by the second. I stuff my collar into my mouth and bite down, tasting the blood that's now smeared all over my T-shirt.

And then I hear a voice I recognize – Susannah St John.

"Josh." Her voice sounds sharp, very clear. I focus on it. "Is that a gunshot wound?"

I nod, trembling.

"Thought so. I heard the shooting; think the whole town did. Still, least it helped me to find you. Now, darling, can you walk?"

Just. Again, I nod.

"That's good; probably nothing broken, then."

"It hurts like hell."

Susannah makes a sympathetic, clucking noise. "I know, dear. Now, listen, before we can take care of that leg we're gonna have to drive some. That fella's on his way to the dock on a boat. Better put some distance between us. That means driving fast. Can you be brave?"

I grit my teeth and nod.

"Give him your hand, dear," Susannah orders Ixchel. "Try to help hold his leg still."

Ixchel gives me a look of deep concern. Slowly, she takes my hand. The car begins to move. Every pothole we drive over is pure agony, forcing a scream from me. But when we're finally on the open road the surface is smooth.

Susannah slams her foot down on the accelerator. "Seatbelts, kids," she shouts above the high-pitched revs of the engine. "We need to get out of here – and fast."

BLOG ENTRY: SOMEWHERE IN MEXICO

ⴲⴻⴶⴲⵀⴰⴳⵉⵥ⵳

This guy who's after me, Simon Madison, keeps popping up when I least expect him. How is he following me? It's as if he knows every step before I do.

When he turned up at this house yesterday where I was visiting someone called Susannah, it crossed my mind that maybe Susannah had set me up.

But then she rescued me from him. She even stitched up my wound. Madison sort of shot me in the leg yesterday. Don't worry! Nothing too serious, as it turns out. Mind you, it was the worst pain I'd ever felt, like my leg was crawling with fire from the inside. Having the wound cleaned and stitched was no picnic, either.

Susannah is a retired nurse. So when she realized I'd been shot, she tossed a top-quality first-aid kit into her car and drove out to find me. We stopped somewhere on the road. In the back of the car, Susannah did a clean-and-repair job on my leg. The bullet had gone straight through – it was "just" a flesh wound. But my jeans were kind of disgusting, so we stopped off somewhere to buy some new ones.

I tried to phone you again – no reply. I guess I always call when you're at Mass. I left voicemail – just want you to know I'm OK. Well, kind of OK.

If I don't tell you anything about where I am, Mum, it's because I've even started to worry that this blog has been compromised. What if somehow the Sect has got into my school, broken into my locker, found the letter to you, guessed the password and is now reading this. . .?

So – no town names, OK? But I can't stop blogging. Cos then you'd worry even more.

All this uncertainty. It's getting to me. I just want the answers – now!

In a roadside restaurant today, I had the most amazing eggs – "Hawaiian Style" with ham and pineapple. The strips of ham and pineapple were arranged in a pattern to make the dish look like a whole pineapple.

I'm finally getting to know this country. And still, I feel completely lost.

Thirty minutes out of Tlacotalpan we stop at the outskirts of a coastal town, Alvarado, where we drink glasses of fresh pineapple juice and eat the most elaborate omelettes I've ever seen. There's an Internet café, so I post a quick update to my blog.

When I'm done blogging, I rejoin Ixchel and Susannah at the restaurant. I take Arcadio's envelope out of my pocket and place it on the table in front of us. Susannah kisses her fingers and then lightly touches the envelope.

Ixchel and I watch her. We can't hide our curiosity. Bluntly, Ixchel asks, "You loved him. Didn't you?"

"Yes, dear, I did" is Susannah's soft-spoken reply. "Which is why it's such an honour to be of assistance to his grandson."

But am I? She keeps insisting that Arcadio's my grandfather, but secretly I wonder if it's the other way around.

My future grandson, travelling backwards in time. . .

I open the envelope. There's a single leaf of paper inside.
The message:

Dear Josh,

*By now you must suspect that your fate is intertwined
with the Mayan prophecy of 2012.*

*As the poet once said, our destiny is not frightful by
being unreal; it is frightful because it is irreversible and iron-
clad.*

*The truth you seek awaits you on the slopes of Mount
Orizaba.*

*A terrible storm is brewing. Yet you will never find peace
until you confront your truth.*

Forever in your debt,

J Arcadio Garcia

I don't know how to react. I gaze into Ixchel's face, and then
Susannah's. They stare back at me with an expectant air.

Finally, I crack. "What the heck is he on about?"

"Mount Orizaba?" Susannah says. "It's there." She jabs a
finger into the air, pointing at the distant snow-capped cone
of a volcano that's just visible on the horizon.

"But what about the rest of it?" I say. "The stuff about
destiny being 'irreversible and iron-clad'. What's that meant
to be?"

"I think it's a warning," says Susannah. "Arcadio sees your fate – whatever that may be – as inescapable. But this is very strange. What's this mention of the Mayan prophecy? What fate of yours could he have known about all those years ago?"

"Maybe he consulted a *brujo*?" Ixchel offers.

Susannah surprises me by nodding at this, apparently serious.

I'm incredulous. "You believe in all that?"

"Of course," she nods. "I've seen remarkable things in Mexico."

"I guess," I say, remembering my own encounter with the *brujos*. "But there's *another* way Arcadio could know about things that are going to happen to me."

Susannah and Ixchel bristle with instant intrigue.

"Go on. . ."

"It's just an idea. . ." I say.

"Yes. . .?"

"Time travel," I say. I ignore their sceptical looks, continuing, "Arcadio could be from the future. My son, or grandson, or something. And that's how he knows what's in my future. In my future – he knows *me*."

I don't mention that he could be Itzamna himself, the very guy who founded Ek Naab. That would be a step too far – and it would break my promise to Montoyo.

"You're so sure of yourself, aren't you?" says Ixchel with a touch of scorn. "Typical macho man – so confident that some woman will give you a son. And a blue-eyed blond, too!"

For the first time ever, I feel actual anger towards Ixchel. "All right, he could be a nephew, then – not that I have any brothers and sisters. Does that make you happy, hey? Sheesh . . . I can't say anything around you!"

Susannah looks mildly amused. "For best friends, you two squabble a good deal."

"We're not best friends," we say, simultaneously.

"Arcadio must be from a future where he knows me," I repeat. "How else could he know my address, that I'd understand the Caesar cipher?"

Susannah smiles behind her hand. "You really think time travel is more likely than a shamanistic vision? Well, maybe we're *tal para qual*, as they say in Spanish – two of a kind – each as misguided as the other."

I want to say more, but I don't. I promised Montoyo I wouldn't leak information from the Ix Codex – but it's getting difficult. I can't tell them about the Erinsi, the instructions to make the Key, the Bracelet of Itzamna, or Montoyo's theory about a time-travel device.

Susannah chops into my thoughts. "Let's get back to the letter, kids. What is this truth you seek, Josh?"

I sigh deeply. "I don't know what really happened to my father. I think he was murdered by some US secret agents, but I can't prove it. And I don't know why."

"And you need to know the truth – why?"

"I've tried forgetting about it. And I can't. It's got into my dreams. In the dreams, Dad tells me that they made it all up, the idea that he died. Him and my mum!"

Susannah says, "Sounds as though deep down, you're looking for someone to blame. Blaming him, anyone, even your mother."

"I dunno. But whoever is responsible – they have to pay."

Susannah shakes her head. "If it really was the secret services, you'll never find out. Never prove it, never hold them responsible. You know that, don't you?"

"That's not true! Read this letter. Arcadio knows that I *will* find out. That's the 'truth' which 'awaits' me. That's what he means when he writes, 'You will never find peace until you confront your truth'."

"OK." Susannah seems to be collecting her thoughts on the matter. "And you're certain that you want to do this?"

Ixchel interrupts, "Even more than getting the Adaptor back to Ek Naab?"

I throw her a bleak look. "I'm the one with a *hole in my leg* that I got from looking after that thing! This is important *to me*. Ek Naab can wait. Anyway, I thought you were the one who wanted to tell Montoyo to get lost."

Susannah looks at both of us in confusion. "Adaptor? Ek Naab? What in heaven's name are you talking about?"

Ixchel and I are instantly silent; something which Susannah notices, logging the fact with another quiet smile.

"I see," she says after a moment's pause. "Not going to talk about that, are you? On that matter you're both *quite* unified."

"We can't. . ." Ixchel begins.

"You wouldn't believe us anyway. . ."

"We're really not supposed to."

Susannah says again, "I see. Well, look: out of respect for Arcadio, I'll drive you to the mountain. There's a small town called Tlachichuca – it's where all the climbers start. You'll have to find a guide – it's a tough hike. And you don't even know what you're looking for. Do you?"

I shake my head. She's right. I've no idea.

"But I'm not coming with you. I'm an old lady – my hiking days are over. I'll wait for you until you come back down. And then – what?"

Ixchel says, "Could you take us to Veracruz? We have transport from there."

Susannah nods. "OK. I'll do it. Now, you, young man, you'd better get some rest if you plan on walking up a glacier with that leg."

I turn away, staring at the distant volcano. The snowcone catches the sunlight for a second, blazing white like a star. It seems I'm long overdue an appointment with one of

Mexico's volcanoes. Mount Orizaba looms like a gigantic pyramid, a colossus, dominating the lives of everyone in its shadow.

Including mine.

Night has fallen by the time we arrive in Tlachichuca. It's cold. There are even isolated patches of snow. Susannah buys us second-hand ski jackets, backpacks and thermal longjohns. She puts us all up in the climbers' hostel. The building is a hundred-year-old soap factory, rebuilt as an Alpine mountain lodge. In the dormitories, bunk beds are stacked across a rough wooden floor. Huge stained pine beams hold up the roof. In the corner, there's an antique oak vat for boiling up lye and lard.

The dining room is crammed with mostly white men and women in their twenties and thirties, Americans and Canadians, fit and healthy-looking. Compared to the local Mexicans – and to Ixchel and me – they all seem impossibly tall.

El Pico de Orizaba is the third-highest peak in the continent of North America. Susannah explained it all on the drive over from Tlacotalpan. It's the highest mountain in

Mexico, an extinct volcano – so far as the past few hundred years go. There are occasional rumbles, but no one's worried. It's not actively smoking and letting off fireworks, like the nearby volcano Popocatepetl.

Apparently, young climbers love to conquer "El Pico". There's a hut on the lower slopes, where people stay for a day or so to get acclimatized. The climb takes you through a field of scree and lava boulders known as the "Labyrinth", because there's only one decent route through. Then comes the Jamapa glacier, which leads all the way to the snow-covered summit. At this time of year, the glacier is usually coated with fresh snow. It's an alpine-style climb, needing ice-climbing gear: ropes, crampons and the right clothes. You need to be fit and strong to reach the summit, but there shouldn't be too much clambering up rocks. Mainly it's a very, very steep hike, into altitudes where the oxygen is so thin that it can give you weird hallucinations.

Susannah doubts we'll even find anyone to take us up there. We're so young, and I'm limping. I keep expecting Ixchel to drop out. I'd happily go alone, except for my leg. But there's no question of her not coming with me. She even seems keen on the idea.

At first, I'm relieved to be able to climb into a bed for the first time in three days. But I toss and turn – can't get comfortable, with the bruises on my ribcage and the deep, dull ache inside my leg. When I finally fall asleep, I dream the dream about my dad.

I wake up dry-eyed, impatient and angry. I've had enough. This isn't how I want to remember my dad, but the dream is beginning to consume my memories. Now, when I think of him, he's always in our kitchen, with that distant air, the one which says, *Hey, Josh, get off my back, OK?*

I put on my ski jacket and go downstairs to the dining room. I buy a can of Fresca from the drinks machine and take it outside, under the inky black of a star-speckled sky. There's a couple sitting close together on folding chairs and sipping from steaming mugs. I wander around to the back of the hostel, find a patch of unspoiled snow and spend a few minutes scrunching over it in my trainers. Then I stand, just gazing out over the lights of the town, across the countryside and to the brooding shadow of the volcano.

What am I going to find?

I expected the postcards to lead to an informer; someone who was willing to leak me the information I so badly need. Since that didn't happen, I don't know what to think.

What could there possibly be on the slopes of a mountain that would explain to me the truth behind my father's death?

I hear footsteps in the snow. "Hey," a voice whispers, right behind me. It's Ixchel. She gives me a wry grin.

"You couldn't sleep either, hey?"

I shake my head slowly, staring at her.

"It's the altitude," she says. "Does strange things to you. We should take a walk tomorrow, get used to it."

Then she gives me a little shove. "So, Josh. How did we end up here?"

"I was just wondering that." My mind goes back to the afternoon that Tyler and I set off to Saffron Walden. Since then I've been disguised as Batman, escaped from a cellar where I was going to be tortured, crossed the ocean in a Muwan, got lost in caves, almost drowned in an underground river, got shot in the leg . . . all in search of the most elusive truth in my life.

What really happened to my dad?

Ixchel's voice breaks across my distant thoughts. "I've been thinking about your theory. The one about time travel."

"Oh yeah?"

Ixchel nods. "Mm-hmm. It's not the first time I've heard time travel mentioned in Ek Naab."

"It isn't?"

"No. There's a rumour . . . I don't know who started it . . . that the Bracelet of Itzamna is a time-travel device. Or part of one."

I struggle to keep my features steady. "Really?"

"Don't get me wrong – there are lots of crazy theories about how Ek Naab got started. Some say we're founded by survivors from Atlantis. Some say we're all that's left of a

305

colony of extraterrestrial visitors. And some say that Itzamna is from an alternative future – one that exists only because Itzamna intervened to save civilization in 2012."

I notice that Ixchel says nothing about Itzamna copying down the writings of the mysterious ancients, the Erinsi – *People of Memory*.

Is that a secret, too?

Ixchel licks her lips in a deliberate way, as if wondering how to say the next sentence. "Josh. You may have the first bit of proof I've ever seen that the time-travel theory is right."

"I thought you reckoned that Arcadio consulted a *brujo*."

"Well, maybe he did. Some of the *brujos* know about 2012. They know a lot more than you imagine."

"So. . .?"

"It's the letter itself. And the instructions from Arcadio. Remember how he told you not to open the envelope, to put it in your pocket? Why? It's as if he knew that Madison would be coming. His advice made it easy to get out of there fast."

"Yeah," I say, spreading my hands on the table. "That's what I've been saying. Arcadio knows me. Or he will know me."

"Which means that whatever we find on the volcano, you'll live to tell the tale."

"It means *one* of us will live to tell the tale," I say.

"I guess. . ." she agrees. "Hadn't really thought of that."

I grin. "You're my witness." Shyly, she grins back, then lowers her eyes.

We sit in awkward silence for a few moments. I sip my Fresca and offer Ixchel a swig. My thoughts swirl with the words of Arcadio's letter.

"*A terrible storm is brewing. Yet you will never find peace until you confront your truth.*"

BLOG ENTRY: SMOOTH JAZZ AT 14,000 FT

⬤ᐊᐱ3ᐱ᙭◻ᐃᐊᕁᐃ

So, we decided to do a bit of climbing. . . I managed to charge up Dad's iPod, and used it on a hike earlier today. We didn't go very far, just trailed after one of the guided groups for a bit, to get used to the altitude. My leg held out pretty well, considering. Mind you, I was fuzzy from the painkillers. And we only walked for two hours.

We bought cold-weather gear and boots for the climb. Susannah spent all morning asking around for a guide to take us up the mountain. None of the registered mountaineering guides will have anything to do with us, because they can't get parental permission. But Susannah found a local indian from a nearby village. He agreed to take us to the second hut and no further. That's still a long way short of the summit, but he reckons that everyone who goes to the summit has to stop at the second hut.

If there's something or someone to be encountered on the slope, hanging around the second hut is the way to find out.

Comment (1) from Eleanor

Josh. You must tell me where you are. I'm going out of my mind with worry. You can have no idea what you've put me through, none whatsoever.

I searched the house for any clue as to where you'd gone. I asked your friends, Tyler and Emmy – Emmy who you said you were staying with? Her parents didn't know anything about it! Tyler admitted he'd talked to you, that he thought you were in Mexico.

But I could hardly believe what Tyler tried to tell me. I finally got your head teacher to give me permission to look in your locker today.

Until I found your letter and this blog, I was ready to call the police.

I can't believe you persuaded your friends to lie for you. Are you really in Mexico, and if so, how? If I find you've used my credit card again, I don't know what I'll do.

Really, Josh. We're going to need to get some professional help. I can't cope with you being like this any more, I really can't.

Stop making up these stories. You simply cannot expect me to believe this. Tell me where you are NOW. I love you, Josh, but I can't take this. It will destroy me.

Ixchel sits beside me at the Internet café, staring over my shoulder at Mum's comment on my blog.

"This looks bad."

"It's pretty bad," I agree.

"How come she only just found your blog?"

"I left her a letter with the Web address and a password to read it. To be honest, the blog was just in case."

"Just in case. . .?"

"In case I never came back. I didn't exactly tell her I was leaving."

"You left home without telling your mother?"

"Didn't have much choice. Madison was after me!"

"So, you going to tell her now?"

"I can't. Not until I know what's on that mountain."

"Well. . ." Ixchel pulls out her Ek Naab phone and gives me a rueful grin. "I hate to tell you this, but. . ."

I groan. "Don't."

"Montoyo's not happy either. Read this text from Benicio."

Ixchel, if you are still with Josh, BRING HIM BACK. Montoyo has ordered us back. If I'm not in Ek Naab with Josh AND you by tomorrow afternoon, we're all in BIG TROUBLE, me most of all, and I will NEVER forgive you.

I close my eyes and sigh. "Just one more day. That's all I need. I've given them so much – what have they ever done for me?"

"Benicio saved your life," Ixchel suggests. "Twice."

"I guess. But to be fair – I was on an errand for them."

Abruptly, Ixchel changes the subject. "Why doesn't your mother believe you?"

"I don't know. It probably all sounds pretty unbelievable. I thought it would be best to be open, but I can't tell any more."

"Have you told her everything?"

"I haven't told *anyone* everything."

"Why?"

I shove my chair backwards, and in frustration, push my hands into my hair until it sticks up. "It's dangerous. What I know is so dangerous. I'm bad luck to be around. Can't you tell?"

"Sounds like you're feeling sorry for yourself."

310

Normally, I'd be irritated with a comment like that. Right now, I can't even be bothered to respond. Mum finding out at this stage was not part of my plan. I don't know what kind of surveillance the Sect has on my house. But for all I know, they're spying on Mum's Web browsing. Which means they now know about the blog, if they didn't before.

If so, I've been found out – again. The blog post doesn't make it clear which mountain we're hanging around. That's my best hope to confuse them. There are four volcanoes between here and the neighbouring state of Puebla. You can climb three of them.

So they have a one in three chance of finding me. With each passing day, those odds shorten. Unless Madison has another way of following me? But I can't figure out what.

I decide that we can't waste any more time. Tomorrow, we'll climb. Ixchel doesn't respond when I tell her the news – not for a few minutes, at least.

Then she heads off, wordlessly. Is she cross? Going to get ready? I really can't tell.

I watch idly as the minutes run out on my Internet access. With two minutes to go, I have a sudden idea. There's still something I can do to decode Arcadio's riddle. I type a line from his letter into the search engine:

Our destiny is not frightful by being unreal; it is frightful because it is irreversible and iron-clad.

The line is a quotation – from a writer and poet named Borges. When I read the line in context, the hairs on the back of my neck seem to prickle with electricity.

The quotation continues:

Time is the substance I am made of. Time is a river which sweeps me along, but I am the river; it is a tiger which destroys me, but I am the tiger; it is a fire which consumes me, but I am the fire.

I don't fully understand the meaning, but inside my mind somewhere, a light goes on, like a dusty old attic being visited for the first time in many years.

This is definitely about time travel.

Arcadio is speaking to me from the future. He's warning me. Somehow, I'm destined to be involved in whatever is coming in 2012. According to Arcadio, that is my inescapable destiny.

I don't understand why or how. But the minute I read those words, I recognize the truth of them.

I'm meant to be here. In some peculiar loop of time – I've already been here. Whatever is going to happen on the mountain, it leads somehow to Arcadio, and to the prophecy of 2012.

I'm light-headed with the weight of destiny. I didn't plan on being led by my dreams again, but it looks as though I have been. It's been there all in along in my dream about my father – the image, over and over again: postcards of Mexico on my fridge.

The postcards – a link with the past and my future.

"What am I doing here?" I say aloud, to no one in particular. "What would happen if I just walked out of here, right now, took a bus to Mexico City and took a flight back home?"

I'm almost ready to do it. But these words stop me: "Time is a river which sweeps me along, but I am the river."

Am *I* the river? What if I choose differently? If that river is diverted elsewhere – will it somehow just flow back to the same spot? Will anything I do make any difference? Have all my actions already been taken into account?

Susannah strolls into the Internet café.

"Ixchel told me that you're both headed up the mountain tomorrow. That can't be right – is it?"

"Uh huh." I'm partly amazed, partly relieved to hear that Ixchel's on board.

Susannah gives the most delicate shrug. "Well, OK."

"You don't think it's too soon to climb?"

"It surely is."

"So. . .?"

"Arcadio gave me some advice about how to deal with you, Josh. Warned me that you'd be impetuous. Told me not to interfere."

313

"But . . . I could get hurt."

It's strange, being around an adult who actually lets me take responsibility, to make my own choices. It takes some getting used to.

Susannah wrinkles her nose. "No, sir. You're gonna live a long life."

"You know that, yeah?"

Susannah nods, and to my astonishment, tears spring to her eyes. A look of deep melancholy crosses her features. Her lips tremble, her chin shakes. She holds out her arms to me in a sudden gesture of yearning.

"Hug me, Josh. Give me a hug for the girl I used to be."

Mystified, I put my arms around Susannah, until a few moments later, she releases me. She's been so great to two kids she barely knows. After our hug, Susannah won't look me in the eye. She stands up, walks briskly to the window, where she stares at the massive volcano, a perfect cone of granite and snow in a green meadow, under a flawless blue sky.

"You'd better go pack your climbing gear," she tells me, still looking away. "It's best to get an early start. There's a jeep leaving for the first hut in an hour or so. An early night and you can be up and about by five tomorrow morning."

39

We wave Susannah goodbye and board the four-wheel-drive jeep that leaves for the first mountain hut. The sun has just set; a heavy layer of clouds rolls in from the Orizaba mountain range, smothering the roads with a film of mist. As we arrive at the hut, the sky is a gloomy, charcoal grey. The plan is to get a decent night's sleep, but it turns out that the hut has been taken over by a group of high-school kids from Mexico City, a bunch of sixteen- and seventeen-year-olds. They want to party until the small hours, by the sounds of it.

Ixchel's in the bunk next to mine, both lower bunks. I roll over and look at her. Like me, she's still awake.

"I wish they'd shut up," I whisper.

Ixchel grins. "Yeah," she hisses back. There's a long pause. After a while it feels awkward. But Ixchel is still gazing back at me. "How are you feeling?" she asks.

"Crummy," I say with a dramatic frown. We both laugh. "The last thing I want to do tomorrow is to climb."

"I'm really excited," she says. "And scared. Josh . . . are you scared?"

I reply slowly, "You're kidding, aren't you? I'm petrified."

"We don't have to do this," she whispers.

"Yeah," I say, nodding, "*I* do."

There's so much at stake, I can hardly bear to think about it. All my questions answered. . .

But what if I don't like the answers?

Before we go to sleep, we dose up on Diamox, to prevent altitude sickness. I eventually fall asleep, but it's not a good night. I'm woken several times by the sound of the older boys talking, laughing. By five the next morning, I'm only vaguely rested. At least the gunshot wound feels better than it has up until now.

Ixchel sits up on her bunk, looking across at me. Like me, she's slept in her longjohns and a T-shirt. In silence, we both pull jeans over our leggings, then dress in the walking socks, hiking boots and the ski jackets that Susannah bought for us.

As we walk out of the dorm, twelve alarms go off. The hut fills with the sounds of teenagers cursing, kicking in their sleeping bags. Their racket does nothing but make me miserable. Everyone else is here for fun. Well, not me.

I'm on the brink of something, I sense it.

Our guide, Xocotli (he pronounces it *Shock-ott-lee*), is waiting for us outside, tying up his horse. He's a slight, wiry guy in his fifties, with a deeply lined face that's straight from the Aztecs and narrow brown eyes which bore into ours. He wears a woollen poncho and a knitted hat. He hands out still-warm *tamales* – steamed cornmeal spiced with green tomato chilli sauce and wrapped in corn husks. Ixchel and I eat them straight out of the husks. Our hot breath billows like fine powder into the air around us.

Xocotli's brown features break into a huge grin. "You enjoy the *tamales*, yes?" he asks, speaking Spanish in a reedy, sing-song voice.

We answer with enthusiastic nods. Xocotli stares closely at Ixchel. "You have Mayan blood, yes?"

She nods, mouth stuffed with cornmeal.

He turns to me. "And you're a *norteamericano*?"

"English," I tell him. "Not a *gringo*."

Xocotli looks us both up and down, sizing us up. He inspects our crampons, ropes and ice-axes. Are we worthy of the mountain? I can't imagine that we look as though we'd make the summit.

"Ever climbed on ice?"

We shake our heads.

"Then it's just to the second hut, agreed? No summit! Well, let's get going. The mountain . . . she can be a dangerous lady."

His words hang in the dry morning air. We make a start on the scree path, carrying chocolate, water and the

317

painkillers for my leg in our climbers' backpacks. I've safely stashed the Adaptor in mine. I'm about to plug in the earphones of my dad's iPod when Xocotli notices and wags his finger at me.

"No. You need to listen, yes?" He gestures at his ears, then points to his mouth. "Listen to every word."

We walk in silence for long while, avoiding occasional patches of frozen snow as we follow Xocotli. He steps as lightly as the goats we pass on the way.

Ixchel asks, "Does the volcano ever rumble?"

"Hardly ever. But she's no innocent," Xocotli warns. "One of these days, she could awaken, just like Popocateptl. Then we'd see."

He nods twice, slow and deliberate; gazes directly into the path that winds towards the distant peak. "Yup. Then we'd see how it is."

The boulders of the "Labyrinth" loom on the path ahead, their long shadows trailing like black tongues over the scree. Xocotli glances at us and points at my dragging leg. "Something wrong?"

Flatly, Ixchel replies, "He was shot."

If Xocotli's surprised by this, he doesn't show it. He just nods. "Then I'll take you up the easiest way. No climbing."

Xocotli leaps forward a few steps so that he's ahead of us. Ixchel draws closer to me. "I know you won't talk about what's in the Ix Codex. So why don't you let me guess?"

I give her a quick glance. She doesn't seem to be joking. "I reckon I can't stop you."

"True, you can't. So . . . if Arcadio is someone from the future – and he's been getting involved in the affairs of Ek Naab – and the Ix Codex is written in English . . . then my guess would be that someone from the future, someone who speaks English, wrote the Ix Codex. Am I right?"

I don't answer, but trudge ahead.

"And that means that there's a time-travel device around somewhere. I think that's what the 'Revival Chamber' is. I bet you get into one of those sarcophagus things and use the Adaptor to start it up. Like a key in a car. Or maybe the Bracelet of Itzamna is the missing part of the puzzle. Maybe the Bracelet acts like the key, turns the Revival Chamber into a time-travel machine."

"Hmm," I say. "Interesting idea."

"I'm close, though, aren't I?"

Truthfully, I say, "I couldn't really tell you."

Ixchel stares directly ahead. In a grim voice she says, "I'm close. And you know it."

Xocotli bears left, leading us across the slope. I stare ahead in trepidation.

No climbing? Yeah, right!

There's no way to get up this mountain without scrambling over some of the huge rocks in our way. Just looking at the route makes my leg ache.

Breathless, I stop and lean against a boulder. "Guys. I need a break."

For the first time, we face down the slope. Beneath us, the gentle incline of scrub and scree falls off towards a far-flung green canopy of pine trees. I turn around and crane my neck, trying to catch a glimpse of the summit. It's there in the distance: a dazzling sunlit cone behind the alpine landscape of snow, ice and rock. All framed in a sky of purest blue.

My ears tingle from the cold. I roll out my thermal hood and fasten it around my head. Soon we'll reach the snow line. It's hard to believe we're still in sunny Mexico.

40

The snow falls all the way to the glacier and beyond. It last snowed two days ago, according to Xocotli. So, not as bad as it could be; fresh powder drains your strength faster. The snow is dry and firm, and where well-trodden, icy. It takes another three hours of slow climbing to navigate the rock field. Every so often we catch a glimpse of what looks like a direct route straight on to the glacier. With hope in our hearts, we point to it. Xocotli always replies with a sad shake of his head. "It looks all right now, but later, you'll see that there's a big drop."

Without Xocotli we'd have had no chance, got hopelessly lost. I reach the point where all I can think about is the agony of my gunshot wound. I don't even want to think about what I'm doing to the healing process, wrenching my muscles again and again. I'm the one slowing us down with frequent stops, turning away from the other two so they won't see me wince in pain. Each time, I eat a square of chocolate and sip from one of my water bottles. I wish

I could be distracted by some music, but Xocotli's made it clear that we all need to focus.

I begin to seriously wonder why I insisted on coming up here. Should I have just caved in and called Montoyo, asked them to come and take me home? That way Montoyo would be happy – as happy as the miserable so-and-so ever seems to get – and my mum would stop worrying.

But me, I'd be back to square one. Always wondering what was up here.

Or who.

I can think of only three possibilities. I seem to remember that Montoyo once told me that my grandfather Aureliano's Muwan crashed somewhere in the Orizaba mountain range. Montoyo reckoned that the wreckage was cleared and taken to the museum of Jalapa. Could some of the wreckage have landed on the slopes of Mount Orizaba itself? That's one theory. But I can't guess at how it would tell me anything about my father's fate.

The second theory is that one of the climbers we'll meet on the way will be a rogue agent from the NRO who wants me to know the truth.

My third idea is the one which really gets my pulse racing. If Arcadio sent the message . . . what if he's coming to meet me himself? I can think of quite a few questions I'd have for a time traveller from the future. Especially if he really is descended from me.

By now we've been overtaken by four groups of climbers, including the high-school kids from Mexico City. Even they walked in relative silence. It's fun for the first hour or two, but after that it's tough going.

I make a point of looking every climber in the eye. Just in case they're the one I'm looking for.

After what seems like a day of total endurance, we reach the edge of the glacier. I check my watch, amazed to see that it's only ten a.m. But then, we have been climbing for five hours. Xocotli tells us that we're now at 16,600 feet.

"You should rest for an hour. We've come up slowly, so you're acclimatizing well. But from now on it'll get harder. The air gets thin, and you'll feel it."

I sit on a low boulder. We can see for hundreds of miles across the farms and villages of Veracruz. Ixchel removes her hood and gloves and smiles at me. Her eyes are damp from the stinging air. I watch as she runs a cherry-flavoured lip balm over her lips. She turns and offers it to me. "Don't worry, it won't colour your lips. Much."

"You feeling faint?" I ask, using her lip balm.

"No. I feel amazing, actually. I've never seen snow, never climbed a mountain, never been so cold I could see my own breath. . ." She breaks into a huge grin. "I've never felt so alive."

"That's great."

"How's your leg?"

I reply curtly, "It hurts." I don't want to say how much, in case I can't stop complaining.

"Take another painkiller. It's about time for another dose."

I don't argue. My head is starting to pound, probably from the altitude. It's getting harder to breathe. Altogether, I'm feeling pretty rubbish.

Xocotli instructs us to fasten our crampons and rope up. There are a few crevasses on the glacier, but even a slip can give you a nasty fall – it's so steep and icy. People have already died this season, he tells us.

The sky is clear, the air still when we begin climbing the glacier. In the next thirty minutes, that all changes. Seemingly from nowhere, an icy wind whips up around us, stinging our faces. I feel sorry for those who are going all the way to the top.

The second hut is just a rescue centre, no more than half an hour's climb from our position. I can see it in the distance, smoke puffing from its chimney. As we approach, I find it hard to catch my breath. I hate the fact that I'm the one slowing the group down. If it weren't for the bruised ribs and thigh wound, I know I'd be most of the way up this mountain by now.

We're about forty metres from the hut when someone comes out, walks to a nearby stack of firewood. I watch in amazement.

This altitude is doing weird things to my eyes.

I pick up my pace, hurrying through the wind towards where the man stands selecting pieces of wood. He's wearing jeans and a grey woollen sweater with a hat pulled down over his ears. He's got a thick beard, and maybe that's what makes me think I'm seeing who I think I see.

"Josh, what's the matter?" Ixchel can't help but notice that I'm rushing ahead – we're roped together. I ignore her and keep moving forward, staring in disbelief at the man.

It can't be. . .

Ixchel catches up with me. "What's wrong?"

I turn to her, face flushed, gasping in wonder. "Can you see that bloke there?"

She looks puzzled. "Of course. . . It's the mountain-rescue guy."

I look back at the man. He turns to us and we stare at each other, face to face. I'm frozen, slack-jawed, my voice blocked somewhere deep inside my lungs.

Ixchel turns to me, then back to him.

"Josh . . . what's the matter . . . what's wrong?"

Dad.

I can barely choke the word out at first. It's no more than a tiny croak. I say it louder, and louder, until I'm yelling. I begin to rush towards him when I realize that something's wrong. Something's horribly, terribly wrong.

The man who looks like my dad just keeps looking at us,

325

but with no sign of any interest. He looks vaguely mystified when I shout, "Dad, *Dad*, *DAD*." There's no recognition in his eyes. None at all.

I must be hallucinating.

Then he speaks. And I know I'm either dreaming or mad.

It's his voice, my dad's, no doubt whatsoever.

"Hey there, pal. Do I know you?"

I stop short, staring at him in disbelief. And yet, I believe him. Only too well. This feels like a waking version of my dream of Dad in the kitchen. Calmly pouring milk as he tells me that he and Mum cooked up a story that he was dead.

"Daddy . . . Dad. I don't understand . . . how come you're here?"

He stares at me, his eyes serious, filling with comprehension and sorrow.

"I'm your father?"

I'm numb with shock. "You don't know me. . .?"

He spreads his hands, palms open, looks helpless. "I've been on this mountain for months. Don't know how I got here. Don't remember anything or anyone. I always figured, you know, that seeing a familiar face might jolt my memory."

He gazes at me. "But . . . I'm sorry . . . I don't know you."

I try to speak, but no words come. All I can do is lick my lips against the blistering cold. Seeing this, the man who is my father takes hold of my arm. "You're gonna freeze up. Both of you – get inside."

Outside the hut, Xocotli exchanges a few words with my father. I don't catch what they say, but Xocotli keeps shaking his head, won't budge. Finally, he comes over to Ixchel and me.

"This man says he'll take care of you now, escort you down the mountain." Xocotli gives me a questioning look. "That's not what I agreed with Señora Susannah."

"He's my father," I say.

"That's something else she didn't mention."

"All right, then; wait with us until we leave."

"We should leave now," Xocotli says. "Bad weather is coming in. Wind rising. Things change fast up here."

"They should stay until the wind goes down," my father says. "I'll take them."

Xocotli gives us a hollow stare. "The mountain is unhappy. It's time to leave."

He watches as Ixchel and I follow my father into the hut. He doesn't come in with us. "I'll wait at the first hut," we hear him yell.

The hut is the size of a large garage. There's a tiny kitchen area with a gas-canister-powered stove and a bowl which functions as a sink. A log fire blazes under a brick-lined chimney. There's a bed, spread with a sleeping bag, a small table with two chairs. On a single pine shelf is a pile of paperback books and a portable stereo.

My dad sits on the bed and invites us to take the two chairs. I stumble, finally find the chair, and sit.

When I bring myself to look again, I can't take my eyes off him. He gazes back with a look that's like a spear to my heart. It's exactly the expression he had in my dream. Bemused, regretful, icily distant.

"So . . . you're my son, hey? What's your name?"

"Josh."

He nods, and I catch a glimpse of a tear in his eye as he grins. "Josh; good, I like it."

There's a painful silence. "You're Andres," I say. "Professor Andres Garcia. You're an archaeologist. You live in Oxford, England."

"Andres. Wouldn't have been my first guess. And England! That explains why I speak such good English," he says.

"Your wife is Eleanor," I continue. "And she . . . and me also . . . thought you were dead."

Andres nods again, eyes down. When he looks back up, I see that his eyes are brimming with tears. He wipes them away with the back of one hand. I rush to his side and hug him. After a few seconds he hugs me back. It feels half-hearted.

"What are you doing here, Dad? How did you get here? And why didn't you come back to us?"

He pulls away and puts his head in his hands for a long moment. Then he stands and walks to the kitchen, where he lights the stove to boil some water.

"I can remember how to speak and walk and . . . all the basic stuff. Which includes speaking English as well as Spanish, apparently. And I seem to know my way around a mountain. I remember everything that happened since I arrived on Orizaba. Most of all I remember the thing that's kept me here – the fear. Someone is watching me. Someone is looking for me, and when they catch up with me, I don't think I'll be coming back.

"One day . . . months ago now . . . I found myself in the rocks on the slope of this mountain. I had a head injury, but nothing more. I was found by a climbing guide, who took me down to the first hut. They wanted to take me to hospital but I wouldn't let them. I was terrified – of people. I didn't want to go where there were many people. This fear was like nothing you can imagine. Completely irrational! And yet it consumed me. I couldn't even stand to see the people arriving in the hut. I looked into each face and I wondered – are you the one who's come for me? So they let me stay in this hut. It's usually an emergency hut, but with me here it's always warm and safe, for anyone who gets caught in bad weather."

Ixchel says, "So . . . you don't remember anything?"

Andres shrugs. "Not so far."

"You don't remember me, or Mum, or Oxford, our house . . . anything?" I say.

"No, son. I'm truly sorry. I don't."

"What do you remember about the people who are after you?"

"Almost nothing. There are some very, very vague memories, like fragments from a dream. And they don't make sense."

"Try us," I say.

"I'm flying . . . and being chased by another aircraft. That's one. I'm in a cage, like a prison. That's another. I'm being shot at, but I don't die and I'm not afraid."

"What were you wearing when you woke up on the mountain?"

"Just an orange jumpsuit. I nearly froze to death. And a piece of really tasteless jewellery." He reaches under the mattress and pulls out a chunky bracelet. Even though I've never seen it before, I know immediately that we're looking at the Bracelet of Itzamna. Dad doesn't miss our unspoken recognition.

"But it's not just jewellery, is it? Even I guessed that much. This has something to do with why I'm here. I think it may even be why those people are looking for me."

Dad doesn't let us touch the Bracelet but instead fits it on to his left wrist, like a watch. It's about twice the width of a fat digital watch, made of a copper-coloured material that shines, but without the sheen of metal. It's engraved with wedge-like symbols, similar to the inscriptions on the Adaptor. Some symbols look like buttons. Just placed to the left of centre is a small dent; a hollow to hold something about the size of a small pea.

"It's got some kind of power source," Dad says, staring at the Bracelet with what I could swear looks like affection. "It hums. Like static electricity. It's not from this world. I'm sure of that. And it's broken."

"Broken?"

"When I look at it, I have one thought, one memory. *Burnt out*."

I give the Bracelet a careful look. "It doesn't look burnt."

"No," he agrees. "It doesn't."

"You don't know how to use it, or what it does?"

He shakes his head. "But I think that once, I did."

"I think you did, too," I say. It's all beginning to make

sense. Montoyo told me that Dad either took the Bracelet from Blanco Vigores – or else Vigores gave it to him. If the Bracelet is a time-travel device, then that explains how Dad escaped from the NRO.

He jumped in time.

Which means that somehow, Dad must have worked out how to use the Bracelet. Or fixed it. Montoyo said they hadn't been able to make it work. But Dad did!

And now all that knowledge is lost. . .

I can't even imagine how long Dad's been away, or where he's been. For me, months have passed. But for him? It might be longer. . . If it weren't for the fact that like me, Dad has dark-brown eyes, I'd even wonder: was Arcadio really my own father, travelling in time?

"Josh . . . do you know what this is?"

"I *think* it's the Bracelet of Itzamna," I tell him, looking at Ixchel for confirmation. She only shrugs. I guess she's never seen it either. "You're right, people are looking for it. Maybe they're even looking for you. The people who captured you were agents from the US National Reconnaissance Organization. It's part military, part secret service. They faked your death, to make it look like you died in a plane crash. They *really* didn't want anyone looking for you, I guess. But what I can't work out is – how did they fake your dental records? The coroner identified the body, said it was you."

Dad shrugs. "Maybe they bribed the coroner."

Open-mouthed, I say, "People can do that?"

"Not without connections, I imagine. But if what you say is right, then this agency must know pretty powerful people within the Mexican government."

"You don't remember anything about me and Mum," I say. "How about something further back. Your mother? Your father?"

"I have these feelings . . . but I can't remember names or faces."

"How about archaeology? You remember any of that?"

"I don't know. Maybe I could remember language. The language part of my memory seems to be untouched."

Ixchel speaks to him in Yucatec, saying something I don't understand. He replies and then looks astonished.

"You speak Yucatec," she says. "Can you also read the writing on the Bracelet?"

"I've already tried. It's a type of cuneiform writing – looks like an ancient Mesopotamian language, but with strange modifications to the symbols. It doesn't make any sense."

Montoyo didn't make a big deal about the links between Itzamna, Ek Naab and the Erinsi – the ancients named with old Mesopotamian words for *People of Memory*. But the Adaptor, the Revival Chamber and now the Bracelet of Itzamna all seem to have a link with ancient Mesopotamia.

How far back does this go?

The sorrow I've been feeling that my own father doesn't recognize me is starting to melt. I sense the beginning of hope. If I can persuade my dad to leave this mountain with us, we can try to get him home. Maybe that will bring back his memories.

Dad stares at me again. "I wish I could remember you. You must be one heck of a boy, the kind of son a man can really be proud of."

I stare back at him wordlessly, feel a lump rise in my throat.

"How did you find me?" he asks.

I tell him most of the story – how I came looking for the Ix Codex, how I found Camila and then Ek Naab, and how eventually I recovered the codex. When I come to the part about Camila drowning, I can't go on. I can see from his reaction that he doesn't remember who Camila is – and I haven't the heart to tell him. So I skip the details – I don't tell him that she was my sister; I don't tell him that she died.

Talking about what happened helps to keep my mind off the utter misery of the situation. I'm talking to my father – and he's rapt with what I'm saying – yet he can't think of me as his son.

Which makes it hard to *feel* like his son. That's not easy to stand.

With help from Ixchel, I tell him about the message in the postcards, from Arcadio. The name doesn't ring any bells with my father. He listens with intense concentration.

At a certain point, I remember that I have my dad's iPod. Maybe he'll recognize an object? Maybe it's just people he can't remember?

I show him the iPod, but he just shakes his head. "As far as I remember, I've never seen one before."

Ixchel says, "What happens if you play something from it?"

I pass Andres the iPod and show him how to hook up the earphones. I select a playlist of Miles Davis tracks, beginning with "Blue in Green".

Watching him listen to the tune that's haunted me for weeks, I almost cry. Within the minute, tears are rolling down his cheeks and into his beard. He squeezes his eyes shut and grips my arm hard. His voice cracks with emotion as he whispers, "I remember this. I do."

Ixchel goes to the kitchen to make tea from the water that's just boiled.

I sit with my father as he listens to the music. I watch him wipe away his tears.

He looks into my eyes. "You've been in all this danger, because of me."

"He got shot, too," chimes in Ixchel, before I can silence her.

"No. . ."

"It's nothing," I say. "Just a flesh wound."

"But it happened because of me."

"No, no way!"

"Yes," he insists, sadly. "From what you've said, it's obvious. I should have found this Ix Codex. Not you. It wasn't your job."

"Well, maybe it was my job."

"No. You completed the mission I started. You succeeded where I failed. Meanwhile I'm holed up in here like a fox, afraid to leave."

"Well, you know what they say . . . it's not paranoia if they really are out to get you."

But Dad ignores my attempt to be funny. "I still don't know how I'm going to get away from here. It's a physical thing. I can't make myself go past the first hut."

"We'll help."

"And I don't even remember my own boy!" He rips the earphones off and stares in despair. "I can remember some lousy jazz track but I can't remember my wife or son."

Ixchel says, "With help, maybe you can get your memory back."

"You say that only because you can't imagine what it's like. To have no memories! Just murky images, impossible to grasp; sounds that bubble up as if from the swamp of dreams."

His voice trails off and he gazes, unfocused, into his hands. Then he looks up at me again. "Did you miss me very much? You, your mother?"

I gasp. "Well, yeah! What do you think?"

To my surprise, he actually shakes his head, smiling. "I think you're managing pretty well without me."

I'm speechless. He continues. "To find the codex, to get all the way here, really, it's amazing. That you don't see it only shows me how normal this has become for you. What high expectations you have of yourself. Someone taught you to believe in yourself like that. It would be wonderful to think I had anything to do with that."

"But . . . of course you did," I whisper. "You're my dad!"

We stare at each other. "Well, your old man's got a dangerous streak too, Josh. I seem to be drawn to trouble."

"No . . . it's not that. It's the adventure you like. You always have."

"Oh," he says. "That must have been rough on you and your mum. Did you mind?"

"Dad! Of course not. That's . . . that's what's so great about you. I wanted – I want – to be just like you."

He ruffles my hair. "You're already better. When I was your age I was just wasting my time, hitting on girls and. . ." Abruptly, he stops talking, becomes deadly serious. I watch his eyes, hold my breath.

"Dad . . . do you remember? Try!"

"There was a girl. God! I wasn't much older than you. We had a baby!"

He stares at me, astonishment mixed with delight. He

grabs hold of my arms. "Josh! I remember something! You have a sister!"

There's a rush of excitement as I realize what this means. His memories are coming back to him. Maybe eventually, they all will. But what a thing to remember first. I feel sick with nerves when I think about it.

I'll have to tell him that my sister, Camila, is dead – murdered.

Outside, the wind whips around the hut, louder by the second. Powdery snow slaps hard against the single window. There's another sound then, one that I can't quite place. It sounds like a low rumble.

The effect on Dad is like an electric shock. He leaps to his feet. "Turn off the gas! Turn it off quick!"

He dashes to an apparatus next to the sink. He picks it up, and staring at it in horror, he crosses the room to where a bulky, granite-coloured North Face ski jacket hangs on a hook by the door. From one of the pockets he takes a walkie-talkie. He barks questions in Spanish, spitting each word. "What readings are you getting? I've got 5.5. Right. How many people are on the way to the summit? How many rescue crew can you spare? OK. OK. I've got two with me. OK."

The second he gets off the radio, he starts to put on his jacket. "Get your jackets back on," he instructs. Now that he's in mountain-rescue mode, a change sweeps through his personality. He's become confident, methodical, precise. "Ropes too. And your backpacks. Get your crampons in place. We're leaving. There's seismic activity."

Ixchel and I reel with alarm. "The volcano . . . is going to explode. . .?"

He hesitates. "No . . . but . . . there's a lot of fresh powder near the summit."

"And. . .?"

Through tensed lips he says, "Avalanche."

My father, Andres, has to lean hard against the door of the hut to prise it open – the wind pressure is so high. Outside, I feel a surge of fear. Occasional gusts blow hard enough to throw me off balance. Metres away, on the glacier, it will be almost impossible to stay upright when those gales blow.

Dad shouts some incomprehensible words into his walkie-talkie and then listens, nodding. The second he finishes talking, he turns to us.

"We're going to go down as fast as possible, OK? Roped together. If you feel yourself slipping, lean back hard, OK? Dig your crampons into the ice. We'll be zigzagging down. Tread exactly where I tread, OK? There are some crevasses, but I know where they are."

There's another rumble. This time I feel it beneath my feet. Terror pours through me like hot water through ice. I can see it in Ixchel's face too.

"Shouldn't we stay in the hut?" I yell above the wind. How is my leg going to hold up?

Dad shouts back, "It's in the path of the avalanche. We need to move."

He leads us out on to the lip of the glacier. We scramble up the two feet of ice, then start walking, first Dad, then me, then Ixchel. We zigzag across, taking tiny steps. One second the air is still; the next, there's a roar of freezing snow.

Another deep rumble. It's strong enough to shake us off our feet. We're thrown back against the mountain. We lean against the slope, scrape our boots into the ice. When the tremor passes, Dad shouts, "That was good. Keep doing that when it quakes."

As I prepare to pull myself to my feet, I glance upwards. I'm slightly surprised to see a light aircraft circling the top of the volcano. I hadn't heard it before, over the wind. I point it out to Dad. He looks up curiously. "Vulcanologists, probably," he says. "They like to take photos of the crater when we get seismic activity around here."

Then, to our amazement, a tiny figure falls out of the plane. It flips and floats around in a crazy, eccentric manner for a few seconds. A parachute opens, a brilliant blue canopy behind the skydiver, yanking him skyward.

"What the. . .?" shouts Dad in disbelief. "That guy is crazy! He's gonna get himself killed!"

The blue parachute floats gracefully towards the summit.

341

Passing the crater, it turns. We watch, paralysed with astonishment.

Attached to the skydiver's feet is a snowboard. The parachute lowers him towards the leading edge of the crater. He suddenly releases the chute. He free-falls and lands on a huge bank of powder snow. There are other climbers close to his position. We're transfixed with horror as a layer of snow begins to crumble and collapse. The skydiver snowboards right through the chaos. Snow billows around him, almost obscuring him completely. He thunders on ahead, leaving a snowstorm in his wake.

Part of me is thinking that it's the coolest thing I've ever seen in my life. Another part notices that climbers are being knocked down in the first wave of rushing snow.

"That's done it now," says Dad. It's the first time I hear real fear in his voice. "Use your ice tool to get a hold on the ice. And hold tight, kids! Hold on tight!"

There's no possible way to make it off the glacier in time. The avalanche doesn't seem to be headed straight for us just yet, so I don't quite understand my father's panic. I hurl my axe into the ice as hard as I can manage. Ixchel does the same. Our eyes meet. We're both white with fear.

The snowboarder sails across the glacier in one long heelside turn. He swerves out of the path of the tumbling snow. He's headed straight for us, getting closer by the second. Dad stares in disbelief.

"This guy is out of his mind. . ."

Only now do I see what's really happening here.

It's Madison.

I struggle to pull my axe out of the ice. Dad shouts at me, "Josh! Stay where you are! Leave it there!"

"We need a weapon," I shout back, grappling with the axe, which won't budge. My leg feels like it's on fire from all my twisting movements. I glance over my shoulder just in time to see the snowboarder careering towards me. In one outstretched hand is a knife.

He carves up the snow between Ixchel and me, cuts through our rope with his knife. He flips around sharply, turning back towards me. In the next second, he grabs hold of my backpack, drags me along behind him. The rope attaching me to my father snaps taut for a second. And then I feel his weight added to mine. The snowboarder slows down. He brakes to a standstill. I can't see his face behind the helmet and snow goggles. Hearing his voice confirms my worst suspicions.

Madison.

"Give me the backpack, Josh," he yells. "I only want the Adaptor."

He leans forward with the knife, slices at my backpack. One strap breaks free.

Just as Madison reaches to cut the other strap, the volcano shakes – the most powerful tremor yet. I wobble for a second, lose my balance and then fall flat on my face.

When I look up, I don't even have long enough to dread its arrival: a wall of snow is plummeting down the mountain, headed right for us. The last thing I see is Madison going over, falling like a skittle.

The roar is deafening. I bow my head and clench my jaw. The snow hits like a massive punch to the face. I'm lifted right off the ground and hurled down the mountain. I'm tumbling, head over heels. Sheer panic floods me. Pain roars like a furnace in my thigh. My mouth and nose fill with freezing dust and snow. I lose all sense of time – my fall could have taken one second or twenty. All I'm aware of is the wild current of terror.

The maelstrom of whiteness dumps me on top of my backpack. I'm somewhere down the glacier, buried in snow. For a few seconds I lie absolutely still, amazed that no bones seem to be broken. I'm covered by at least one foot of snow, but the fact that I can still see sunlight through it gives me hope. I scratch and carve my way out. I push my head and shoulders through the crust of snow, searching for signs of Ixchel, my father and Madison.

I'm almost at the edge of the glacier's tongue. Another twenty metres and I'd have been flung into the rock field. The snow has settled over everything. The entire glacier is blanketed with an eerie silence. It's partly because I'm still muffled with snow. I use my fingers to scoop snow out of my mouth, nose and ears, and spit out the rest.

I can't see anyone else near my position. Much, much further up the slope I spot some movement. One or two of the climbers who fell in the first little avalanche seem to be emerging from the snow. I feel a stab of anxiety. That was the group of high-school kids. Where are the rest of them? I look over at where the second hut had nestled against an outcropping of rock. It's gone – buried in a deep slew of snow.

I manage to stand up. That's when I realize that the rope is still around my waist. It seems slightly loose. I tug at it, gently.

It tugs back, slowly at first. Then with a violence that sweeps me off my feet, it yanks hard at me. I'm pulled right under the snow and dragged along for a second. I'm screaming all over again; my mouth jams up with snow.

Then I fall. Into the ice.

A crevasse.

The idea is so blood-curdling that I clutch at the walls of the cleft in the ice. I fall about two metres before my hands find an ice axe sunk deep into the wall. It isn't mine or Ixchel's, and the handle is slippery, frozen. I grip hold of the top of it. My feet scramble in a furious attempt to find a foothold.

The rope pulls at my waist, even harder this time. The downward force is relentless. It takes all my strength to keep from falling. I can't see anything below me but snow.

But I know that someone's down there, further down the crevasse. Either Ixchel . . . or my father.

I try calling out. "Dad. . .? Ixchel. . .?"

There's no answer.

My cheek numbs, frozen against the wall of the crevasse. I daren't move an inch, in case I lose my balance. I'm trembling from the effort. I don't even dare use energy to yell. The snow silences everything. I channel every ounce of strength I have into not slipping further into the crevasse. The ice axe is saving me – it's so deeply buried that it supports my weight. But I can't climb – can't move. The rope around my waist squeezes and pulls at me, as if it might tear me in two. Gradually, I come to the shattering conclusion that whoever is on the end of my rope is hanging freely. Possibly unconscious, possibly even dead.

And when I realize that, I realize who it must be.

If it were Ixchel, I think I'd be able to take her weight. I think I'd even be able to drag her up.

This weight is overpowering me. It has to be my dad.

The idea sends me into a wild panic. I can't help myself screaming, "Dad! Dad! It's me, Josh! I'm up here! I'm on the rope!"

There's no answer. I feel tears of frustration welling up. If only I had a knife, or could spare a hand to free myself of the rope. . .

But the only thing stopping my dad from falling deeper

346

into the crevasse – is me. Just below me, the gap in the ice narrows. Snow has collected around the bottleneck. The rope disappears into that snow. I can't see anything beyond.

I can do nothing but cling to that ice axe. And pray.

Then I hear his voice. It sounds icy, cold as the layers of frozen dust which separate us.

"Josh. Listen to me. Can you climb up?"

"No . . . no," I say. My voice quavers. "I can't move, Dad."

There's an agonizing silence.

"I'm gonna cut the rope now."

I scream. "Dad, no!"

"Listen!"

I force myself to be silent. Already I'm struggling with tears. I'm beginning to lose sensation in my lower limbs, where the blood supply is choked off by the rope.

"Rules of the mountain, Josh," I hear him say, wearily. "I may have forgotten everything else but . . . I remember that much. I won't pull you down with me."

"No . . . Dad. . ." I sob.

"There's no other choice for me. Now be brave."

"Please. . ." But I'm barely whispering now.

And then in a voice which seems to cut like a knife through the freezing air he says, "Josh . . . this isn't over."

Without any warning, the pressure around my waist goes slack.

347

The fear of being torn apart vanishes.

The weight pulling me down has disappeared. I cling tightly to the edge, my mind racing with horror. I listen for any sound of my dad at the bottom of the crevasse.

I hear nothing.

Dad's cut himself loose.

My father saved me. But where is he now? I feel useless, utterly lost.

A wave of blank despair hits me. I want to give up right now. Hard on the heels of that thought is another, older, colder voice.

Stop crying, you baby. Get out of this place while you still can. Or else what he did will be for nothing.

I blink my tears away, angry. I drag myself up, sniffing. The crampons on my boots scratch deep into the ice. I feel a foothold higher up and inch a little higher. My fingers hunt around for a handhold, until I find a small crack in the ice. I finally get the nerve to let go of the ice axe, and scrabble upwards until I can lodge a knee on to the axe. That helps me to push a little higher still. Finally I stand on the axe. At a stretch, I can just reach the lip of the glacier.

I crawl out of the crevasse. Every movement of my wounded leg against the ice is pure agony. But I manage to ignore it. I keep crawling on my belly until I'm far enough away from the edge. Then I turn on to my back, sit up and pull on the slack rope that now dangles into the crevasse.

There's something at the end of the rope.

I hear a faint rattling sound as some object scrapes the ice on its way up. I pull even faster, threading rope through my hands. Until every centimetre of rope is there.

There, tied to the end of the rope, is the Bracelet of Itzamna.

There were twenty-four climbers known to be on the slopes of El Pico de Orizaba when the earthquake hit. Twenty-five if you include Simon Madison.

Twenty of us made if off the mountain alive. Including me and Ixchel.

They found only three bodies. My dad's was the first. He was at the bottom of an ice crevasse, his neck broken. They sent a climber down after him, attached to a winch, and pulled his body up. Two other bodies were found a day later, buried deep under the snow. Their jackets had avalanche detection systems. They were both high-school students from Mexico.

They still haven't found the third high-school kid. I've overheard comments about waiting until the snow melts, in spring.

There was no sign of Madison. No one saw him come down the mountain; no one saw him alive again on the glacier. He simply vanished into the clouds of snow.

If my dad hadn't cut himself free, I'd have fallen with him. Maybe the fall would have killed me, maybe not.

Someone asks how I'm feeling.

I don't feel anything.

It's as though everything poured out of me on the mountain. I'm emptied, exhausted, numb.

At least no one wants to *tell* me how to feel. We're all in the same boat. Sixteen-year-old boys hug each other and cry for their lost friends.

Dark words are spoken about how the weather conditions had looked dangerous. Everyone's wise after the event. No one's sorry for the lost snowboarder. The avalanche, they reckon, may not have been his fault, but he sure made it worse.

I'm staying at a fancy hospital for a few days to recuperate. Montoyo arrived with Benicio, only hours after the rescue operation. Tomorrow, Mum will be here.

Ixchel was one of the first to be found. As soon as Madison cut her rope, she ran off the glacier, towards the hut. She was caught by the edge of the avalanche that hit the hut, but wasn't buried too deep. Like me, she was able to dig her way out of the loose snow. By the time she surfaced, some of the high-school kids were on the surface of the snow. One of their party radioed for help. Ixchel called Montoyo.

I suppose I should feel something more than relief at seeing Ixchel. But that's just the problem.

I feel nothing.

It's as if the air around me has been sucked away, replaced with dead space. Between me and everyone else, there's this vacuum. When I try to talk, everything gets swallowed up. It comes out monotone, monochrome.

I hardly notice when Montoyo comes to see me. I'm lying on my bed in a hospital in Veracruz. During the avalanche, my leg wound opened up. It bled pretty badly. They had to stitch and bandage it all over again. Susannah has been sitting with me ever since they brought me down from the mountain. She says very little, but strokes my hair and tells me that I'm very brave.

Brave? What does that even mean?

Montoyo asks for time alone with me. He won't let me lie on the bed, just staring into space.

"Sit up, now. You can do that much."

I can't meet his eyes. He stares at me for a long time, and then pats my back and sighs.

"This is gonna be a tough time for you, Josh. Believe me, I know."

I turn slowly to face him. "What do you know?"

"You're in pain. That's something we all go through."

I shake my head slowly. "This is something different."

Montoyo nods. "This is shock. And it, too, will pass." He pauses. "What you need to understand, Josh, is that your father's fate is something beyond you. It's out of your hands."

I gaze at Montoyo. "He didn't even know me. Did Ixchel tell you? He sacrificed his life for me. Even though he couldn't remember I was his son."

"He sacrificed himself because it was the only thing to do. He knew the hazards of the mountain. Most importantly, he *knew you*, even if he couldn't remember. You can be sure that knowing you were his son would have made that choice much easier. A father doesn't think twice about a decision like that."

"I want to cry. . ." I say in a low voice. "But I can't any more. Why?"

"You spilt a lot of blood and tears on that mountain. It's enough. Don't cry too much for the dead – they see it. And it hurts them."

I glance up in surprise to see Montoyo nodding solemnly. "How can your father's spirit leave this place," he asks, "if you won't let him go?"

"What about my mother?"

Montoyo sighs. "Well, that's another matter. I will help you there. I believe the time has come for her to know – about everything.

"Your father lived a marvellous life. He was greatly respected in his field of work. He had a wonderful family. A son he can be really proud of. He discovered Ek Naab – and through him, we discovered you. Through him and you, we have the Ix Codex; we can prepare for 2012. Think about that. It's a life to celebrate."

Slowly, I nod.

"And you . . . you did amazing things, Josh. You found the Adaptor, found the Revival Chamber – the one written about in the Ix Codex. And you found your father. I underestimated you. I didn't think you were ready for all this. Well, maybe you are."

But he's so wrong. Madison almost killed me, three times. If he really wanted me dead, I probably would be. I don't know how to defend myself properly. I do things without thinking them through.

"I don't know how . . . but I led Madison to that mountain," I whisper. "He as good as killed my dad, and those kids."

"The avalanche was an accident waiting to happen," Montoyo says, shrugging. "With all this strange weather we're getting – there's not usually so much snow. People who climb mountains take great risks."

I'd never really considered the risks. All I can remember is how badly I needed to know: what happened to my father? Who killed him?

I feel a distant sense of regret, thinking that if I'd just ignored those postcards, or Arcadio's letter, my father might still be alive.

"Josh," Montoyo says, "one of the rescue workers returned your possessions." He hands me the iPod, my UK mobile phone and a watch. I take them, hardly looking at them as I mumble my thanks. "Was there anything else?" Montoyo asks, with care. "Did your father give you anything?"

I stare at Montoyo, make my decision.

He's not getting his hands on that bracelet.

"He didn't know me," I say blandly. "Why would he give me anything?"

Montoyo examines my eyes closely, then nods a few times. He pats my back again. "OK, Josh. Take it easy. We're gonna take care of you. And your mother too. We're gonna take good care of you now."

He leaves me then, and I lie back on the bed, wincing at the constant pain that spikes through my entire body.

The Bracelet of Itzamna lies safely hidden under my mattress. No one knows I have it. Except maybe Ixchel. She knows I'm holding something back. When we told Montoyo about how we found my father, and what he told us, I was careful to point out that Dad didn't offer to let us touch the Bracelet. As far as Montoyo knows, the Bracelet is still somewhere on the volcano. Discarded, lost in a deep fissure of ice.

Maybe Arcadio sent me up the mountain to get the Bracelet. If I'd never showed up, my dad might have stayed there for ever, never remembering who he was. Or maybe he'd have died in an avalanche. The Bracelet is the only part of any of this which makes any sense to me. Until I decide what to do with it, that bracelet is mine.

The day of Mum's arrival from England, I'm a bag of nerves.
I know I'm in big trouble with Mum – and I can't blame her.
I've made sure not to actually lie to her in any of my texts or
phone messages, but I know her well enough to know that
she'll see it as deception.

She flies into Veracruz after a connecting flight from
Mexico City. The doctor on the mountain-rescue team won't
give permission for me to leave, so Montoyo goes to pick her
up. He promises to ease her gently into the whole Ek Naab
situation.

"I'll drive," he tells me. "We'll talk about your father,
how he came to the city, how you followed in his path.
Everything. I'll tell her the whole history."

"She won't believe you," I say.

Montoyo looks impassive. "We'll see."

At that moment I can't imagine how anyone could accuse
Montoyo of making anything up. His face always has this

drawn, sombre quality. His eyes have a weary gaze, like he's seen and heard too much, like he knows there's more to come.

I don't know exactly what he tells Mum, but when they arrive, around ten at night, Mum seems not only exhausted but in shock. She says nothing when she first sees me, just hugs me for a long, long time.

When finally she faces me, her eyes glisten with tears.

"I'm sorry," she whispers. "I should have listened to you."

Her apology floors me. A sob threatens to choke me. It's the most powerful feeling I've had for two days.

Then she starts to cry properly. The way she did when we first thought Dad had died. I put my arms around her. The dead air around me finally crackles with energy. Her grief gets through to me in a way nothing else has. It's like her heart is breaking.

Then after just a minute or two, suddenly, she stops. She dries her eyes and wipes her nose. She even forces a smile.

"They've told me all about what you've done. I don't even know what to say. Josh – it's incredible!"

I stare in stunned silence. Eventually, I manage to say, "You actually believed what Montoyo told you?"

"Not at first, no. I asked him to let me out of the car. I refused to go anywhere with him. I was about to call the British Embassy. Then he called your friend Benicio. . ."

I interrupt. "He's my cousin," I say, trying to be helpful.

"Yes, thank you," she says with a grave smile. "I'm still trying to get used to all that. Your cousin Benicio. Who arrived in that flying machine."

"The Muwan?"

"Yes. Difficult to argue after seeing that."

"Wait until you see Ek Naab," I murmur.

"Some of your blog, I really loved," she says. "It made me feel close to you, sweetheart. It made me feel I was getting to know a different side to you."

I blink rapidly, staring at the blanket. I try to laugh. "Well, that's good."

"Yes. . ." Mum says. Her voice trails off.

"I'm sorry too, Mum. Sorry that I couldn't tell you what I was doing. That I got involved. That. . ." My mouth goes dry. The words seem to stick in my throat. "That Dad died because of me."

"You mustn't say that."

"But it's true."

"He gave his life to save yours. It was a split-second thing. Things like that happen on mountains."

"I shouldn't have been there."

"But you were. And that's how it goes, you know, Josh? Things happen. If you hadn't gone to the mountain, your father might still be there, still unable to remember us. Or he might have died in the avalanche."

"That's what Montoyo said."

"Well, he's right. And. . ." She hesitates for a moment, adds, "You might want to give a moment's thought to God's part in all this. Maybe it's all part of his plan for you, for your dad, for us."

I don't have the energy to argue with her. And right now, I have to admit that the idea seems tempting. It would be nice to believe that I'm going through all this for a reason.

Right now, the only reason I can believe in is the Bracelet of Itzamna.

If it's a time-travel device, then maybe I can find a way to make it work. Maybe I can go back in time – and change how things turned out.

Maybe there's a way to save my dad after all.

For reasons that he doesn't explain to me, Montoyo tells Susannah all about Ek Naab.

It's getting to be a free-for-all, this Big Secret.

After three days of it, I'm fed up of lying on a bed whilst sad-eyed women come and visit me. I drag myself out of the hospital room and join Ixchel in the restaurant.

"Try the tortilla soup," she says. "It's not bad. The spaghetti's OK too. And those pink-frosted doughnuts are the best."

"Is this all you've been doing?" I say. "You'll get fat."

Ixchel sticks out her tongue. "Huh, what's it to you?"

I actually laugh. "Thanks."

"For what?"

"For being normal. My mum's being all sensitive. Montoyo even. They're all on eggshells around me. It's good to be with someone who isn't. Makes me feel like I might be normal too."

"Oh, what's so great about *normal*? I wanted to try being a normal Mexican girl – look how that turned out."

"Well, that's cos you're such a weirdo," I say with a faint grin.

"Listen to who's talking."

"Yeah, about that, it's *'look who's talking'*."

"Really? You're sure?"

"I think I know my own language."

She has a little laugh, probably at my expense. Then we stop smiling and she gets a serious look in her eye again.

"You've got the Bracelet of Itzamna, haven't you? It's OK – you don't have to tell me. It's just that I've been thinking it through. Putting it all together. Arcadio had some kind of gift of prophecy – he could predict the future. How? Your dad escaped from those US agents who captured him – and he used the Bracelet."

We stare at each other. I say nothing.

She continues. "Those agents haven't found your father to this day. But they'll get to hear about it. They can't be complete idiots. They know that the Bracelet has some strange energy and power. They want it. If they find out that your father has died here . . . they'll come looking for you."

She's right. Ixchel must notice the anxiety on my face, because she adds quickly, "It might be OK. Susannah and I told them that your name is Josh Gonzalez, and that your father's name was Pedro. It's going to be in all the local papers. No foreigners were killed, so hopefully no one outside Mexico will be interested in the story."

I shake my head. "I dunno. Don't those intelligence services sweep *all* the news?"

"Even so, they'd be looking for the name 'Josh Garcia' or 'Andres Garcia'."

Doubtfully, I say, "I guess."

"And there's been no sign of Madison. If he survived, he made it off the mountain without anyone noticing him."

"No one noticing the bloke who started the avalanche? I doubt that." I pause. "Or he could be dead."

"We can hope. But at least now, the Sect can't find us. Not so easily, anyway. Because I found their tracer."

I'm astounded.

"When Madison found us in Tlacotalpan, I really couldn't figure it out. I guessed he'd been following in a car. But when he tracked us to the mountain . . . it had to be something more. And then I remembered – your fight with those girls in the caves."

I'm open-mouthed. "They planted something. . .?"

Ixchel nods. "At first I thought – our clothes. But we changed out of them for the climb. It had to be something we'd carried since we met them."

At the same time, we both say, "*The Ziploc bag. . .*"

"I took it off you in the ambulance," she says. "It was a tiny micro-transmitter, stuck to the outside of the bag. I threw it away. It's somewhere on the road now. Near Orizaba."

I take a few seconds to absorb this.

"So . . . you have the Bracelet." It's not a question, but a statement. I try to return Ixchel's steady gaze, but I can't.

Eventually, I cave in. "Yeah."

"I won't tell."

"Why?"

"Because that's why we were there. Isn't it? Arcadio predicted that you would find the Bracelet. '*You must suspect that your fate is intertwined with the Mayan prophecy of 2012.*'"

I look away for a second, then back, to find her eyes burrowing into mine. I can see we're on the same track now. She's reached the same conclusion as me – Arcadio must be a time traveller. I say quietly, "You're pretty smart."

"You too, Josh. I know you're planning something. Whatever it is, you need me to help you."

"I can't. It's probably dangerous. It may be my fate; doesn't have to be yours, though."

"Hey, don't forget we're promised to each other," she says, attempting a grin.

"Don't. Don't talk about that."

She swallows. "I know. It's all a little . . . what's the word. . .?"

"Creepy."

"Yeah."

Neither of us speaks again for a long while. I tear Ixchel's pink doughnut in two and chew my half slowly.

"Montoyo wants us all to go live in Ek Naab," she says.

"Good for him. Still telling everyone what to do."

"Your mother says she won't allow it. Not until you're sixteen."

"Course she won't. That's just asking too much."

"So what will you do?"

"We'll be OK. I'll get stronger, train harder. I'll take care of her."

Softly, Ixchel says, "But, Josh . . . the Sect want to hurt you. Remember what that Professor woman said. They want you for their experiments on the Bakab gene."

"They'll have to catch me first."

"But . . . you're all alone."

Hearing Ixchel say this, I feel a sudden rush of fear. I sense my argument collapsing.

"You could ask Montoyo to send someone to you."

"What. . .?"

"To protect you. Someone from the city, to be, like, your bodyguard."

"You're right," I say, seriously impressed by the suggestion. "That could work."

"I'm glad you like the idea. So, actually, Benicio already

asked Montoyo to send him. He's gonna send Benicio to be a student in Oxford."

I smile to myself. I guess our fly-by of the dreaming spires of Oxford really impressed him.

Ixchel continues. "Maybe so you can investigate the Sect?"

"Maybe," I agree. But I can't help wondering, would Montoyo do that? Actually let me do something risky?

"But Montoyo and Benicio – they don't know you have the Bracelet." Ixchel gives me a wary look. "Do they?"

I stare back. "No."

There's a long pause before her next words. Like she's really not sure whether to speak out or not. "Have you thought about what your father said . . . about *burnt out*?"

Actually, I have. But I don't respond except to watch Ixchel closely. "I've had a lot of things on my mind. . ." I say evasively. "But obviously you have. . ."

Ixchel eyes gaze almost imploringly into mine. "*Burnt out!* Not the whole Bracelet . . . but some part of it, maybe?"

"Some part of the Bracelet," I say slowly. "Like what?"

"Like a crystal. A control circuit, perhaps?"

"Why a crystal?"

Ixchel cocks her head to one side. "Come on now, Josh. This is me."

Tight-lipped, I stare back into that challenging gaze.

Eventually I say, "There's a little hole in the Bracelet. It's empty. I wondered . . . what with all that talk of a Crystal Key . . . if maybe it needed some kind of crystal."

Ixchel smiles, and then through closed lips, she laughs. Quietly she says, "You got it."

Truth is, I was just guessing. It couldn't be the same crystal, could it? But the fact that Ixchel's had the same thought makes my pulse race.

"Josh, let me help fix the Bracelet. I don't want you just blinking out of existence. Like Arcadio."

"You think that's what happened to him?"

"That's what Susannah says. Isn't it? One day, he just didn't turn up. Poor Susannah; I think she's been waiting for him ever since."

"That's pretty rough."

Ixchel murmurs, "Sure it is."

"So, what about you? What will you do?"

Ixchel sighs and licks pink frosting off her thumb. "Back to Ek Naab, I guess. So much for my freedom! To the Tec, to study ancient languages."

"Start with Sumerian," I suggest.

"That was my plan. . ." she says with a slow grin. "So you'll let me help?"

"Could I stop you?"

Ixchel grins and nudges my elbow with her knuckle. "Nope."

I go up to the food counter, fetch a plate of spaghetti in a sticky tomato sauce, and a can of Orange Crush. Ixchel watches me eat. I try to avoid thinking about tomorrow. Montoyo is driving us all back to the outskirts of the surface part of Ek Naab. We'll be going in through the orange groves, to the cemetery on the hill.

And we'll bury my father. I don't know how Montoyo persuaded my mother, but she's agreed to it. It's vital that we cover up the whole thing about how my dad didn't really die in that plane crash. We have to keep his actual death and burial a secret. Anything to stop the word getting out that Professor Andres Garcia finally turned up somewhere on Planet Earth.

Maybe Mum finally understands just what the NRO – and the Sect – are prepared to do to get their hands on the secrets of Ek Naab.

Mum and I waited six months to say goodbye to my father. When we finally did, it was for the third time. There'd been the first funeral in Chetumal, alongside the one for Camila. Goodness knows whose ashes we saw off that time. The second time was the memorial service in his Oxford college. I sat through the whole thing in a daze.

And now here we are again. This time with a coffin, on a cool December morning, two days before Christmas. By a pristine white church surrounded by orange trees.

All members of the ruling Executive of Ek Naab are there with their families, except one – Blanco Vigores. Everyone lines up the church to give the *pesame* – condolences – to Mum and me. I look along the line but can't see Vigores. It doesn't seem like a polite question to ask right now, but still I wonder, and not for the first time:

Where is Blanco Vigores? Where does a blind old man disappear to on all these important occasions?

In case anyone is spying on us via satellites, everyone dresses like regular Mexicans. As far as the outside world is concerned, this is supposed to be a private chapel on the huge ranch of some rich Mexican family. The men wear black suits; the women dress in smart black skirts and dresses, their heads covered with black lace mantillas. I'm always amazed at how many people can put their hands on a sharp-looking black suit at the shortest notice.

They even find something to fit me.

"You look really nice," Ixchel whispers to me as her turn comes to kiss my cheek.

"So do you," I mumble. She does, too. Sleek black hair pouring over her shoulders, her eyes and lips lightly made up, she looks as elegant as you like. Talk about scrubbing up nice.

It's the craziest scene, straight out of a Mexican soap opera. Everybody dressed up to the nines and wearing fancy cologne. I can hardly believe that these are the same people who lined the underground streets of Ek Naab a few months ago in their traditional dress and watched me go to be installed as the Bakab Ix.

My mum looks amazing. She's getting good at being the grieving widow. She and Susannah really stand out with their fair hair under the black mantillas. In front of all these strangers from Ek Naab, Mum is elegant and charming. Not a tear in sight.

Susannah is calm the whole time. I don't expect her to be moved – she didn't know my dad, after all. What's a bit odd is that she also seems perfectly at home in these surroundings. I've never met anyone who could take so much weirdness in their stride. Nothing fazes her.

The priest – a woman – even wears robes of liturgical purple. All a bit bizarre. My mum doesn't say anything, but I'm sure I notice her pursing her lips.

Inside, the church is crammed with hibiscus flowers. Pride of place in the church goes to a statue of the Virgin Mary. Statues of saints line the pews. Candles burn in hanging chandeliers. Dad's coffin, draped in white, stands in front of the altar.

The service is in Latin, sung by the priest and two robed attendants, who stand with their backs to the congregation for most of the time. A choir chimes in with music which sounds just like the kind of thing you hear in the chapel of an Oxford college. I have to watch everyone else to know when to stand, sit or kneel. It's obvious to me that at least half the people there are as clueless as I am. Carlos Montoyo stands on the other side of my mother. I'm between Mum and Ixchel. I find myself wondering about Montoyo. Does he have a family? Does he do anything, apart from quietly run Ek Naab?

I'm strangely disoriented. The whole experience is so odd, it's hard to believe this is actually happening. I seem to go

371

through everything on automatic pilot. Sit, stand, kneel, listen to prayers; what is it all for? How can the guy in the coffin really be my dad? How can the choir be singing a mass straight out of sixteenth-century Spain? I feel like I'm existing in the past and in the present; in Mexico, Spain and Oxford, all at the same time.

The priest talks about redemption. Whatever my father ever did wrong in his life, she reckons, his sacrifice at the end will redeem everything. He's a hero in everyone's eyes. I wonder why no one blames me, but they don't.

As we process out of the church, the choir, high in their stalls at the back of the church, throws hibiscus petals over the coffin. Falling on the simple white coffin drapings, they look like drops of blood against snow.

Outside, the sky is flat and grey like a beach pebble. High above the clouds, the air stirs, preparing for a storm. We bury my father on the slope of the nearby hill, in the shade of a tree. It feels like reaching the end of a very, very long day.

As I watch the coffin being lowered into the ground, I clasp my hands together hard, to stop them shaking. It doesn't work. Ixchel moves closer to me, her fingers reaching for mine. Her hand is small and hot. She's trembling too.

At the touch of Ixchel's hand, my mind flicks back to the memory of my dad in his hut on the slopes of the volcano, listening to Miles Davis on his iPod whilst Ixchel made the tea. How his eyes filled up with tears.

I sense Ixchel next to me, our shoulders touching. She turns to me, but I can't bear to look at her. I blink rapidly; tears sting my eyes as I stare directly ahead. In my chest there's an almost unbearable ache.

"You'll get through this, Josh," Ixchel whispers, and squeezes my hand.

I was desperate to have all my questions answered. . . . I never imagined it would end like this. But I guess it has. Now I really do know how my father died . . . he was saving my life.

Meanwhile, pieces of the puzzle keep falling into place; the human race still has an appointment with the superwave in 2012. As to how things will turn out for me and my family . . . I'm still in the dark.

On my wrist, under the sleeve of a crisp white shirt and the suit jacket, the Bracelet of Itzamna fizzes gently against my skin. I find myself focusing on the sensation. It's as though the Bracelet were communicating with me:

This isn't over.

Acknowledgements

I'd like to thank good friends and expert consultants: Reba Bandyopadhyay for astrophysics, Kate Salesse for forensic science and Barry Clarke for codes and ciphers.

Thanks also to all the wonderful team at Scholastic, especially my editors, Elv Moody and Jessica White, and publicists, Alyx Price and Camilla Allen.

Also to my agent, Peter Cox, for a truly brilliant suggestion and steadfast enthusiasm. Finally to my husband, David, and daughters for their support and patience… It's not easy keeping Joshua's secrets…